CURVY GIRLS CAN'T DANCE

KELSIE STELTING

To Michelle, whose light dances even when she's standing still.

ONE

"IT HAS TO FIT!" I told my mom, who was attempting to help me into my dance uniform. The one we were forced to order two sizes too small because it didn't come in the extra-large size I needed. The one our studio director insisted I fit into for the qualifier.

Tears stung my eyes as the mermaid costume caught on my hips and wouldn't budge up another inch. I sniffed, wiping at my nose. This was a nightmare.

"Don't cry!" Mom ordered in a hushed voice so none of my teammates would overhear us in the dressing room. "You'll ruin your makeup!"

I fluttered my false lashes quickly, trying to stem

the tears, and made another effort to flex my legs and suck in my stomach to give myself even a millimeter more room. With a hard yank and the sound of a few popped threads, the bottom made it over my thighs.

I gasped. "Did it rip?"

Mom was silent for a moment. "I'll get a needle."

I closed my eyes, trying to stay calm. We didn't have another choice at this point. It was either wear the costume or forfeit the chance to dance at nationals. No way would I give up a chance at gold or an opportunity to dance in front of the top dance recruiters in the country.

Everyone from college drill team coaches to the New York Ballet would be at the Dance Dance National Competition, looking for their next crop of talented dancers. I swore I would be one of them, size extra-large or not. Sausage casing mermaid costume or not.

Why Galina forced me to purchase this exact costume was beyond me. Especially when my mom offered to custom make mine in more forgiving materials.

Mom came back through the curtain and began

working around the back waist of my pants. A needle pricked through the fabric and poked my back.

"Ouch!" I hissed.

"Sorry, but I'm rushing," she whispered back. "We need to get out there."

I gritted my teeth as I endured prick after accidental prick until finally, she stood, stretching her back. "It should hold for the dance," she said. "Just be careful on your tilt."

Just thinking of the standing splits made me cringe. "Mom, I can't take it easy today. These are the qualifiers, and Galina's been on my back all month."

She shoved the needle and thread back into her sewing kit. "We just have to make it through today, Adriel. Just one day. Okay?"

I nodded. We'd been working on this, waiting for this moment for years. Ever since I first stepped foot in Emerson Dance Academy as a four-year-old girl, unaware of the massive yet subtle differences between a *temps de poisson* and a *temps de l'ange*. We'd come too far, put in too many hours and too much money, to give up now.

Mom's sleek blond bob was askew for what

seemed like the first time ever, and she tucked the loose strands behind her ears before turning toward the dressing room curtain and taking a deep breath.

I followed her out into the craziness that was a pre-show dance room. In one corner of the room, Isabella and Tatiana partner stretched, while Benjamin and Alejandro warmed up their feet. Several other girls worked through the routine moves in unison.

Each of them wore their dance uniforms like they had been made for them. The material wasn't stretched to the hilt like it was on me, and they moved freely as if they weren't uncomfortable in the slightest. I rubbed my hands over my tight costume, wishing it fit like theirs.

Benjamin nodded at me and walked my way. Not only did he dance in the group routine, he was my partner for the couples' dance portion of the competition. Out of everyone at the studio, he was the one I felt most comfortable around.

"How are you feeling?" he asked.

I shrugged, trying to work out the kinks in my neck. "I'll be better when the group dance is over."

He chuckled. "Great attitude, teammate."

I smiled and shook my head. "You know I'm ready." I wanted to tell him about the costume issue, but guys didn't get it. And I hated for anyone to know more about my issues with Galina than necessary. It just made me look weak and took our heads out of the most important game.

Besides, I had a different costume for the couples' dance—one that fit—and I couldn't wait to change into it.

A hush fell over the room, and I looked up to see Galina walking through the door. My shoulders immediately straightened, and I held my chin high. Her steely black eyes scanned every dancer with the precision of a hawk going in for the kill.

"Isabella, you call that a *tendu*?"

Isabella shifted her gaze down and redoubled her efforts.

Galina turned her eyes on Alejandro. "For the love of god, how many times have I told you? Square shoulders."

"Yes, ma'am," he said, correcting his posture.

"Ruby." Galina merely shook her head. "Benjamin. Fix your hair."

He nodded and walked back to a mirror to fix what already looked like a perfect hair style.

Galina stepped to me, her eyes taking me in, from the tight bun atop my head to the even tighter pants. Her eyes met mine again, contempt and disappointment warring with each other.

"I see the diet is not working," she said.

A hand touched my shoulder, and I saw Mom stepping to my side.

"We have a doctor's appointment for her on Monday," Mom said quickly. "We'll find out what has been holding her back."''

Galina gave my mother an even harder stare than the one she had given me before walking away to make the rest of her assessments.

My shoulders eased, and I took a breath. Once she had finished walking the room, she stood by the door and said, "We are set to go on stage in five minutes. Follow me."

We fell into formation, dancers marching likes soldiers behind our merciless leader. But there was a reason we all danced with Galina at Emerson Dance instead of going to another studio in Brentwood or even LA. She was the best—exactly what we all wanted so desperately to be.

The closer we got to the stage, the better we could hear fast-paced dance music. Through gaps in the curtain, I watched beautiful dancers in stunning bejeweled costumes move their bodies in unison. I quickly became transfixed on the dance, on the beauty of the steps. My body hummed with energy, with anticipation for my turn on stage.

"Dancers," Galina said harshly. "For the last five years, we've competed at Dance Dance Nationals. Participated." Her eyes fell on each of us, making my skin feel cold. "No longer am I satisfied with being second, or third or fourth best. This year, we will win, and I will do *whatever it takes* to make sure of it. Do you understand?"

"Yes, ma'am," we all responded.

"Now. Remember your steps. Hold your chins high. Your reputation is on the line, as is mine."

The music on the stage faded to a close as the dancers struck their final pose.

Over the speakers, an eager announcer said, "Now, we welcome to the stage five-time Dance Dance National competitors, Emerson Dance!"

"Go," Galina ordered, although she didn't need to.

We each squared our shoulders and lifted our chins before sashaying to our positions on the stage. The harsh lights hit me, but even so, I could see the people I loved in the audience. My mom, sitting with her husband, Ted, and the rest of the studio parents. Each of my four closest friends sitting in an aisle all their own.

My heart lifted at the sight of them, giving me just what I needed to take a steadying breath as the music fell over us.

We'd practiced the routine so many times that my body took over without needing my mind to follow along. Suddenly, all my worries, the audience, my insecurities about the costume and how it fit faded away.

I moved through the steps, feeling the music just as much as hearing it. The volume rose, and Benjamin took my hand for our across-the-back roll. My back steadied against his, and I cartwheeled my legs through the air, just like Galina taught. But there was one thing I hadn't prepared for: the loud rip as every seam popped in my pants.

My heart froze, and I fell off Benjamin's back, dropping onto the floor in a heap in front of Ruby. She tripped over me and stumbled forward, crashing into Alejandro, who hurtled to the ground with a thud even louder than my own.

Although blood rushed to my eardrums and my cheeks got hot, the music kept playing. My teammates kept dancing.

And me? *I felt a breeze.*

I clenched the back of my split pants together and

ran off the stage as fast as I could. Tears blurred my vision as I sprinted away from the music, away from the stage and toward the safety of the dressing room.

Except it wasn't as safe as I thought.

Only moments after I walked through the door and ripped my shimmering pants the rest of the way off, the door was opening again, my mom and Galina rushing in.

A million Russian swear words were flying through Galina's mouth until she was only inches away from my face, her lips curled back like a dog ready to bite.

"You ruined me, you fat pig!" she hurled, each of her words landing like fists on my face.

"I'm sorry!" I cried, shimmying my sweatpants the rest of the way up. "I promise the couples' routine will be better!" I was scrambling, grasping for anything that would make this moment any less painful than it was. Because right now, it felt like a knife was ripping through my chest.

I'd never had a mistake like that in a routine before. Sure, I might have missed a step or stumbled, but I'd never caught other dancers in the crossfire. Never been *exposed* on stage.

My mom stood behind Galina, frozen, like even

she didn't know how to operate in this new world where something so horrible could happen.

"Couples' routine?" Galina spat. "There will be no couples' routine!"

"What do you mean?" I stammered.

Galina rose to her full height, her shoulders squaring, her mouth set in a snarl. "You will *never* dance with my studio again."

My mom sprang into action then, stepping forward and taking Galina's shoulder. "You can't mean that! It was an honest mistake. If you hadn't insisted on ordering uniforms that didn't fit her—"

"Do not blame me for her lack of willpower! She has had every chance to lose the weight and has chosen not to." Galina's coal-black eyes consumed me with self-loathing. With guilt. "You chose food over your future, and now you will have to live with that for the rest of your life."

My mouth fell open in a silent sob. "Galina, no, you can't do this!"

Mom's voice wavered right along with mine. "Do you have any idea how many hours she's put in? The dieticians we've worked with? We even have a doctor's appointment on Monday! If more money is what it takes, we've got it. What do you need?"

The door opened behind us, and the other

dancers, my former teammates, began walking cautiously into the room.

Galina gave them half a glance before turning all the hatred in her gaze on me. "Leave, Adriel. And don't *ever* darken my studio doors again. Your dancing days are over."

TWO

I HAD REPLAYED the moment so many times in my head that I didn't think anything could make it worse. Not hearing my mom explain through sobs to her husband what had happened. Not the text from Benjamin telling me not to worry about him because he had danced with Tatiana and it went *fine*.

But when my four best friends came over and their phones went wild with notifications, I realized my humiliation was far from over. There was a video on YouTube of my pants ripping, with *thousands of views*...

My eyes were glued to Des's phone as the whole event played over again, but this time from another angle. I watched in horror at the wreckage I'd caused and the way the entire routine had been derailed. Then I read the caption: FAT GIRL RIPS PANTS AT DANCE COMPETITION – HILARIOUSLY RUINS ROUTINE

The comments underneath it were even worse.

"Can you have YouTube delete it?" I asked, desperate.

Des frowned, pouting her berry red lips. "I can report it, but I don't think it's going to do anything."

"Are you sure?" I asked. "They can see my butt! Doesn't that count for nudity?"

Nadira scoffed. "There's way worse on YouTube than part of your butt."

I collapsed back on my bed, covering my face with my arm, and Faith comforted me by patting my shoulder. But it was no use. The amount of views on that video was larger than the entire population of Emerson. No way could I show my face around here again.

"Look at me," Cori said, her dark brown eyes narrowed. "If anyone even thinks about bringing it up at school, Ryker and I have got it covered."

Her boyfriend was a powerful ally, but people at Emerson Academy were sneaky. Even if they didn't say anything about the video outright, it would be there. In the way they looked at me. In the way I would never ever being wearing pants again. I was a skirt-only girl from now on, with multiple layers of spandex underneath. Better yet, put me in a burka for the rest of my life.

I covered my face with a pillow, and Nadira and Faith rubbed my back on either side of me. They were two of the kindest people I knew, but kindness couldn't take away what happened. Couldn't bring me to the national stage to dance in front of the country's top recruiters.

"It'll be alright," Faith said gently.

"It won't be alright," I moaned. I pulled up and looked at her, devastation and humiliation warring with each other. "Every day after school, I go to the studio and dance. From four until nine at night. And on the weekends? Eight to five. It's more than a hobby or a team to me. It's my *life*. I just cost myself everything that matters to me."

"You're wrong," Nadira said on my other side. She had her bushy black hair pulled back with a headband, making her face that much more serious. That much more severe.

"What do you mean?" I asked.

"You didn't cost yourself dance," she replied evenly. "A teacher with bad practices humiliated you in front of an audience. You can still dance, no matter what anyone says."

She was right. I could dance, but I needed more than that. "What's the point in playing a sport if you can't join the team?" Her dad was a basketball coach. She had to understand.

Nadira shook her head and smiled softly. "I think you'll have to figure that out."

A gentle knock sounded on my door, and I looked up to see Mom standing there. Even in her jogging suit, she looked perfectly put together. "Sorry to break up the fun, girls, but it's dinner time for us."

I wished my friends could have stayed for supper, but it was probably best that they left. Spending an awkward dinner with Mom's husband wasn't the most pleasant of things.

Des leaned across the bed and gave me a hug. "We'll see you Monday, and we'll figure this out."

I stood and walked them to the front door. Out of the corner of my eye, I could see Ted leaning against the kitchen island, his laptop open in front of him. I turned away from him and gave each of my friends a hug before they walked down the side-walk to their cars.

With the door shut and locked, I had no excuse

to avoid Mom and Ted any longer. On the nights we were home, Mom made a point of eating together, since dance and my mountains of schoolwork rarely allowed us the option.

I walked to the table and sat in my usual seat. Although, typically instead of eating here, I was trying to catch up on mounds of Academy homework I'd fallen behind on.

Mom brought a big bowl of salad to the table, and I looked at it hatefully. Just as hatefully as the grilled chicken on a platter and bland brown rice I was supposed to stomach with it.

"Am I seriously still dieting?" I asked her. "What's the point?"

She wouldn't meet my eyes. "Don't give up on Galina yet. She has a hot temper, but she's loyal. She wouldn't just dump us like that."

I shook my head, grabbing chicken to put on my plate, although I didn't feel the least bit hungry.

"Maybe it's a good thing," Ted said, taking a seat at the table.

Both Mom and I swiveled our heads toward him at the speed of light. I could practically feel the daggers extracting themselves from my cornea and hurtling toward his head.

Without seeming bothered, he began helping

himself to the food and said, "Adriel's spent her entire life dancing, and you've spent your adult life watching her. Maybe it's about time you both took a break." He added, "Plus, we can finally take our honeymoon, Glenda."

I looked out the corner of my eye to see how Mom was reacting to this nonsense, but she didn't seem as bothered as me. In fact, she didn't seem bothered at all.

"It has been three years since we got married," she said, a small smile growing on her face.

"Wouldn't Mexico be nice?" he asked, reaching for her hand. "You, me, the beach."

I gawked between the two of them. Were they really planning a vacation on the back of today?

Her smile was brighter than the chandelier now. "A couple of margaritas."

Ted nodded. "And Adriel's already eighteen. It's not like she can't spend some time alone."

I glared at them openly now. I *hated* when they talked about me like I wasn't even there. Picking up my plate and drink, I said, "Why don't I start right now?"

THREE

WHEN MOM CAME to my room the next morning, I was still asleep. I couldn't remember a day when I hadn't gotten up at six to do my morning stretches. Not when my parents divorced in the sixth grade. Not when my dad remarried in seventh grade. Not when Mom married Ted in ninth grade. Not when my grandpa died in tenth. Not even when my dad had his replacement child, my half-brother, in eleventh.

But today, I groggily blinked my eyes open to see my mom staring at me in concern. The put-together kind of concern though, with eyebrows furrowed under perfectly curled bangs.

"Are you feeling alright, honey?" she asked.

"No."

She stepped forward and put her hand to my forehead. "You don't feel warm. What hurts?"

"Nothing," I answered honestly. In fact, I felt numb. Everything I had ever cared about had just been stripped from me, so what more was there left to feel?

"Sit up," she demanded, her voice taking on an edge. She pulled back the blanket and repeated, "Sit up!"

"Okay, okay," I replied, begrudgingly getting up. Mom never talked to me like this—the shock was enough to at least get me moving. "What's your deal?"

"My 'deal'?" she asked, tilting her head. "My *deal* is that you are not a quitter. You are going to get up, you're going to get dressed, and we're going to speak with a doctor about what's causing your weight gain."

"And then what?" I asked. "I'll be a slightly thinner dance reject?" I lay back down. "Pass."

Now she pulled the blankets off, leaving me bare in short shorts and a tank top.

"Hey!" I cried.

"No!" She pointed a finger at me. "The day after your father left me for some twenty-six-year-old cliché in heels, I got up and took you to dance. You made me. Do you remember?"

I pulled my knees to my chest, wishing I couldn't remember that day. Mom had been a complete mess, sobbing in her bed, still wearing mascara from the night before. Of course Dad had taken her to some restaurant in the mall to break up with her. Less chance of causing a scene and ruining his precious reputation. No worries about destroying a family.

"Now, I'm doing the same thing for you," she said. "One mean person isn't going to ruin your life. Get up. We're going." She stormed out of the room, bringing the blankets with her, and I watched in awe. How did a woman in lavender capris hold that much emotion?

Still in a state of shock, I got up and put on my Emerson Academy uniform. This was usually the fastest part of my morning routine—one I rushed through after spending as much time as possible on my stretches. But today, I took my time.

After making sure my skirt was securely zipped and my crisp white shirt was free of stains, I went to the bathroom. My box of hair supplies was still open on the counter from the night before. I gently touched my weathered curling iron, wondering when I would be able to use it again. Prom maybe?

But then I realized I had more time this morning—especially since my doctor's appointment wasn't until half past eight. Instead of my usual bun, I began winding sections of my hair around the barrel, forming loose curls that twirled midway down my back. I wound my fingers through my hair to pull the excess hairs that always shed when I put my hair into more than a bun and did a quick-once over with hairspray.

Although my hair looked beautiful compared to my typical tight bun, my eyes looked hollow. No amount of eyeliner or mascara or under-eye concealer hid the loss I'd experienced.

"Adriel!" Mom yelled down the hall. "It's time to go!"

A tear threatened to slip down my cheek, but I blinked quickly and unplugged my curling iron. It was time to face my life without dance.

I slipped on my sensible heels and walked out of my room. Mom took me in approvingly. "Good," she said. "Look good, feel good."

I wanted to ask if it had worked for her after the divorce, but I wasn't sure I wanted to know the answer.

We left through the side door and went to the garage, where her wedding gift from Ted, a pearlescent Mercedes, waited for us. It beeped twice and the lights flashed as she unlocked it—though why she kept it locked in our own garage, I had no idea.

I walked around to the passenger side and got in, then put in my earbuds as she pulled out of the driveway. Contemporary French music filled my ears, drowning out the sounds around me to something I preferred. Something lighthearted, fast-paced, and...happy. Something so at odds with how I felt inside.

Within thirty minutes, we'd picked up a protein smoothie (aka liquified cardboard) for my breakfast and were checked in at RWE Medical for my appointment with Dr. Edmonson. A girl named Chloe with Winnie the Pooh scrubs walked us back and weighed me.

Mom and I both stared at the scale. I'd gone up five pounds from my last weigh-in.

"Can you check again?" Mom asked.

"Sure thing," Chloe said happily, letting me step off and back on. She carefully ticked over the scales until it leveled on the same weight.

As I got off, I felt Mom's eyes hot on my head. "Have you been sneaking food at school?"

"No!" I cried. "I only eat that garbage Ted's chef packs for me."

"And you don't get any snacks from your friends?" Mom demanded. "I've seen them, and they're nice, but they're not the fittest—"

I gave her a stare that could melt glass. "Don't even go there."

Chloe looked between us like she was completely lost. "Let's go into the room instead!" She walked ahead of us, her ponytail swinging, to room seven. "Dr. Edmonson should be in shortly." As quick as humanly possible, she left us there. Alone.

"Five pounds?" Mom breathed.

"Apparently just enough to split the ass of my pants," I said sourly.

"Honey, I didn't mean—"

"You never do!" I cried. "It's always all about dance or Ted. Can't you be my mom for one second instead of my handler or Ted's wife?"

"Adriel—"

A knock sounded on the door, and an old, balding man walked in. Great, just who I needed to talk to about women's health.

"Ms. Pruitt," he said to me, then turned to my mom. "Mrs. Pruitt."

"Anders," Mom corrected him. "Mrs. Anders."

"Ah," he said, glancing at the papers on his clipboard. "Need to get these reading glasses checked." He chuckled. "Now, I understand we're here to talk about Adriel and her weight?"

"Yes," Mom said before I could even jump in, which was probably best. "She's an active dancer, has been on a dietician-approved diet, and for some reason, she can't seem to lose the weight."

"Hmm." He tapped his chin. "I've seen this in a few girls your age, Adriel. Let me ask you a few questions."

He worked through a mental list, including everything from my haircare routine to my acne and menstrual cycles. "And what about your depression medication?" he asked. "Does it still seem to be helping?"

I nodded. After my parents divorced, focusing on the good things in my life got harder and harder. When I wasn't dancing, I was spiraling. Galina was actually the one who convinced my mom to put me on medication. She said my dancing lacked its typical *joie de vivre*. Little did she care that my family had just been ripped apart.

"It could be a couple of things," he said, "but I don't want to give you any false fear—or hope—

until I run some panels on you. In the meantime, I know you dance, but have you tried any strength training?"

"You want her to lift weights?" Mom asked.

He nodded, going to a wall full of brochures. "Weight training often helps women burn calories more efficiently and can strengthen their bone density. Very important for dancers." He pulled a copied flyer from a manila envelope and handed it to me. "Why don't you try some of these at your school gym? If you find yourself gaining weight or bulking up after a few weeks, you could always stop. No harm no foul."

I glanced up from the handout to see the wheels in my mother's head spinning. We weren't even out of RWE Medical before she said, "I'm getting you in at Ted's Gym tonight after school."

FOUR

THE GOOD PART about having a morning doctor's appointment was missing the walk into school. It would have been like swimming in a school of fish, moving past sharks and hoping someone else would get eaten.

Mom pulled along the curb, reached into her purse for Dr. Edmonson's note, and handed it to me. "Be sure to bring this to the office."

"Sure." I unbuckled my belt and bent for my bag, but she put her hand on my arm.

"It's going to be okay, sweetie. We'll get you lifting in the gym, and you'll be back on the team in no time. You'll see."

Her words unsettled me in various ways, but

instead of targeting in on one, I said, "What about your honeymoon?"

She smiled at me, missing the venom behind the words. "Cabo isn't going anywhere, but you, my darling, are."

My heart softened—if only slightly—before I got out of the car and walked across the empty courtyard to Emerson Academy. A broad swath of stone steps led up to the brick building with our school's motto embossed into the stone.

Ad Meliora.

Toward better things.

The words had always left me with a sense of purpose before. Like I was a part of something bigger than myself. Even if I wasn't the best student, I had a goal, a mission. Now... I just felt lost.

I walked to the main office, handed them my doctor's note, and waited for a late pass to chemistry. I wished the woman would hurry up because missing Mr. Cho's class was not ideal.

When she finally handed me the slip, I hurried down the empty hall to Mr. Cho's room and walked inside. As I opened the wooden door, every eye turned from the whiteboard to me.

Mr. Cho said, "Late slip goes on my desk. You go with Mr. McCormac."

My lips parted as I looked from my teacher to the guy sitting by himself in the third row.

"Quickly," Mr. Cho said, snapping his fingers. "We have a lot to get through before we start experiments tomorrow." He was already looking back at the board.

I marched to his desk, leaving the paper slip in the middle where it was sure not to get lost or misplaced. Then I took a deep breath and turned toward my class. Toward Carter.

His golden eyes met mine, and my heart skittered around my chest, forgetting how to beat. Then his full lips quirked into a soft smile, and my brain went AWOL too.

As a dancer, I was aware of my body in ways most people weren't. I didn't trip or stumble. I didn't slouch. But as I made my way toward him, I felt clunky. Out of place.

Since when had simply walking become such a challenge?

After what felt like a decade of putting one forgetful foot in front of the other, I reached the table.

As Mr. Cho continued his lecture at the whiteboard, Carter leaned closer and whispered, "Don't worry, you haven't missed too much."

Worry? How could I worry with his beautiful face that close to mine?

This was exactly the reason why I sat in the front row for most of my classes—less distractions. The more focused I stayed, the faster I could get my homework done and focus on what really mattered: dance.

Just the thought had my chest aching again.

"Can I borrow your notes tonight?" I asked. "To copy them down?"

"I'll send you a picture after school... here." He passed his notebook toward me. "Write your number?"

My hands shook as I took his mechanical pencil. Had Carter McCormac, acclaimed bodybuilder and complete hottie, just asked for my number? I carefully wrote down each digit, not wanting him to accidently message the wrong person, all while fervently reminding myself that this was just for school.

For so long, I'd avoided relationships because I'd seen how dating had hurt my dance mates' perfor-mances. My mantra had been that love could wait until after I was where I wanted to be. But now that dance was over...

I handed his pencil back and reached for my own notebook in my backpack. For the rest of the hour, I tried not to look at the beautiful guy beside me and instead focus on electrons and protons and whatever inscrutable things Mr. Cho was writing on the board. The hour dragged on until the bell finally rang, and I began packing up my things.

"I guess I'll be seeing you tomorrow," Carter said. Judging by his smile and the tone in his voice, he wasn't upset about it either.

I tried not to be giddy. "Same time, same place."

He nodded and began walking away, but then he turned back and said, "By the way, I like your hair." His eyes lingered on my face for a moment. "It's different."

While fighting a blush, I said, "Thank you," and resolved to wear it down every day for the rest of my life.

Ryker's threats must have worked—whatever they were—because I didn't hear more than whispers about me in the halls between classes. Still, when lunchtime came, I kept my head down and walked straight to the table where my four best friends sat. I couldn't believe it had only been a few months since our guidance counselor, Mrs. Bardot, had the brilliant yet hare-brained idea to get all the plus-sized senior girls together. What I'd thought was an embarrassing support group had quickly become some of my best friends.

Des looked up at me, her red lips pulling into a knowing smirk. "What happened to make you so smiley?"

I shook my head. How was I smiling after what had happened just two days ago? "It's nothing, just, do you guys know Carter McCormac?"

Cori's eyes widened. "The body builder? He is so—" Her boyfriend, Ryker, shot her a look, and she finished, "not nearly as attractive as my totally insecure boyfriend."

Ryker chuckled at the jab, but Nadira said, "Boy is *fine*."

"Fine?" Faith giggled. "I don't think I've ever heard you use that word before."

"Me neither," I said, "But I agree."

"Carter McCormac calls for it," Nadira said. "Not sorry."

"Mhmm." Des nodded, taking a sip of her Diet Coke. "What about him, A?"

"He asked for my number this morning!" I

practically squealed. "Just to send me notes for class, but I've never had a guy ask for my number before."

Ryker raised his eyebrows. "Seriously?"

I rolled my eyes. "No one was exactly lining up for my contact info before I made a humiliation of myself at the showcase. And now..." I gestured at the boys the next table over who were staring at me and their phones.

Des giggled. "Maybe they just needed a little show."

"Stop!" I hit her shoulder, my cheeks even redder than before. "Don't make me laugh. I'm supposed to be sad."

"Oh, right," Des said, hunching her shoulders. "Just think of Jude Santiago. That'll bring you right back down."

"What about him?" I asked. He was one of the hottest new singers coming onto the social media music scene. In both looks and popularity. If anything, that would bring up my mood.

Des sighed. "Maybe the fact that he's completely gorgeous and completely out of my reach?"

On Des's other side, Faith patted her arm, but I just shook my head. "Speaking of things that are out of reach…my mom wants me to start weightlifting."

Ryker leaned forward, as if excited there was finally a topic he could chime in on. "That could be good. I keep trying to talk Cori into getting in the weight room."

"Why?" Nadira asked, like weights were a dirty word. "So she can get MRSA from the dumbbells?"

"Lots of reasons." Ryker shrugged. "Gaining strength could help with rebounding, defense, everything."

Cori bobbled her head along with his words. "And I keep telling him that he should come lift cans with Knox and me at my dad's store and see if he thinks I need *another* workout."

I giggled and shook my head. "Well, wish me luck. Mom's taking me to Ted's Gym after school."

"Your stepdad's mega-gym?" Faith cringed. "I'd hate to work out in front of anyone."

"I've already split my pants in front of hundreds of people," I said, pushing my lettuce around. "How much worse could it get?"

FIVE

WORSE. Way worse. That was the answer.

Raf, the personal trainer my mom hired for me, led me from the front desk to the powerlifting area, where we turned the corner to see Carter lifting at a weights station, wearing only shorts, a cut off T-shirt, and Chuck Taylors.

Why was my mouth watering?

Oh yeah, because I was a complete weirdo. A complete weirdo who was about to be embarrassed in front of the only guy in school who bothered to talk to me—aside from my teachers.

Raf gave me a strange look out of the corner of his eye. "Are you okay?" he asked, continuing around the corner.

"Are you sure we can't focus on some cardio first? Maybe the elliptical?" I knew I couldn't mess that one up.

"Nope," he said simply, walking toward the station right next to Carter's. "I'm under strict orders from Ted to teach you Olympic lifting. Sorry, but he kind of writes my paycheck."

I glared toward the ceiling. "Let's get this over with." Sometimes I really wished my mom hadn't married someone who owned multiple gyms across the country.

Movement caught my eye as Carter lifted a weight bar loaded with colorful plates from the ground. His muscles bulged as he swung it to his chest and squatted low. He stood steadily until his legs were straight and dropped the bar to the ground.

We were only feet away now, and panic rose in my chest. Was I going to talk to him? I had to, right? It would be awkward not to say anything at all.

I opened my mouth to say hello at the same time Raf said, "Nice lift, man. Remember to keep your chin up."

Carter nodded, then his eyes landed on me.

They narrowed a bit, as if he were confused. Taking note, Raf jerked his thumb toward me. "Ted's stepdaughter's taking some Olympic lifting lessons."

A grin spread on Carter's face. "Is that so?"

Raf nodded, which was good since I was completely disarmed. If not by Carter's smile by the bulging muscles on his bare arms and the confident way he carried himself in the gym.

"Carter here is one of the best lifters at the gym," Raf said. "How many comps have you won now?"

"I don't keep track," Carter said, turning his gaze away from us. Was he...shy? It was so adorable, my heart almost burst.

"Modest." Raf clapped his back. "Any tips for the new girl?"

Carter took me in, his eyes trailing from mine down to the brand-new gym shoes Mom insisted I wear. When his honey eyes met mine again, I almost shivered.

"Form is everything," he said, his warm voice just as sweet as his gaze.

I swallowed, trying to make sure my voice wouldn't crack. "I'll keep that in mind."

While Carter resumed lifting, Raf led me to the closest weight rack and showed me what each item was called and how much each color of plate weighed. He started me with a forty-five-pound bar doing different types of squats.

"Watch yourself in the mirror," Raf said. "Make sure your knees stay even with your toes and don't slope inward."

I nodded and looked in the mirror, catching Carter's gaze instead. I quickly averted my eyes, focusing instead on the task at hand. I'd thought dancing was a hard workout, but after an hour of learning lifts and trying repetitions at different weights, my arms and legs felt like jello, and my skin slicked with a thin sheen of sweat.

Part of me wanted to take off my tank and just finish the workout in a sports bra like I would at the dance studio, but with Carter so close, I didn't exactly feel like putting my stomach on display. It was the largest part of me, marred with purple stretch marks and thick cellulite. And next to his chiseled form? I would just look worse. He'd erase my number before he even had a chance to send me the notes.

When my time was up, Raf said, "I'll go get a

rag and spray bottle." I nodded, making a mental note to tell Nadira we were sanitizing, and sat on the floor to stretch. If I'd learned anything, it was to never forget stretching after a workout.

"That was good," Carter said.

I glanced over to see him sitting against a wall with a towel around his neck, holding a water bottle.

"Thanks," I said. For a moment, quiet hung between us, and I asked, "How long have you been weightlifting for?"

Carter shrugged. "Ever since I told my grandma I didn't want to play football." He chuckled. "She said I needed to do something with my body instead of living in my head all the time, so she signed me up for a gym membership."

I chuckled. "Sounds like a good grandma."

"She is," he agreed. "I didn't think so at the time, though. Pretty much sat in the lobby and worked on homework until Raf came by and offered me a free session." He shrugged. "Once I started lifting, I was hooked."

Although Carter and I had gone to the same school for as long as I could remember, I couldn't recall a time when he hadn't been strong. When his muscles weren't apparent, even through an Academy blazer.

"What do you think of it?" he asked. "Weightlifting?"

I shrugged. "It's different. No rhythm to keep pace with. No dancers to work around. Just the same repetitive movements. I guess it's kind of like barre work, but with weights." I immediately regretted bringing up dancing. If Carter hadn't seen the video yet, he surely would soon.

Blind to my turmoil, he chuckled, dropping his head and then looking back up at me just in time for Raf to get back and hand me the rag and spray bottle. Had Carter been about to say something more?

I tried not to focus on it too much as I wiped down the bars and plates Raf and I had used during our session. When we had it all clean and put away, Raf gave me a high five and said, "See you tomorrow, same time."

"Tomorrow?" I asked.

He nodded. "Ted booked you a slot, Monday through Friday, for the rest of the month. But I better meet my next client."

I gaped at Raf as he walked away. An entire month?

But then again, what else did I have to do? It wasn't like I was dancing anymore.

Carter lifted his chin. "Looks like I'll be seeing you around, Addy."

I smiled at him as he walked away, realizing I was actually looking forward to coming back.

SIX

THE NEXT MORNING, I got up and showered, but the drain must have been clogged because I ended up standing in two inches of water. As I got out and wrapped myself in a bath towel, I yelled, "Mom!"

She came to my room, wearing a billowy white shirt, pink capris and camel leather booties. How was she always more fashionable than me? Oh yeah, probably because I lived in leggings or my school uniform.

"What's going on?" she asked.

I shook my head, remembering the unpleasant feeling of my feet soaking in my own dirty water. "I think the drain's plugged. Can you call a plumber?"

"You know," she said, "Ted can handle that sort

of thing." She winked. "One of the perks of having a man around the house."

"Ugh," I said out loud, even though I meant to only think it. That kind of dependent thinking was what got her in such a mess with my dad in the first place. Not mutual love and respect. If Dad would have had that, he never would have cheated on her then left her to raise a child by herself. I still remembered moving to an apartment while he and his new wife took the house I used to call home. I wouldn't wish that torture on anyone.

Mom gave me a look and then said, "I'll drive you to school this morning and to the gym, but you'll have to ride home with Ted."

An entire car ride with Ted? By myself? There had to be a way to get out of this. "Doesn't he get off at six?"

"Six thirty," she said. "But there's internet there. Maybe you can get some homework in while you wait."

I frowned. "Great."

As if she hadn't heard me, she turned and left my room. I took my time getting ready, blow-drying my hair and pulling out the loose strands that hadn't come out in the shower. Then I wrapped the curling iron around the strands, remembering the sweet way Carter's lips lifted as he told me it looked nice.

God, I was pathetic.

I promised myself I was looking nice for me, for a change of pace, as I finished getting ready.

On the car ride to the parking lot, I asked, "Do you know when my car will be done at the shop?" Mom—or her husband, really—had gotten me a new car last year. A brand-new car, one that practically screamed *I'm trying to buy your love because your mom wants me to*. But it had been at the dealership for a few days getting a tune-up.

"Just a couple more days, I think," she said. "But it will be good for you to spend some time with Ted. He wants to take you out to dinner."

I froze, my hands clenched in my lap. "The three of us?"

"Just you two," Mom said. "I have a date with Janet, so I thought this could be a great chance for the two of you to bond."

"Great," I said flatly, looking out my window. The school building was approaching, and we couldn't get there soon enough. As she pulled along the curb to drop me off, she said, "He's making an effort. Please, just, be easy on him?"

I got out of the car, dragging my bag along with

me. "As if he's the one who needs protecting." I shut the door and walked toward the school.

Ted never had children, and he had no idea how to talk to young women. At all. His conversations always focused on sports teams I couldn't care less about, new research around health and fitness, and, of course, vacations. He wanted to take my mom to see the world, and I was happy for her—I was—but being constantly reminded that I was the reason she couldn't travel didn't feel the best.

As I reached the steps, I heard a squeal behind me. "Adriel!" Cori yelled.

I turned to see her pulling her boyfriend along behind her, her hand firmly in his.

"Hey, you two!" I said, thankful for the distraction. "How's it going?"

"Good," Cori said easily. "You look hot. I'm loving your hair this way."

I shrugged, readjusting my backpack. "Having time in the morning makes a difference."

"I hear you," she said. "I can't believe basketball is starting in a week!" She leaned her head against Ryker's shoulder before we all started up the stairs. "I'm going to miss seeing him, though."

Ryker laughed. "Sure you are." He spoke to me.

"She's been going crazy without basketball, and she knows it."

"Not as crazy as you've been without football," she pointed out.

"Yeah?" I asked.

Again, Ryker shrugged. As we crested the stairs, one of Cori's basketball teammates called her aside, and Ryker and I stood together.

"How do you manage?" I asked, suddenly desperate for an answer.

His gray eyes studied me. "Manage what?"

"Not playing." I'd seen him at enough games to know he loved football like I loved dance. But every year, the football team had an off season, where they didn't play at all. I'd never experienced that. Until now.

Ryker dipped his head for a moment, rubbing his hand over his mouth. "Are you doing okay, with...everything?"

Tears stung my eyes, and I blinked them away. "If I was doing okay, do you think I'd be asking?"

He chuckled sadly. "I guess not."

I waited for his answer, holding on to hope that he might have some secret I didn't know. Finally, he looked at me and said, "I guess the thing that's always helped is knowing that eventually, I'll have the chance to play again."

"But I can't," I said.

He raised his eyebrows and looked me over.

"What?" I asked, feeling naked under his scrutiny.

"I'm looking for some kind of injury that makes you incapable of hearing music or moving your body. I'm not seeing one."

My eyebrows drew together. "It's not that simple."

"Isn't it?"

"No," I said, becoming angrier by the second. "I had a partner, a team, a teacher, a studio to go to, and now... nothing. How could you even—"

Cori came up to us, her smile quickly fading. "What's going on?"

"Nothing," I said and walked away. It was the truth.

SEVEN

I WAITED on a bench out front for Mom after school. Countless students poured from the building, going to their cars in the parking lot, catching rides with their friends. And here I was, getting ready for another day at a gym where I didn't belong to fix the weight that wouldn't stop coming.

Someone sat beside me, and I glanced over to see Cori.

She smiled softly at me and put her arms around my shoulders.

I leaned into her hug, then sat back up.

"I'm sorry," I said. "About earlier."

"Sorry about Ryker," she replied. "He can be a little rough around the edges."

"Compared to how he used to be?" I said. "He

was a dream this morning. It wasn't his fault—he just said something I didn't want to hear."

She nodded, sitting back up. "So, everything's okay?"

"As okay as it can be without dance," I said with a smile that fell flat.

"We'll get through this," she said, rubbing my shoulder. "Why don't you and the girls come over Friday after the basketball game? We'll have a movie night and..." She gave me a slow smile. "Celebrate me signing with a college team."

My mouth fell open. For a moment, all my distress was forgotten as I took in Cori's eager smile and what her words meant. "What! You already decided where you're going?"

She nodded eagerly.

"Where?" I asked.

A car pulled along the curb, and Mom said through the open window, "Hi, Cori!"

Cori waved back and whispered, "Guess you'll just have to wait and see."

I glared at her as I walked to the car. "I hate you," I called.

"Love you too." She grinned and turned away.

As I got into the car, Mom said, "What was that all about?"

"Cori figuring out her life," I said. "She's deciding which college to play for."

"How wonderful!" Mom said, then paused as she waited for me to put on my seat belt. "And what about you?"

"What about me?" I asked, getting my cell phone from my front backpack pocket.

"Have you given any colleges some thought?"

I closed my eyes, trying to focus on the smooth feeling of my phone screen underneath my thumbs. Of the small crack in the corner where I'd dropped it. "Already, Mom?"

"It's November," she said and rattled off a list of deadlines for Ivy League and state colleges I had no interest in attending. Dance had always been Plan A. There'd been no backups. At least, not for me. My mom, on the other hand...

"How did you find out all that?" I asked.

"I can work a laptop," she reminded me. "And you need to, as well. That was the deal. You'd apply to *at least* five colleges for Plan B. You can even apply to major in dance. Janice's son barely got into two colleges last year for theater, and he applied for ten!"

"Well, Janice's son is also an idiot," I muttered.

"Don't say that," Mom said. But she didn't

disagree.

We were quiet for a moment, and I got out my phone to check my messages. I hadn't heard from anyone at the studio except Benjamin, but even he hadn't sent me a text today.

My fingers hovered over the keyboard, trying to decide what to send him. I didn't want to be forgotten, but at the same time, maybe I didn't want to be remembered either. Not for how I'd embarrassed everyone.

I closed the screen as a new message came in. A photo of yesterday's chemistry notes and a message from Carter saying he'd see me at the gym.

"You're smiling big," Mom said.

And you better believe I wasn't smiling after that. "No, I'm not."

"Is a boy texting you?"

"God, Mom." I trained my eyes toward the ceiling, surprisingly wishing I could be at the gym.

"It's good you're talking to boys!" she said, as if I were worried about her chastising me. "You've been so focused on dance. Maybe you should live a little, date around, enjoy what's left of your senior year."

I gave her a look. "Dance *was* how I enjoyed myself."

"Past tense," she said, turning on her signal.

"Until you get me back in with Galina, right?" A small spark of hope that didn't want to be buried shined in my chest.

"Maybe... maybe it would be good to find something new." She parked in a space close to the gym reserved for staff.

"What do you mean?" I asked. "What happened to me lifting weights and slimming down and getting back in at the studio?"

She leaned her forehead against the steering wheel and let out a heavy sigh that shot straight through my chest. When she met my eyes, I already knew what she was going to say before she spoke the words.

"Honey," she said gently. "I went to the studio today. Galina isn't changing her mind."

Even though I'd known it was a long shot, my eyes still burned.

"Oh, honey, I'm so sorry." Mom reached for a hug, but I reached for the handle.

"I'm fine," I said. "Fine." I grabbed the gym bag she'd packed for me and walked inside. Through the open window, she called, "Remember, you're eating supper with Ted!"

Great. Just great.

EIGHT

FOCUSING on the lifts instead of the cute, ripped guy next to me was easier than ever. Why bother when there was no way he could possibly be into me? I was an overweight, disgraced dancer with thinning hair and a bad attitude.

When the hour of lifting was done, Raf gave me a high five and said, "Great focus, Pruitt."

I slapped his hand and went for my water bottle. As I took a swig, I noticed Carter watching me from the corner of his eye. What did he see when he looked at me? I wondered.

But I shut that thought down. I probably didn't want to know.

After Raf and I wiped down the equipment, I grabbed my bag and went to the locker room to change back into my school uniform. Knowing Ted, he'd probably take me somewhere ridiculously fancy that I'd probably need an app just to know what to do with all the silverware.

I think that was one of the things Mom liked about him. He spoiled her, treated her how Dad treated his mistress.

I finished freshening up my hair and left the locker room to wander around the gym. The clock on my phone told me I still had another half hour until he'd be ready to leave. Maybe Carter was on to something with using the Wi-Fi here to work on homework.

But each of the tables in the lobby area were filled with couples drinking liquid cardboard smoothies from the drink bar, so I kept walking. This place was huge. There had to be somewhere for me.

I walked past the rows of ellipticals, treadmills, and stair climbers to the open gyms. On one court, middle-aged men played basketball, sweat darkening the backs of their shirts. In another gym, a game of club volleyball had players sprinting about the court in an intense game of "don't let the balloon touch the floor."

I pushed forward, noticing the lights off in one

of the racquetball courts. Opening the door, I decided I could hang out in here until someone decided to play. At least I'd get a few minutes of peace and quiet.

My footsteps echoed off the floor, and I realized it may be too quiet.

I slipped off my heels and set my backpack on the ground. I got out my phone, switching to my favorite playlist of French pop music, then set it down too and rolled out my neck. That workout had been hard, just as difficult as any of my dance practices.

I worked through my shoulders and hips, and slowly the stretching transformed to dancing. I closed my eyes and moved with the beat, letting the rhythm take me wherever it wanted. My body moved me across the floor in a way that felt like coming home.

My mind registered the lyrics I understood, but my body registered the beat. Each passing second saw my breathing grow heavy and sweat bead on my forehead. I pushed myself harder, my emotions bubbling under the surface, my pain building in my throat, in my eyes.

As the song drew to a close, my body slowed, and my dancing became more lyrical. More heartfelt. I lowered to the ground, until finally my body stilled in a heavily breathing heap.

The opening chords of the next song played, blending with slow clapping.

I jerked upright to see who was there and found Carter dropping his gym bag on the floor. My cheeks immediately heated, but he stuck his hand out.

I slipped my hand in his and let him help me up, not quite meeting his eyes.

"Don't be embarrassed. That was incredible, Addy." His voice told me he believed it, but I couldn't get over the fact that he'd just seen me dance.

"I didn't have a routine," I said. "That was just..."

"Amazing?" he finished.

"Spontaneous." I rubbed my arm, not sure what to say. I settled on, "Thanks."

He smiled. "You're welcome. And I'm sorry. I was just walking by and I saw..." He smiled abashedly. "I should have given you more privacy."

"It's okay," I found myself saying. "It felt good, you know, just to dance."

"Yeah? What's your plan next? Are you finding another studio?"

Not meeting his eyes, I walked back to my heels and slipped them on, still leaving me a few inches shorter than him. "I don't think so."

"Why not? You're not just…stopping…are you?"

I shook my head, sliding down against the wall. Following suit, he sat beside me.

"I don't know," I said. "My mom's been pressuring me to apply for colleges and Emerson Dance isn't taking me back, and there's no way I can swing an hour commute to LA and stay in school, so I don't have a lot of options."

He frowned. "In weightlifting competitions, we have something called open class, where anyone can register to compete. Can't you just compete on your own?"

"If I qualified, yeah, but there's only a couple of qualifiers left that I could actually get to. And I can't compete as a solo dancer."

"Why not?" he asked. "That was amazing."

I softly snorted. "It was okay, but other girls are incredible. I've been a partner dancer all throughout high school."

"So, you just need a partner?" he asked.

I laughed out loud, reaching for my backpack.

"What?"

"'Just' a partner?" I said. "You make it sound so easy. Ben and I had to dance for months together before we even had enough chemistry to be competitive. Of course, it didn't help that he was gay. A lot of partners end up falling in love with each other because it's *that* intimate. And I don't know if you've noticed, but there's not exactly anyone lining up to dance with me." I gestured at the empty racquetball court with scuffs on the floor and smudges on the wall.

He chewed on his cheek for a moment, and then his lips spread into a smile as he turned and looked at me with dark golden eyes. "I wouldn't be so sure about that."

I almost asked him what he meant, but he hitched his bag over his shoulder and said, "See you at school, Addy."

The door had already closed when I managed to echo, "See you at school."

NINE

AROUND HALF PAST SIX, I walked to Ted's office, thinking about Carter the entire way. His smile and stunning eyes were way more appealing of a subject than the impending hour (or more) of "quality" time with my mom's husband.

He had the kind of office that was entirely glass walls, so I could see him pacing the floor with his sleeves rolled up and his cell phone to his ear. Ted was a hard worker, and it was one of the things Mom loved about him. He wouldn't feel neglected while she was at the studio with me.

I couldn't help but wonder what would happen to Mom and Ted when I was gone. The plan had always been for me to dance in New York. Never for Mom to come with me.

Ted caught sight of me through the glass and held up a finger. That could mean one minute or ten. So, I sat on a purple bench along the wall and reached into my backpack for *The Abolition of Man* by CS Lewis. I'd barely finished a page when Ted came out and said, "Ready to go?"

"Sure." I put the book back into my backpack. He offered to carry it, but I declined.

"Where do you want to eat?" he asked, undeterred. "I was thinking Halfway Café or La Belle?"

And there were the fancy options. "Halfway Café," I said. At least I wouldn't feel so out of place there. A lot of Emerson Academy students hung out there or even wealthier college students.

We walked to his car at the far back of the parking lot. He said he liked the extra exercise, and he felt like it was the boss's job to put himself last. All noble characteristics, until you walked alongside a girl in heels with a twenty-pound backpack...who had just turned down help carrying it.

Ted unlocked the car, and I got in. Even though he had it detailed regularly, it always smelled a little like the gym. Not that I was a stranger to the smell of day-old sweat. Mom and I had been dealing with it for years.

The radio fired up along with his car, playing the top forty, just like it did all the time.

"How was school?" he asked as we pulled out of the lot.

"Good," I answered.

"And how are you friends doing?"

"Good," I said again.

He tried to hide his sigh by looking out the window, but I caught it. The problem was, I wasn't trying to be a jerk. I just didn't have anything in common with him, and I had another hour to look forward to.

"How was work?" I asked, knowing it would get him going.

He launched into a story about someone who had been stealing one kettlebell at a time from the gym until they realized more than twenty were missing. Even though all the staff had been asked to keep an eye out for the kettlebell bandit, no one had seen the guy—or girl—who had stolen more than five hundred pounds in weights.

"How do they get out the door with them?" I asked.

Ted shrugged. "Gym bags. We're thinking of installing a metal detector."

"That seems a little excessive. Wouldn't you notice someone walking funny with a heavy gym bag?"

"Apparently not," he said with a sigh. "So, if you see anyone suspicious..."

"I'll let you know," I replied with a smile, thinking how ridiculous Carter would think this whole debacle was.

My eyes widened as I realized I wanted to tell Carter about it before my friends. What was going on with me? Had the world just turned upside down? Odds were yes, considering Ted and I were going out to dinner by ourselves.

He pulled into an angled spot in front of Halfway Café and got out of the car. I followed suit, walking behind him to the glass door. All the walls in the café were windows, so we had a clear view of people inside.

Ted leaned over and whispered, "Is that Ryde Alexander?"

I followed his gaze to the pair of guys sitting in a corner, drinking from the oversized café mugs. "It is!" I said excitedly. "And his boyfriend."

"Boyfriend? When did that happen?" he asked.

I immediately launched into the story of how

Ryde and his friend Ambrose came out in front of everyone at Ryde's latest movie premier. I'd been watching the red-carpet fashion commentary on TV when they kissed each other with cameras flashing all around.

We moved forward in the line as I spoke until we reached the front and had to order.

"That's brave of them," Ted said, walking toward the dining area.

I nodded. "Especially being in the public like that. It's not like they just had to deal with their families—they have the whole world to worry about."

Ted agreed, sitting back in the modular chairs that were more stylish than comfortable. "Speaking of being in the public eye... how are you doing?"

My stomach bottomed out as I remembered the dance, crashing into my teammates, and the YouTube video my friends had shown me afterward. "I'm alright."

"No one's said anything at school?" he asked.

"I haven't really been around the people who would." Isabella and Tatiana to be specific. They both danced with the studio and were some of the more popular girls in school. Steering clear of them had worked wonders. "Plus, one of my friend's boyfriend is kind of like a god at the Academy. I'm pretty sure he'd put out a hit on anyone who brought it up."

Ted chuckled. "I'll have to start calling you Garth with all your friends in low places. Now if I could just get the word out about the kettlebell thief…"

I laughed too. Between Ryker and Cori, they'd have caught the bandit and made them carry all the weights back into the gym before sunset. They were an unstoppable couple, and I couldn't wait to see what Cori's decision would be for college. If they would get to go together.

"What about you?" he asked. "Have you been seeing anyone?"

I nearly choked on my own spit. Not because it was a ridiculous question, but because an image of Carter McCormac's smile immediately filled my mind. "With what time?" I reminded him, and myself.

"You have time now," he said easily.

Before I could argue, a waitress in a slinky dress brought out two smoothies and bowls brimming with artfully crafted salads.

I began eating, realizing how starving I was after lifting weights the last couple of days, and glanced around the room. Ryde and Ambrose were standing up, and I was about to ask for their autographs, until I saw the family sitting behind their table.

My eyes landed on my dad and a woman only a handful of years older than me. And then their two-year-old child. My half-brother they never bothered for me to know.

Ted followed my gaze and started coughing, realizing who it was. Dad's sharp brown eyes snapped toward me, and I wanted to duck under the table, to hide, but there was no point. Not with him standing up and pushing his chair in. Not with him walking toward Ted and me.

"Hi, kiddo," Dad said with a grin.

"It's Adriel." My hands shook, and I put them in my lap.

"Of course." Dad gestured at an open chair nearby. "Mind if I?"

"Of course not," Ted said, at the same time I said, "Yes, I mind."

Ignoring me, Dad sat down, readjusting his tie. "How's dance going?"

I narrowed my eyes at him. "Is that a joke?"

Dad looked between Ted and me, clearly lost. What little food had hit my stomach quickly soured. My own father didn't know about the worst, most embarrassing day of my life?

It wasn't like he bothered to call and check in—or do more than write a monthly check, but the blow hurt nonetheless. Not only did my chest ache from the loss of dance, it hurt all over again from the loss of my dad.

From across the room, his two-year-old, Toby, escaped his mother's grasp and came sprinting over. "Daddy! Daddy! Who's this?"

Dad chuckled uncomfortably. "Beau, baby, it's your big sister. Remember Adriel?"

I stared at my blond-haired, blue-eyed replacement in horror as he shook his little head. "Nope. Can I have a cake pop, Daddy?"

"Oh my god," I whispered. My own brother didn't even remember my name. Without waiting for Ted or my dad, I moved. I walked away from the table and away from the man who'd first walked away from me.

The second I hit the sidewalk outside, footsteps came after me. Maybe part of me had been hoping for my dad, because when I heard Ted's voice, my eyes began to sting.

"Adriel," Ted called. "Wait!"

"No." I shook my head, continuing toward the car. "I don't want him to see me cry."

In his first fatherly move, Ted simply nodded, led me to the car, and drove us away.

TEN

THE NEXT DAY I was more thankful than ever for our "Curvy Girl Club." At the beginning of the year, our guidance counselor, Mrs. Bardot, set up a weekly support group where five of us ate a catered lunch in the AV room ever Thursday.

Today's menu was Mexican food from *Viva Los Gordos*.

Which was kind of offensive if you thought about it, but I wasn't offended at all. I was too busy staring at the greasy, salty tortilla chips and the Styrofoam bowl of chunky salsa. I swore I could hear it whispering, *Adriel, eat me. Just one bite. Tomatoes are vegetables, after all.*

That food was making way too good of a case. I tried to focus on the taco salad in front of me. A little bit of a splurge, even with a gluten-free tortilla bowl and fat-free sour cream. I was jealous of the way my friends could eat with abandon, without hearing the mean words that always echoed in the back of my mind when I ate.

I glanced away from the salsa, trying to distract myself, and noticed Nadira was wearing her math-letes jacket. "Do you have a meet today?" I asked.

"Yep!" she said happily. "We're leaving after lunch."

"Where is it?" I asked.

"LA. Should be some pretty tough teams there," she answered, reaching to dip another chip in the salsa.

Cori gave her a look. "No way are they better than you. You practically inhale math equations and exhale answers."

"And you," Nadira replied, "spout hyperbole."

"Not hardly," Cori said. "Right, Des?"

Des put her hands up. "Don't draw me into this! But..." She gave Nadira an apologetic look. "She's kind of right."

Nadira rolled her eyes.

Faith put her fork down. "Nadira's good at other things too."

"Thank you!" Nadira said.

"Like what?" Cori asked. "Being perfect?"

"Oh please," Nadira said.

"Come on," Cori replied. "When's the last time you got in trouble?"

Nadira glared at her. "Never. Now can we change the subject?"

I toyed with some soggy lettuce in my tortilla bowl. "We can talk about how my half-brother doesn't even know who I am."

Faith gasped. "What?"

I nodded and told them about the whole ordeal with my dad the evening before.

"That's cold," Des said. "I can blast him on YouTube if you want. My commenters can be harsh. They'll put him in his place, for sure."

I laughed. "No need to send the mob on him. I just want to forget I even share his DNA."

"Done," Cori said. "Let's think about snacks for tomorrow night. I can get some things from the store?"

"We're eating right now!" Nadira said. "And you want to talk about food?"

"Duh." Cori laughed. "So... chocolate-covered peanuts? Kettle corn?"

"Yes and yes," Faith said.

I giggled. "Speaking of kettles... are you guys up for a mission?"

Des grinned. "Now we're talking."

"Apparently someone's been stealing kettlebells from Ted's Gym. Anyone want to stake out the place on Saturday and catch the guy?"

Faith's eyes lit up. "I'm in. That's way better than shining shoes at the church for the choir."

The rest of my friends agreed to come and help, and Cori said, "Let's make it a sleepover! I haven't had one since I was a kid."

"I haven't had one ever," I admitted.

Each of the girls gasped at me.

"You're kidding," Nadira said. "I've done something you haven't?"

My cheeks heated as I cracked off a piece of my tortilla bowl. "I was always too busy with dance. But now..."

Cori gave me a sympathetic smile. "No worries. We'll make it the sleepover to end all sleepovers." She grinned. "Bring a sleeping bag and a flashlight."

Des giggled. "I've got the face masks."

Faith lifted her hand. "I'll bring the nail polish."

Nadira shook her head with a smile. "I'm braiding hair."

I grinned, thankful for my friends and thankful for something, anything, to look forward to.

Carter had been in chemistry, but I didn't see him in his usual weightlifting spot at the gym. A disappointed feeling settled over me. Even though it had only been a few days, I was already used to his steady presence.

Raf kept me busy though, learning new lifts and incorporating the ones I had already learned. Weightlifting was quickly becoming second nature, and I found I enjoyed the way I could focus on posture and form like I had in dance. The way it challenged my muscles and kept my mind focused on nothing but getting out from under whatever was holding me down.

After the session, Raf said, "I think you might just be a lifter yet, Pruitt."

I shook my head. "I'm not so sure."

He flexed his deeply tanned arm, making his large muscles ripple. "Would you believe I used to be a string bean kid?"

"Not at all," I said. "So, what happened? Weights?"

"Puberty," he answered with a smirk. "But weights helped."

I shook my head. "I'll just be happy if I drop a few pounds."

"You'll see more benefits than that," he said. "Extra strength, endurance, force, and eventually improved bone density and a boosted metabolism that works even when you rest."

I lifted a corner of my mouth. "You have so much faith."

"Because I've seen it before, in Carter actually. Just trust the process."

Now that Raf brought him up, I didn't feel like a complete creep asking. "Where is he today?"

Raf shrugged and finished re-racking the forty-five-pound bar. "I saw him check in and walk toward the studios, but I have no idea what he's up to."

"Ah," I said, trying my hardest to be casual. Raf's suspicious look told me I didn't completely pull it off.

"See you tomorrow," I told him and walked away. Toward the studios.

When I got to the hallway, a class had just let out. Women poured from the room, wearing leggings and sports bras. Through a small window, I saw a bar along a mirrored wall. And then I almost walked smack into Carter.

Thankfully, he was faster than me and stepped out of the way.

"I'm so sorry!" I said.

He chuckled. "No big deal. What are you doing over here?"

I glanced around, and my eyes landed on a door across the hall that said Zumba.

"Um, that," I said, pointing.

He looked from me to the sign. "Are you teaching?"

I snorted. "Of course not."

"Mind if I join?"

Glancing back at the sign again, I stammered, "Um, not at all." And together, we walked into what was sure to be the most embarrassing hour of my life.

ELEVEN

A MIDDLE-AGED WOMAN in neon spandex, leg warmers, and a thick sweatband stood at the front of the room. On the front mirror in neon marker, someone had written EIGHTIES NIGHT!

I looked around in horror as I realized everyone around us was coming into the room dressed in similar garb.

"This should be fun," Carter chuckled.

"Are you sure you don't want to go?" I asked. "I don't see any other guys."

"Nah, I'm kind of a trailblazer." He winked at me, then laughed.

I covered my face in my hands. This was going to be painful.

The opening chords of "Hungry Like the Wolf" played over the speaker, and the woman up front called, "Welcome to eighties night, ladies!" Then she waved at Carter. "And gent! What a sweet boyfriend you have!" she said to me.

"We're not—" I began, but she was already marching in place up front.

"Tonight is all about the eighties! The clothes"—she ran her hands over her spandex suit —"the hair!" She zhuzhed her hair. "The music."

"Oh, for the love of god, she just did jazz hands," I mumbled.

Carter chuckled, wiggling his hands like she had. "What's wrong with that?"

I laughed out loud, and she gave me a look in the mirror. "Ladies, let's show these young'uns what the eighties are all about!"

She pressed a button on the remote in her hand, and the music switched to "500 Miles" by the Proclaimers. She began marching to the beat. "Bet you two didn't know this came from our genera-tion!" She pointed her thumbs at her chest. "That's right! Now, let's warm up!"

She picked up the pace, marching in place, then adding a shuffle step back and forth.

Next to me, Carter whispered, "I actually didn't know that. Did you?"

"No, but don't tell her that," I said.

Carter added a spin to his steps and said, "Your secret's safe with me."

I was too busy gaping at him to think. "Look at you! You have some moves!"

"I'm full of surprises," he said, waggling his eyebrows.

From the front, the teacher called, "LESS TALKY, MORE DANCEY!"

I laughed to myself and easily fell into step with the rest of the class. I could only imagine the things Galina would say about these moves and the women in the studio. It made being here that much more fun—like a form of rebellion against the strict dance regimen I'd grown up with.

The music changed, and the teacher called, "Welcome to the late eighties!"

As the lyrics began, I recognized it as "Listen to Your Heart" and giggled. Who knew I'd have so much fun in a class like this?

She added new steps back and forth, and I could feel my muscles becoming more limber, working harder. I was honestly a little surprised this actually felt like a workout, but here I was, sweat beading on my forehead, dancing next to Carter, enjoying it.

The teacher shuffled through "St. Elmo's Fire," "We're Not Gonna Take it," and "Kiss" by Prince, before she changed it to "Love Shack."

Carter laughed out loud. "My mom used to sing this to me in the car."

"Alright!" the teacher called. "Grab a partner and let the music take you. Remember, the eighties were about breaking all the rules and having FUN! Now's your chance, lover boy!"

My cheeks heated as she singled out Carter, but he extended his hands to me, and I couldn't help but slip mine into his. They were large, warm, and he drew me to him just as assuredly as any trained dancer.

We moved back and forth to the music, and he sang the words out loud to me, making me giggle. As the chorus hit, he spun me away from him and back. I almost lost my balance but caught myself by placing a hand on his muscled chest. It was firm. Solid.

His eyes heated on mine as he swayed back and forth to the music, and thank goodness I had dancing as an excuse to use for my breathlessness.

As the chords came to a close, clapping erupted

around us, and Carter and I looked up from our trance. Everyone in the class was cheering for us as the teacher changed the music to "Africa" by Toto for the cool down.

"Great job, everyone!" she cheered. "Remember, next week we'll be voting for December's dance theme!"

Carter slowly let go of my hand, and the absence of his warmth was sharp against my skin. My cheeks flushed as I stepped away.

"That was fun," he said. "But then again, you're an incredible dancer."

"You're not so bad yourself," I said. "Who taught you to dance?"

He nodded his head toward the front. "Karen, of course."

"Is that her name?" I asked.

"No," he chuckled, "but I could totally see her asking for the manager."

I laughed again as I walked with him toward the door. Being with Carter was so easy. Easier than spending time with Benjamin, even though we'd spent hours together.

As we reached the door, I froze, seeing my mom. "Oh my gosh! You were going to pick me up."

"That's right." She looked between Carter and me, stepping out of the way so the other students could walk past us. "Looked like you two were having fun though."

If I'd been blushing earlier, it had nothing on what my cheeks were doing now. The smoke alarm would be going off any minute now.

"It was fun," Carter said, extending his hand. "I'm Carter—Addy and I go to school together."

Mom was positively beaming now. Meanwhile, my eyes were darting around for a hole to hide in for the rest of my life. This was *so* embarrassing.

"How would you like to come by our place for supper, Carter?" she asked.

"I'd love to," he replied, "but my grandma's making a roast tonight. Can't let her eat it by herself."

Mom smiled. Even she seemed to be taken aback by his charm. "Rain check, then?"

"Definitely," he agreed, and then said, "see you at school, Addy."

After he got a few feet away, Mom leaned over and whispered, "Addy? Is that his pet name for you?"

I cringed. "Can we go now?"

"Of course, *Addy*."

"You're the worst," I muttered.

She giggled, walking alongside me. "Love you too."

TWELVE

DURING THE REQUIRED volunteer period Friday afternoons, I went to the grade school for music classes. Part of the fine arts curriculum was to learn different types of dance, and I'd been selected to help the teacher.

For a few hours each week, Mrs. Florence and I taught dance to the kindergartners, first, and second graders. She let me in on the back side of the elementary school, closest to her classroom, and then we got to work.

Helping the kindergartners was mostly about crowd control. Making sure their hands were in the air instead of their noses. By the end of my time with the young ones, I always felt like I'd been through several hours of practice.

The first graders were a little better, but I lived for teaching the second graders. There were twenty students in the group, and ever since Ryker had told them football players had to learn ballet, they'd been some of my most devoted pupils.

After the first graders left and before the second graders arrived, Mrs. Florence pulled me aside and said, "I've been thinking of having the seconds do a dance routine for the winter showcase. What do you think?"

"To go along with the song they sing?" I asked.

She shook her head. "No, a ballet piece."

My eyes lit up. "Really?"

Her earrings jingled as she nodded. "I know we usually just have them sing at the showcase, but they've been working so hard, and the showcase is supposed to feature some of their best work."

"They've been so good," I agreed.

"But I want to showcase you as well."

My eyebrows rose, not quite following. "What do you mean?"

"You, my dear, are going to choreograph the dance." She grinned wide, her coffee-yellowed teeth on full display.

"Me?" I could have hugged the woman. Maybe this would be the distraction I needed. Something that could keep me involved in dance without completely giving up such a major part of my life.

The second graders grew louder as they neared the door and walked inside.

"Think about it," Mrs. Florence said, just in time for the kids to maul me. They ran up, hugging me and welcoming me to their class.

I loved being a senior around little kids. They acted like I was royalty.

"Can you do an arabesque?" Anna asked.

I grinned at her. "An arabesque? That's just showy. You want difficult, I'll do a grand adage."

"Like math?" her friend Bailey asked, eyebrows scrunched.

"No." I giggled. "It's a difficult move that can take years to master."

Mrs. Florence clapped her hands together. "Let's start the class with the grand adage, and then we'll get to work on your dance moves!" she told the students. "You may stand in first position, second position, or third position!"

The students lined up, each pointing their toes in different positions. Mrs. Florence walked the rows, examining them and making slight adjustments. When she reached the last student, she said, "Wonderful! Adriel, let's see the grand adage."

I smiled and went to the CD player in the corner of the room and hit play on the same tracks we'd listened to in the last class. As the evenly measured beats played over the speaker, I balanced on one leg and slowly lifted it in the air with control and poise. I pointed my toes as I'd been taught and kept my arms firm and my face soft. Then I lowered my leg and brought it behind me, bending into my back while keeping my standing leg straight.

The students oohed and ahhed, and it felt nice to be royalty, if only for a moment.

While I walked the students through a variety of poses and the freestyle dance portion at the end of class, I thought of the winter showcase and what I could have them do. I promised myself I would be different from Galina.

Instead of belittling them into compliance, I would encourage them, build them up, make them believe in themselves the way my mom had always believed in me.

As the class drew to a close, I gave my students hugs goodbye and promised Mrs. Florence I'd have rough choreography planned for them by next Friday. Since the exit was right by the classroom, I slipped into my jacket and walked outside.

The final bell rang as I walked from the elementary campus to the high school, and I began seeing students pouring out of the building. Among the first were Isabella and Tatiana. I glanced around for a bush, a bench—anything to hide behind—and came up short.

Besides, they'd already seen me like predators sniffing their prey.

Isabella fluttered her fingers at me. "If it isn't our YouTube star."

"Yeah," Tatiana said, pretending to search through her backpack. "Can I get your autograph? Be sure to sign it from 'Complete Failure.'"

I glared at them, wishing that Ryker and Cori were anywhere in sight, but they usually took a different path from their volunteer hour. No, the closest students were more than twenty feet away and wouldn't be able to hear the mean words coming at me like arrows.

"What do you want?" I asked, my voice bitter.

Isabella shrugged, folding her arms over her chest. "Just wanted to let you know I was keeping Benjamin nice and warm for you. Galina said she's never seen such a talented couple."

Her words hurt, no matter how much I wished

they didn't. Why couldn't I just let things roll off my back like my friends seemed to?

"What?" Tatiana asked. "You're not going to cry, are you?"

I hardened my gaze at her and then kept walking. This was a big courtyard. They couldn't hold me back to torment me.

"Bye!" Isabella said cheerfully. "I'll tell Benjamin you said hello."

I kept walking. They'd already said more than enough.

THIRTEEN

I COULD PROBABLY COUNT on one hand the number of high school basketball games I'd watched in my life. Partially because of dance, but also because I just didn't fit here. As I walked into the big gym, looking for my friends in the stands, I felt so out of place.

Parents stood around talking, kids ran down the bleacher seats, the echoing of bouncing balls filled my ears, racketing inside my head. I looked over the court and saw Cori with the rest of the team in navy-blue jerseys and flyaway pants. She stood at the free-throw line, practicing shot after shot as the clock counted down the warm-up.

"Adriel!" Nadira called.

I glanced around, finding her about midway down the court, a few rows behind the scorekeepers' stand. The others hadn't arrived yet, so I scooted in next to her and offered her some popcorn.

She reached into the paper bag and took a handful. "Thanks."

"So, I might need you to translate," I admitted.

"No problem. My family basically breathes basketball," she said.

"Why don't you play?" I asked, watching as Cori and her team started making baskets one after another.

"Let's just say I'm better at coordinates than coordination." She shuddered. "I played once in fifth grade, and it did *not* end well."

I laughed. "Your brothers must have taken all the athleticism while you got the brains?" Terrell and Carter were pretty popular in the school because of their skills on the court.

"Yep," she said. "They're the family's pride and joy."

My heart ached for her, and I searched for a change in subject. "Has Cori told you where she's planning on attending college?"

"Nope," Nadira said. "I even tried to bribe her with chocolate chips."

"And she didn't give?" I asked, shocked. That girl would do just about anything for a bag of chocolate chips.

Nadira shook her head. "Didn't budge even a little."

I laughed. "Well, then I guess we'll all have to wait. When is she announcing it?"

"They're bringing out a table so she can sign over halftime. Making a big show of it."

I smiled. "That's awesome." Cori definitely deserved her fifteen minutes of fame, however it came. She was a great friend and an even better person.

Over the PA system, they asked us to rise for the national anthem, and Des stepped to the middle of the court, holding a microphone. Even though I'd heard her sing all throughout football season, her voice still sent chills to my spine and rose goosebumps on my arms.

When the final note rang throughout the gym, I clapped hard along with everyone else there. As the applause died, Nadira said, "Girl's gonna be famous someday."

I grinned. "She definitely is."

They began announcing each of the starting players, and a little farther down the aisle, I heard Faith excusing her way toward us, holding a Mt. Dew and a tray of nachos.

"Just in time!" I said.

She grinned and sat beside me. "I didn't want to miss seeing Cori tipoff."

"Should be good," Nadira said. "The girl from the other team is a little taller, but Cori has a good vertical."

Was this what it sounded like when I talked about dance? What was a tipoff? And why was Cori's vertical important?

The girls lined up on each side of the court, acting like their spots had been taped off for them, but I didn't see any black Xs on the floor.

Cori and another girl stood toe to toe in the middle of the big circle, and a ref stood between them holding the ball in her hand.

Faith gripped my arm excitedly as he tossed the ball into the air and the girls jumped as high as they could to get it. Cori snagged it with her fingertips and sent it to one of her teammates before running down the court to stand by the basket.

"Translation?" I asked Nadira.

She giggled and began talking me through all the basketball information I never needed to know. Which positions did what, what happened when the ball went out of bounds, and what a foul was.

Des joined us halfway through an intense first quarter, and by halftime, the score was even. In the front row, Ryker started a chant for the girls, and soon we were all standing and cheering for the last ten seconds of the half.

The seconds ticked down until Cori tried to shoot and a girl pushed her down.

"What the heck?" I cried.

The refs blew their whistles, and Nadira said, "Good, that's a foul."

"Good?" I asked as the players lined up for some sort of synchronized event.

"She gets to shoot two free throws now," Nadira explained. "Better chance at making those than the first shot anyway."

The referee passed Cori the ball, and she dribbled a few times before shooting. It sailed through the net with a crisp snap, and we all cheered for her.

Everyone quieted as she prepared for a second shot, and just like the first, it flew through the hoop, putting Emerson two points ahead.

"That was so intense!" Faith said.

"I know!" I agreed. "I'm starting to think I should have watched more basketball."

Nadira nodded. "And wait till the guys' game. Cute guys *and* suspense."

I grinned. "And their faces won't be covered up by a football helmet."

"Exactly," Nadira agreed. "None of that thinking a guy is cute and then seeing him take his helmet off to be disappointed."

As I giggled, my eyes caught something on the court. A couple of volunteers were carrying a folding table to center court, along with a few chairs. Cori's parents walked onto the shiny wooden floor from the doorway—her dad had even changed out of his banana-yellow work shirt and into a plaid button-down.

The grin on Cori's face looked so sincere it brought a smile to my own face. Over the speaker system, Mr. Davis said, "Today, Cori Nash will be signing to play with a collegiate basketball team!"

Cheers erupted throughout the crowd as Cori and her parents walked to the folding table with a purple shirt on one side and a green shirt on the other. Cori sat in one of the chairs while her parents stood beside her, her dad wrapping his arm around her mom.

Mr. Davis continued with some statistics on Cori's time playing at Emerson Academy and then said, "We've had five seniors already commit to college athletics, with Ryker Dugan playing football at Brentwood U, Grant Haymish playing at Kansas State University, Shianne Young playing volleyball at Penn State! Our cross-country runners, Elizabeth Jenkins and Frederick Pennington, are studying at Duke University and Harvard respectively.

"Now, we get to hear Cori's decision between Brentwood University and University of Hawaii!"

Nadira, Faith, Des, and I held hands as we waited. With a signature Cori grin, she lifted her hand over the shirts and then put on the purple Brentwood University shirt with BASKETBALL printed on the front.

My mouth fell open, and I cheered along with everyone else as a woman in a sharp black suit entered the court, holding a microphone.

"We are so excited for you to join the Brentwood University family, and I can't wait to have you as one of my players," the woman said, Cori's new coach. She placed a piece of paper and a pen on the table, and Cori signed it with a flourish.

As the cheering died down, Ryker jumped from

his seat in the front and ran to her, picking her up and spinning her in an excited circle.

I might not have had my own happily ever after yet, but watching hers was almost as good.

FOURTEEN

SINCE MY CAR had gotten out of the shop that morning, I was able to drive to Cori's house without bumming a ride from my mom or anyone else. I parked along the street, in front of their **Eat Ripe** yard sign. Then I grabbed a brand-new sleeping bag, another bag with clothes for the next day, and my hair and makeup bag.

I was a little disappointed I hadn't heard from Dr. Edmonson yet on my results, but I hoped this sleepover would help me forget it. At least for a little while.

Before I got to the door, it swung open to Cori's twin sisters.

"Hi there," I said, a little surprised they'd seen me coming.

"Cori's back in her room," they said. The one on the right had a sour look. "No 'little kids' allowed."

I smiled. "Maybe I can talk her into bending the rule, just a little."

Their eyes lit up, and the one on the left said, "Thank you!"

"Of course." I winked at them and walked back to where I knew Cori's room was. I'd never had siblings myself before my dad had a son who didn't even know me—and I wished I had some growing up. Like built-in best friends. I hoped Cori didn't take her sisters for granted.

Cori's door was shut, so I knocked. As soon as she told me to come in, I opened the door to find her and Nadira on her bed, already dressed in pajamas.

"Go change!" Cori said, throwing a pillow at me. "We're making the most of your first slumber party."

I giggled and got my pajamas out of my bag. "Whatever you say, party queen."

After changing in the hallway bathroom, I went back to Cori's room to find Faith and Des there as well. Faith had a pan of scotcheroos with four pieces already cut out of it. My mouth watered at the sight of chocolate.

"Take one," Faith said.

I looked from her to the pan, ready to give my custom response that I was on a diet and training for nationals, but those lines fell flat before they ever left my mouth.

I'd been eating salads and grilled chicken for months with no slips, no splurges. And for what? I still let down my dance team. I still gained weight.

Why not at least enjoy myself?

I reached for one and took a bite, then moaned. It was so good.

Cori giggled, "Want us to give you some privacy?"

"Better hurry," I said, going for another bite. What else had I been missing out on all this time?

Cori stood on her bed, teetering on the soft twin mattress. "I dedicate tonight to Adriel. May we stay up too late, eat too much junk food, and have the best time ever."

"Hear hear," I said, raising the small bit that was left of my scotcheroo.

"Where do we start?" Nadira asked.

Des grinned evilly. "Boy talk?"

Faith groaned. "Good thing you broke it off

with my brother after homecoming. I would have barfed."

Des giggled, "You can't break something off that never started." She rubbed her hands together. "Cori, you go first."

Cori sat down, leaning back against the wall. "You guys already know who I'm dating."

I smiled, thinking of her and Ryker. "Was he thrilled about you going to BU?"

"Definitely," she said. "You should have seen the kiss he gave me after the game."

Nadira smirked. "Now I know what took you so long to get here."

"You were here before her?" I asked.

"Oh yeah," Nadira said. "But the twins and I hung out for a little bit, so it was fine."

Cori nodded. "They're finally relaxing about the whole acting thing. Cara was being a real prima donna for a little while, but I think knowing they have a year to wait until the premiere helps."

Des glared at her. "I thought we were talking about boys?"

"Right." Cori zipped her lips, then mumbled, "Who's next?"

"Not me," Nadira said, going for a second

scotcheroo. "My calculator gets more action than I do."

I giggled. "You don't have a crush on anyone?"

"Not at all." She shook her head. "I think MIT might be my time to shine."

Des shook her head disappointedly. "Maybe we should go to Spike tonight, meet some guys, have fun."

Spike was the under-eighteen club that I had only been to one time before. And that was only because someone threw up all over the dance studio and Galina had to cancel lessons until it could be cleaned up. Going out tonight sounded like fun to me, but Cori said, "Absolutely not. Tonight is a girls' night." She looked at Faith. "Any luck in the boy department?"

"Not in the slightest," Faith scoffed.

Des looked at me desperately. "*Please* tell me you have some news about that slice of man meat in your chem class."

My cheeks immediately warmed, and Des squealed, pointing at me. "You like him! You like him!"

I picked up a pillow from the bed where I sat and threw it at her. "Shush! He'll hear you at this rate!"

Completely undeterred, Des clapped her hands together and said, "Tell us *everything*."

"Sure," I agreed, then winked at Nadira. "But only if you braid my hair."

Nadira came to sit behind me, and for the next hour, it was like something out of a movie. I talked about the cute guy who lifted weights while Nadira plaited my hair into a million tiny braids. My stomach was even starting to hurt from all the junk food.

"Do you think he'll take you to the winter dance?" Cori asked.

I shrugged, trying not to get my hopes up. "I don't know."

From behind me, Nadira shook my shoulders. "He better ask you! He is *cute!*"

Laughing, I said, "Maybe. But you guys will have to help me find a dress."

"Please," Des said as if I should be ashamed for ever doubting her. "We will find *the* dress."

My lips spread into an easy smile as I realized for the first time in a long time, I was excited for something other than dance. My friends had given that to me, and it was priceless.

"Can I just say I love you guys?" I asked.

Des smirked. "I hate to break it to you, but I don't like you like that."

Cori picked up a pillow and whammed Des with it, then cried, "Pillow fight!"

We each grabbed one and bounced around the room hitting each other with pillows like children. Playful, *happy* children.

"OH MY GOSH," I groaned from my spot on the floor. My whole body hurt, and my eyelids felt like sandpaper on my eyes. "*Why* did we stay awake so late?"

Next to me, Cori's sleeping bag rustled, and she responded with a sleepy, "It was a slumber party, remember?"

On Cori's bed, Faith groaned. "I don't remember doing much slumbering."

"Come on," Des said, already out of bed and fully dressed in sleek black workout gear. "What happened to catching the kettlebell bandit?"

I threw my pillow at her. "You're just excited to see shirtless guys at the gym."

"And?" she asked.

I laughed—as much as a girl who got two hours of sleep could laugh.

"Besides," Des said, "Cori's mom made a breakfast casserole, and you *know* how I feel about Anne's casseroles."

"Fine," Cori said, pushing herself off the floor.

I squinted my tired eyes at Des as I got up. "How do you feel about her casseroles?"

"Like you feel about Carter," she answered. "I want to eat them up."

I rolled my eyes and walked to the door. "I'm going to the bathroom. To vomit."

"Whatever," Des giggled and waved at me.

In the bathroom, I splashed water over my tired eyes and began pulling out the tiny braids Nadira had put in my hair. Each strand came out with little kinks, and I used some of Cori's hairspray to hold the little waves in place.

I actually didn't look too bad. Which I had been a tad worried about. Did Carter go to the gym on weekends? Who did he spend time with when we didn't have school? He'd mentioned his grandma signing him up for the gym, but he'd also said his mom sang "Love Shack" to him.

A knock sounded on the door, and Cori said, "Please tell me you're not actually sick."

"I'm fine," I said. But my breath wasn't. I put some toothpaste on my finger and rubbed it over my teeth until my mouth tasted more like mint and less like decaying sugar.

Outside of the bathroom, the air carried hints of savory and sweet flavors. My mouth instantly watered, and I followed the scent to the kitchen, where my friends all sat around the table.

"Good morning," Anne said cheerfully to me. How were moms so happy in the morning? I swore my mom got out of bed with perfect hair and a pant suit.

"Morning," I replied. "Please tell me you have coffee."

She grinned and moved from the stove to the coffee pot. "Of course." She poured me a mug, and I drank deeply, not caring how hot it was.

I sat at the table between Nadira and Faith, eating an egg and potato casserole that tasted like the gods had made it themselves. Then Anne pulled out a French toast casserole for "dessert" that tasted even better.

"This is so good," I moaned.

"See?" Des said. "You almost wouldn't believe there's no sugar in it."

No sugar *and* it tasted good? "Can I live here?" I

asked, only half joking.

Anne laughed. "If you're always this flattering, you're more than welcome to take Ginger's bed."

"I might have to," I said, working my way through the rest of my food. I wondered if I could talk to Mom about backing off on my diet a bit. Once the costumes became an issue, we'd gotten so strict, but now...

"Are you ready to go?" Cori asked.

I took a last bite of the French toast casserole. "Absolutely."

We decided to take my car to the gym. But first, we made a coffee stop. I needed more caffeine or this operation would quickly turn into a nap. Dance competitions had made me a pro at finding places to sleep.

With each of us holding our steaming coffees with extra espresso—except for Des, who preferred hers on ice—we drove up to Ted's Gym and parked the car.

As we walked inside, I gave them the lowdown about the thief. Which was basically nothing. "We have no clue if it's a man or a woman or what time they steal or anything. But I think if we each station ourselves around the gym, we can get enough eyes on people to find out."

Des eyed the weight benches where a group of what looked like college guys were working out. "I'm over there."

I laughed, deciding I would take one of the stationary bikes. There was a TV in that area, playing what looked like a baking show. Not great for someone trying to lose weight, but for my purposes, it worked just fine.

For the better part of an hour, I moved my legs on the lowest resistance possible, taking sips from my coffee. This whole thing was beginning to feel a bit pointless. Why would a kettlebell thief come during the busiest part of a weekend? Wouldn't a Wednesday at midnight be a better bet?

My friends didn't seem quite as bored as I did, though. Des was chatting up some shirtless hunk. Cori had made herself a launch pad of resistance bands to make pull-ups super easy. Faith hung out at a table by the smoothie bar, and Nadira bounced on an exercise ball while doing something on her phone.

I decided we could give it another hour and then call it a day. Or night. The slumber party had been fun, but I was ready for some more sleep.

To my right, a friendly voice said, "Coffee and cardio? Nice."

I glanced over to see Carter settling into the bike next to mine. My cheeks heated as he set his water bottle in the holder and adjusted the resistance.

"Do you always come here on the weekends?" I asked, putting my coffee in the drink holder. Then I realized I'd just asked a lame variation of *come here often?* And cringed even harder.

"Yeah," he said. "Sundays are my rest days, though. Grandma makes sure of it."

"Does she live with your family?" I asked, my curiosity getting the better of me.

"She *is* my family," he answered, starting to work the pedals with his muscular legs.

"Oh, I'm sorry, I didn't—"

"It's okay," he said lightly. He glanced over, giving me a sad smile before facing the TV again. "My parents were political activists—they died during a riot when I was eight. It's just been Grandma and me ever since."

My mouth fell open in horror. "That's awful."

"It was," he agreed. "But the settlement took care of my grandma, and she took care of me. Someday, I'll pay her back for all she's done."

"That's sweet of you," I said, then realized I was gushing, and faced forward again. Could I not put my foot in my mouth every two seconds around him?

After a moment, he said, "Addy, I've been meaning to ask you something."

"Yeah?" My voice came out breathy as I imagined him asking me to the winter dance and going on a dress shopping spree with my friends.

"THAT'S HIM!" Des shouted.

I followed my friend's voice to see her pointing at a guy in a hoodie. He had a big backpack on and was sprinting toward the door.

I tried to get out of the bike but tripped and fell, face-planting on the rubbery floor. So much for grace.

Feeling my cheeks burning, I scrambled up and chased the person too. I yelled at the front desk people, who stood around like a normal day at the gym included screaming girls and running boys. "THAT'S THE THIEF, YOU IDIOTS!"

At least one of them sprang into action, getting out the phone, but it was too late. The guy had gotten out the doors, and by the time Des and I reached the parking lot, he was already gone.

With a groan, I got out my phone and called Ted. When he answered, I quickly launched into what had happened. As I was telling the story, Faith,

Nadira, and Cori followed Des and me out to the sidewalk surrounding the gym.

I switched my phone to speaker mode so my friends could hear. Ted chuckled. "You and your friends are regular Nancy Drews."

"Who's that?" Des whispered.

I rolled my eyes. "Well, I'm sorry we didn't catch him."

"No, but maybe you spooked him," Ted said, like that was good enough. "Adriel?"

"Yeah?" I asked, trying to quell my disappointment. I'd really wanted to get the guy. Not just come up with another empty lead.

There was a smile in his voice as he said, "It means a lot to me that you tried so hard."

My stomach bottomed out. "You're not getting sappy on me, are you, Ted?"

He cleared his throat. "Not at all."

"Good. I'll talk to you later." I hung up the phone, and my friends and I decided it was time to go home.

It wasn't until I'd pulled into my driveway that I remembered Carter had been about to ask me something. That freaking kettlebell bandit hadn't just hurt Ted's bottom line; he'd interfered with my life. This...was war.

SIXTEEN

MONDAY MORNING, I took extra care with my hair and makeup. My mind had gone wild imagining what question Carter may have wanted to ask. A part of me hoped the winter homecoming dance had been on his lips, but I didn't want to get ahead of myself.

After grabbing my backpack, I went down the hall to get some breakfast. Mom sat at the table, her computer open in front of her, and when she saw me, she quickly slammed it shut.

My eyebrows drew together. "What was that about?"

"Nothing," she said lightly, standing up. "What would you like for breakfast?"

"Yogurt with granola..." I said slowly. "Really,

what were you looking at?"

"Nothing," she repeated, this time more firmly. She began rummaging through the fridge for the ingredients. "I think there are more strawberries in the freezer in the garage... I'll go get them." She set the container of yogurt on the counter and rushed by me, as if she couldn't get out there fast enough.

The second the garage door closed, I sprinted to her laptop and lifted the screen, finding the internet browser open to the website of an adoption agency. On the page, there were rows of images of orphaned children.

My mouth fell open, and I immediately shut the laptop, trying not to feel the ache in my chest. Mom wanted to adopt? Were both she and Dad ready to move on from me? To have a second chance?

Aside from Mom, I didn't have anyone. Dad's parents were just as absent as their son, and both of Mom's parents were gone now. Suddenly, it felt like the floor was opening up on me, threatening to swallow me whole.

The garage door opened, making me jump, and Mom breezed in with a bag of frozen strawberries. "I should be hearing from Dr. Edmonson this morning," she said.

"Really?" I asked.

She nodded. "As soon I find out the results, I'll call you on the school phone so we can get on top of this."

I nodded. "Thanks."

Going to the counter, she poured me a bowl of yogurt and granola, then put the strawberries in the microwave so they'd thaw. I wanted to ask her about the adoption agency, but I couldn't, not without giving away the fact that I'd violated her privacy.

So I settled on asking her a different question. "Have you ever thought about going back to work?" Mom used to be a stylist, before she met Dad and had me. That was how they met each other—she redid his wardrobe for his new high-paying corporate job, and he found more than good clothing in the store. I used to think it was sweet. After all, didn't all the fairy tales end with Prince Charming taking the princess away from a life of work and introducing her to a life of leisure for happily ever after?

Now, I knew better. Even though trends had changed since Mom was first employed, she'd kept up with fashion in her own wardrobe. And maybe if she was busy working, she wouldn't be able to get busy replacing me.

She lifted a corner of her mouth. "I don't

know," she answered honestly. "My favorite job has always been being your mom. But I can't exactly follow you to college."

I smiled softly. "They might frown on that."

"Exactly." She handed me the bowl and said, "Sit. Eat."

I obliged her, sitting at the counter even though I didn't much feel like eating.

About halfway through my bowl, Mom said, "You should probably get going. Wouldn't want you to be late."

"Yeah." I went and scraped my bowl in the trash.

"Will you be taking another Zumba lesson with that boy?" she asked with a sly smile. "Or should I expect you home at six?"

Despite my reddening cheeks, I rolled my eyes. "I'll let you know." I wouldn't mind another hour with Carter, especially one as fun as that Zumba class had been.

After setting my bowl in the sink, I grabbed my backpack and told Mom goodbye.

All through first hour, I couldn't get the adoption website off my mind. Or the fact that my lab results should be coming soon. How was I supposed to decide what to panic about?

By the time I got to chem class, I was already on edge. I smiled at Carter as I sat down, but I could hardly listen as Mr. Cho lectured about acids and bases for an upcoming experiment. I maybe made two or three notes before an office aid knocked on the door and said, "Adriel Pruitt has a call."

Mr. Cho's perpetually disappointed face creased more deeply as he gestured his fingers for me to go. "I trust you'll get your notes from Mr. McCormac."

Carter smiled at me. "Don't worry, I've got you covered," he said, mistaking my hesitance for not wanting to miss out on chemistry.

I hurriedly put my notebook and pen in my bag, then followed the office aid down the long, tiled hallway. Each step I took led me closer to answers about my health, but what if I didn't want them? What if the issue I had was incurable?

Finally, she led me around the front desk and said, "It's on the right line. Just lift the receiver."

I nodded and picked up the black plastic phone with shaky hands. "Hello?"

"Honey?" Mom's voice came through the line. I tried to read it but couldn't.

"Yes?" I asked.

"I heard from Dr. Edmonson."

"And what is it?" I wanted to tell her to just spit it out, to let me have the bad news sooner so I could begin dealing with it.

"He thinks you have hypothyroidism. Basically, your thyroid isn't producing enough hormone, and it's affecting your metabolism and cholesterol and even your mental health."

"What?" I asked, still trying to take it in. If there were a chair by the phone, I would have sunk into it. Instead, I rested my free hand on the counter, letting it hold my weight.

"He said we were probably seeing the symptoms long before we brought you in—hair loss—"

"Lots of people lose hair," I said.

"Not enough for Ted to find as much as he did in the shower drain," Mom said. "You also had high cholesterol for someone your age on your kind of diet. He even thinks your thyroid may be a contributing factor to your depression."

I looked around, desperate for a chair, and dragged one over from the wall. "So, what?" I couldn't remember when we covered the thyroid in health class—or if we had.

"It's simple!" she said, seeming almost giddy. "There's a medication—synthetic thyroid hormone—and once you're on it, your symptoms should start to clear. Of course, it may be a bit before we find the right dosage, but... that's good news, right?"

I could tell she wanted me to be happy, but all I could hear was that there was something wrong with me. Something I hadn't chosen that had ruined the one thing that really mattered to me.

Tears stung my eyes, and I swallowed. "Yeah, that's... great."

"Good," she said. "I can't talk too long, but I'll have your medication from the pharmacy ready for when you get home tonight. Whether it's before or after your dancing with Carter," she teased.

I managed a smile so my voice wouldn't be completely off. "Thanks, Mom. I'll talk to you later."

After hanging up my phone, I took my late pass and left the office. But instead of going back to class, I went to the bathroom, sat down, and cried.

SEVENTEEN

WORKING out at the gym had never felt more pointless in my life. Sure, there were benefits to lifting weights, but why was I doing it? I wouldn't be able to get back on the dance team. We'd figured out why I was gaining weight. So what was the point?

I missed dance and how we always had a goal to work toward—a performance to ace or a new skill to learn. Now, I felt like I was drifting. Sure, I could try to lift heavier weights, but for what? The sake of lifting heaver weights?

Out the corner of my eye, I watched Carter blow through repetition after repetition with the focus I used to have for dance. Sweat beaded on his forehead, and his cheeks quivered with the force of his exhalations. Maybe after we got done working out, I could ask him his secret. I needed something, anything, to focus on now besides my diagnosis and the team I missed so desperately.

Luckily, I didn't need to ask him. As soon as Raf and I finished cleaning off the weight rack, Carter said, "Come with me?"

I would have followed him anywhere, but I still asked, "Where?"

"It's a surprise," he said with a small smile.

Smiling myself, I followed him down the hall, past the basketball and volleyball courts until we stood outside the racquetball court where he'd caught me dancing. It felt like months ago since I'd danced with such abandon. Today, I just felt heavy.

"Here we are," he said.

"What's going on?" I asked, confused.

"Come in." He pushed through the door into the court where a small speaker was plugged into the wall. "Your new dance studio." He gestured around like we'd entered the Taj Mahal, but all I saw were echoing floors and dirty white walls.

"What?" I managed.

"I thought maybe I could help you get to Dance Dance Nationals. Without Emerson Dance."

"What?" I asked again, my voice barely a squeak.

"You said you needed someone to dance with you, and I had a lot of fun dancing in Zumba class. Besides, I don't need to start training hard for the next bodybuilding competition for two months. You'll be done with nationals by then and I'll be in great shape for when the off season is over."

"You're in the *off* season?" I asked. I didn't know why that stuck out to me, but it had. Maybe because he already looked like he was in such great shape.

He nodded. "Just trying to keep muscle tone while I bulk," he answered, then he watched me for a long moment. "What are you thinking?"

"I don't know." I glanced around the gym, picturing myself dancing with Carter.

"I saw the look you had in your eyes when you were dancing. It's the same way I feel when I'm lifting. If I ever had that taken away from me, I have no idea what I'd do, but I hope you would do the same thing for me."

The heartbreaking thing was that I wouldn't. "I hardly know you" I said. I mean, I knew he was nice and cute and fun to be around, but enough to put in the hours of work it would take to even begin dreaming of qualifying for nationals? "Why would you do this? I don't understand."

His eyes met mine for a moment. "Why don't you leave that to me to worry about?"

I folded my arms across my chest. "So I'm just supposed to believe you're willing to practice for hours every day?"

He nodded.

"And that you would let me teach you to dance?"

Again, he nodded.

"And that when it gets hard, you won't just give up?"

"I can deadlift five hundred pounds, Addy. You don't get that strong by giving up."

My eyes widened, remembering my own hundred-pound deadlift. "Five hundred?"

"Don't change the subject." He stepped closer, his broad shoulders squared to me, his eyes hot on mine. "Are you in, or are you out?"

I chewed on my bottom lip. I knew Carter had talent, could tell from the one class we'd taken together. And I knew he was strong, but would it be enough? Without taking time to think it over, I backed up and said, "Catch me."

Without pausing to let my fear take over, I ran toward him and jumped into his arms.

He lifted me into the air, smooth and steady as he balanced me in his arms, looking up at me with hard honey eyes. But instead of leaving it at that, he spun me in a low circle and lowered me, ever so slowly, to his chest.

My lips parted, and even though he'd been the one doing all the work, my breaths came out in short gasps.

"So we have ourselves a deal?" he asked, his face inches from mine.

I nodded, clearing my head. "But it happens on my terms."

"And those would be?"

"Two-hour practices every night, then you practice your steps on your own." The last qualifier within driving distance was in two weeks, and we had a lot of work to do if we even wanted to have a *chance*.

"I can do it," he said. "I promise."

"We start tomorrow." As I walked away, I hoped, with all my heart, that he was right.

EIGHTEEN

WHEN I GOT HOME, Mom and Ted were at the table in the middle of what looked like a serious conversation. But the second they say me, they jerked apart, as if sitting too close would clue me in to what they were talking about.

I had a feeling I already knew.

"Hi, honey," Mom said, standing and brushing nonexistent crumbs off her shirt. "Hungry?"

I nodded slowly, dropping my backpack by the island. That was one of my favorite spots to post up and do homework because I could stand when I got too antsy. Sitting still didn't come naturally to me.

"How was the gym?" Ted asked.

"It was good," I answered with a smile as I leaned against the island. I couldn't wait to tell him and Mom about Carter and what we were going to do. It was crazy, but excited, nervous butterflies tickled my stomach at the very idea. I'd only ever gotten that feeling when performing, and I couldn't wait to get it back.

"You know," Ted said. "It's been so great having you and your mom home more." He gave Mom a loving look. "I missed you two when you were at the studio all the time."

It took all I had not to throw up, that was until Mom said, "I know. I never thought I'd enjoy being at home so much. Janice even convinced me to sign up for an online styling class. I never would have had time for this before, especially with qualifiers and nationals coming up."

My eyes flicked toward the quartz countertop. Everyone was doing better without dance. Except me. How could I ruin this for them without knowing it was actually going to work?

"Isn't it nice?" Mom asked me.

"What?" I glanced back at her where she stood by the stove, putting a pot of water on the burner.

"Being a teen for once in your life," she said. "Meeting cute boys, not staying up all hours of the night to catch up on homework? Knowing you can go to college and just *enjoy* yourself?"

"Yeah," I said lightly. "I'm actually tired... can I just take supper to my room?"

"Go ahead," Mom replied. "I'll bring it to you. And take your pills with you." She gestured toward a white paper bag on the counter, stapled to an informational paper covered in fine print. "You'll take one in the morning on an empty stomach."

I nodded, grabbing the bag and my backpack.

From the table, Ted said, "See you tomorrow."

Somewhat surprised, I said, "see you," and continued to my room. Inside, I dropped onto my bed and ripped apart the paper bag to see the orange bottle inside. There it was, my name, right by dosage instructions and Dr. Edmonson's name.

I set the bottle down, making the pills rattle inside, and looked at the paper handout. It outlined the side effects of Synthroid—fevers, irritability, sweating, nausea, hair loss... the list went on, and I couldn't help but wonder if being fat and tired was that bad.

But hypothyroidism had taken so much from me, I wouldn't let it take any more. Not if taking this medicine could make me a healthier, better dancer and person.

I laid back holding the paper and closed my eyes, imagining Carter and me dancing at nationals.

We would be the most mismatched pair—him with his bulky muscles, me with my round midsection. I grinned at the thought of Galina watching us dance. Of us beating one of Galina's pairs for the gold.

I clung to that dream instead of my fears. My fears of not being good enough. Of taking away from the life my mom could live with her husband. My dad had definitely found more happiness after leaving me behind.

My eyes burned with tears, and I blinked, knowing I needed to get up, to move, to do something to occupy my mind.

I reached for my backpack because Emerson Academy always gave us *something* to work on. My chem notes were ready to read for the quiz tomorrow, and I read over everything I had written before checking my phone for Carter's notes from earlier today.

His handwriting was neat, measured, but not showy. As my eyes traced each letter, I wondered how something so simple could be so captivating. So endearing.

I began copying his notes into my own notebook, thinking of him as my dance partner. What would it be like to dance so close to him, without letting my attraction to him get in the way? Dancing with him meant nothing could happen between. But I would give up a chance at a relationship any day of the week for a chance at nationals.

If my parents' marriage—and subsequent divorce—taught me anything, it was that you couldn't count on love. Someday, you could be alone, and if you never focused on yourself, on your dreams, you wouldn't have anything left. You'd be in your mid-forties signing up for styling classes and looking at adoption agencies.

I closed my eyes against the thought. Mom had done everything for me, and I was glad she was finally doing something for herself. It was about time.

NINETEEN

THE NEXT DAY, I lifted weights beside Carter for an hour, wondering whether or not he was going to go through with this. I'd gotten my hopes up already, and I didn't want to have them crushed now. Not when this was my last chance to dance at nationals, to impress a recruiter for a dance company.

When Raf and I got done washing off the weights, Carter rubbed his hands together and said, "Are you ready to do this thing?"

"This thing," I said, shaking my head and picking up my dance bag. "Let's go."

"Okay, boss," he said, following behind me.

I smirked, but my smile quickly faded. "This is going to be hard, you know?"

"Why wouldn't it be?" he asked.

I pushed into the racquetball court, meeting him face-on. "Dance isn't something you can just 'pick up' and be incredible at. It's hard work. Hours and years of practicing technique. Time that we don't have. I'm going to have to choreograph around your ability, and you're going to have to make up for what you lack in skill with how you emote."

His smiled faded slightly. "You don't think I can do this."

"No." I smiled then. "But I think it will be fun to try."

I bent and connected my phone into the speaker, turning to the first song in my favorite playlist. Then I folded my arms and stepped back to the wall. "Let me see what you have."

He raised his eyebrows.

"Dance," I said. "Without a crazy eighties lady telling you what to do."

He chuckled, then stilled, closing his eyes. His fingers tapped his leg to the beat, then his head moved side to side with the rhythm. As the music swelled, his movements came to life. His dancing wasn't polished—it was instinctive, like the notes told him what to do and he only listened.

My eyes transfixed on the muscles on his arms. The slow swing of his hips. The way his lips moved without knowing the words. It was captivating.

Distracting.

I turned off the music, and he jerked as if coming out of a trance.

"So?" he asked.

I folded my arms over my chest, trying to get the butterflies in check. "You have a lot of work to do."

His expression fell, sending an arrow straight through my heart.

"But I think we can make it work," I said, which seemed to lift his spirits. "We can't just go with the routine Benjamin and I had, but you need to work on form anyway. That will give me some extra time to work out the choreography." I'd have plenty of practice, considering I now had to come up with a routine for the second graders' winter showcase *and* qualifiers.

Since we didn't have a barre in the racquetball court, I had him rest his fingers against the wall and said, "The first thing a dancer learns is posture... May I?"

He nodded.

I lifted my fingers and gently touched his chin.

His skin was smooth, and he responded instantly to my touch, straightening his spine and lifting his neck. I moved my hands to his muscled shoulders, feeling electricity as I slightly arched his back. My fingers practically shook as I pressed them to his stomach, engaging his core, and I stepped back, catching my breath.

He cleared his throat. "Like this?" he asked, holding the shape.

"Exactly," I breathed, then repeated, more firmly, "Good."

I led him through a series of exercises so he could get used to moving his body in the way a dancer did. I'd trained in ballet, jazz, tap, and contemporary for years, and any routine that had a chance of competing in the contemporary category at nationals would be a unique blend of multiple styles.

My phone began ringing, and I said, "You can take a break, Carter."

He gave me a tired smile. "You're tougher than Raf—thought I'd never get a break."

I rolled my eyes as I answered my phone.

Mom's voice came on the other end. "Is every-thing okay?"

"Yeah, why?" I asked, pulling my phone away

to check the time. My eyes widened. Carter and I had already been at it for two hours. "Sorry, Mom, I lost track of time."

"With that boy?" she asked.

My cheeks flushed as I glanced to Carter, who was drinking from a green water bottle.

"At the gym," I said.

"With the boy at the gym?" she asked, making me blush even harder.

"I'll be home in half an hour."

"See you then," she said. "And your friend is welcome to join us for dinner."

"Rain check," I quickly replied. I hung up before she'd give me another chance to get embarrassed.

"Need to get home?" Carter asked.

I nodded.

"Me too."

He bent, picking up my duffel bag, and gently slipped it over my shoulder. It was a sweet gesture that made me smile way too big.

"See you tomorrow," he said.

"See you tomorrow," I repeated and walked away before he could see just how happy I was.

TWENTY

FOR THE REST of the week, I divided my time between school and the gym. When I was at home, I caught up on homework and ran a million possibilities for choreography through my mind. By the time my volunteer period came around on Friday, I had a rough idea of what I could have them do and the first day of practice went alright.

My friends made me promise to go out with them after Cori's game, but I almost didn't want to do that. Carter and I had so much ground to cover before the qualifying meet. I compromised on meeting Carter at the gym and leaving when my friends texted me.

As Carter and I took a drink break between

exercises, I said, "I'm sorry I'm taking you away from the basketball game."

He shrugged. "I don't usually go anyway."

I leaned back against the wall, letting cool ice water fill my mouth, and swallowed. "What does your grandma think of you being out all the time?"

"She's thrilled."

"Really?"

"Yeah." He chuckled. "I told her I was dancing with you, and I think she's just happy I'm spending time with a girl."

"You haven't spent time with a girl before?" I asked, my curiosity way too strong.

"Too busy," he said easily. As if it wasn't the biggest news of the night. "Between the Academy and bodybuilding, dating just seemed like an inconvenience, you know?"

I knew all too well, but it didn't help the sinking feeling in my chest. "If this is taking too much time away from—"

"No," he stopped me short. "It's not." His smile seemed genuine as he turned his honey eyes on me. "This is good for me. I'm betting I can use the dancing I learn for posing at competitions."

"Posing?"

"Yeah, at bodybuilding competitions, all the

guys line up on stage, and you have to pose to show the work you've done on your body."

I lifted my eyebrows. "Like you flex?"

He chuckled. "Something like that."

"Show me," I said.

"Seriously?"

"Yeah."

Seeming hesitant, he got off the ground and stood in front of me. "So, there are a few basic poses... The Arnold." He lifted his arms over his head, flexing and making each of his muscles bulge. I'd thought they were big before, but now...

"Wow," I said.

"And this is another classic." He bent slightly, bringing his fists together in front of him.

My eyes traced the ridges of the muscles I could see outside of his cut-off shirt, imagining how much work must have gone into making them look that way. What his abs would look like underneath the fabric...

"And now, I can always add a little booty pop." He mimicked one of the moves I'd taught him and laughed.

My cheeks went red as I laughed along with him. "Ha ha, very funny."

"I thought so." He grinned. "Have you been working on any other moves? For our routine?"

"As a matter of fact..." I stood and went to the speaker. "I wanted to see what you thought."

I turned on the music and danced several eight-counts, trying to remember the moves I'd practiced in my bedroom at night when Mom and Ted couldn't hear me.

"What do you think?" I asked when I got to the part I'd memorized.

"It's good," he answered. "Will I just do the same?"

"No, it will be more complex than that... Want to see your part?"

He nodded, and I closed my eyes, getting in touch with the beat and the way I saw our dance playing out in my mind. When I felt ready, I launched into his part, working through the moves I knew would amplify his strength and personality.

When I opened my eyes, he was nodding as if impressed. "It's good. Are you sure you can't dance both parts?"

I rolled my eyes. "You'll be just fine. Want to try it?"

"Sure." He stood, and I helped walk him through

the moves. Without dance training, he picked up on the movements slower than we'd been expected to in the studio, but after a little while, he had them down well enough I could switch to my part.

I started the music over and counted us in. Our bodies moved in sync, not perfectly, not like Benjamin and I would have, but it was okay. It gave me hope that we could get there someday.

"Good job." I grinned.

He raised his eyebrows. "I have a great teacher."

I pressed my lips together to still my building smile. "You think so?"

Carter came closer, gripping my hands in his large grasp. "I know so."

My heart sped as I could feel the heat coming off him, smell the mix of cologne and sweat on his skin.

Then, my phone chimed, making me jump away and ending the moment. As I went to it, I did wish, for the shortest of seconds, that I could be like other kids. That my biggest worry was passing midterms and showing up on time for school. But wishes like that were dangerous, so I shoved them down as I checked my phone.

Des: On our way to Waldo's. See you soon!

I looked up from my phone to see Carter reaching for his bag. "I better get going too. Can I walk you to the parking lot?"

I nodded and slipped on my sweater, my stomach dancing with butterflies... or hunger. Definitely hunger.

We walked quietly beside each other, and for a moment, I realized I didn't know what to say.

"What are you doing this weekend?" he asked. "You know, other than teaching me to dance?"

"I don't know. Last weekend's plans to bust the guy stealing kettle bells failed miserably, so I might not be the best at making plans."

"Is that what you and your friends were doing?"

Embarrassment flooded me as I realized he'd seen it all—me falling off the stationary bike and screaming at the front desk people. I quickly launched into an explanation, and he nodded.

"Kettlebells are the worst anyway," he said.

"What do you have against kettlebells?"

"They're basically overhyped milk jugs."

I laughed. "That's actually a really good point. Maybe I'll tell Ted to buy those instead."

"Why do you call your dad Ted?" Carter asked.

"He's not my dad," I said quietly, coming to a

stop beside my car. "Mom married him my freshman year."

"Ah," he said with a nod and looked down. "Well, I'm embarrassed now."

"Not by the booty pop?" I asked, raising my eyebrows.

Chuckling, he said, "Touché."

With a smile, I reached into my gym bag for my keys. But before I hit unlock, I said, "You know, I'm really thankful for what you're doing. Even if it doesn't work...it means a lot."

He tipped his chin down in the most adorable way, then looked back at me. "It's worth it. And it's going to work. You're too good for it not to."

I blushed, looking down, and he put his fingers under my chin, guiding my gaze to his eyes. For a moment, they searched my own, and he slowly leaned in, his curly lashes coming together as he closed his eyes.

My heart pounded quickly, and my body wanted to fall into his. If ever there had been a guy worth dating, it was Carter. But my future was on the line. I had to remember that.

I backed up, parting from his gentle touch. "We can't," I said, trying to ignore the rejection in his eyes, the longing in my heart. "Nationals is...every-thing right now."

"And after?" he asked.

My lips twitched into a smile. "After..." I pushed the unlock button on my car and opened the door. "I'll see you tomorrow, Carter."

He backed away, his lips forming the most adorably crooked smile. "Bye, Addy."

TWENTY-ONE

THE WALDO'S Diner parking lot was just as full as it was after any football game. I found a spot along the street and walked past all the cars overflowing from the parking lot. Through the big side window, I could see my friends in our favorite booth, and Ryker had pulled up a chair to sit at the table.

They were talking to Betty, who was laughing right along with them. Our friendship seemed to have its own gravitational pull, like their kindness was so contagious it just drew people in.

I walked into the restaurant and past a couple paying at the register, then waved at my friends. They returned the gesture, and Faith and Nadira scooted over so I could get in beside them.

"Hi, sweetie," Betty said warmly. "What can I get you?"

"Sweet potato fries?" I asked. "And a tea?"

"Absolutely," she said.

As soon as she walked away, I turned to Cori. "How was the game? Did you win?"

"Yeah." She shrugged. "It was alright."

Ryker scoffed. "'Alright'? If you call twenty points and twice as many rebounds 'alright.'"

I reached across the table and shook her arm. "That's amazing!"

She blushed and took a sip of her chocolate shake. "Can we talk about how Des did at the national anthem?"

Des rolled her eyes. "Please, how differently can I sing the same song?"

Pulling out her phone, Nadira looked at the screen and said, "According to your YouTube subscribers..."

Des pushed down on Nadira's screen. "Oh, hush."

Faith gave them an exasperated smile and shook her head before turning to me. "How was the gym?"

Despite myself, my lips were spreading into a

telling grin. Carter had almost kissed me. Would have kissed me if I hadn't backed away.

"What?" Des asked. "Find some man candy?"

"Um..."

Ryker mumbled, "Man candy? I'm going to sit with my friends."

Cori squealed. "You did! Tell us everything!"

I watched as Ryker put his chair away and walked down the aisle toward some of the guys from school. How did I even begin? "There's something I haven't been telling you. It was just so new..."

Des's eyes widened. "You're dating Carter?"

"No," I said. "No, I'm *dancing* with him."

The disappointed looks on their faces didn't do the enormity of the situation any justice.

"I thought you got kicked off the dance team?" Faith asked.

I cringed. "I did. But then Carter had this idea. He said he would dance with me at qualifiers, and if we get to nationals... well, even better!"

Des's excited grin was back. "You know, they say you can tell a lot about a man by the way he dances." She waggled her eyebrows suggestively.

I rolled my eyes, even though butterflies were

dancing in my stomach. If Carter's dancing said anything, it screamed he was a natural.

"This is a big deal," Cori agreed. "He wouldn't be dancing with you if he didn't like you."

"What does that mean?" I asked.

Nadira sighed. "Even *I* know that dancing is just a cover to spend more time with you."

My cheeks were growing redder by the second. Maybe Nadira was right... "He tried to kiss me tonight."

"Tried?" Des squealed.

"Obviously I said no," I replied.

Faith's jaw dropped open. "A cute guy wanted to kiss you, and you said... no?"

"We have to focus on dance," I said. "I'm not letting some high school fling ruin what slim chances I have at nationals. You know my mom is making me sit down with her tomorrow and apply for colleges? It's getting desperate."

"What's wrong with applying for colleges?" Nadira asked.

Of course, my MIT-bound friend wouldn't understand. "I don't want to go to college and study business and just become another person who *used to* dance," I explained. "I want to be there, on stage, doing what I love."

Cori nodded. "Yeah, but you can study dance at college, right? There are performing arts schools, and it's not like they can kick you out like Galina did."

"No," I said. "They probably just wouldn't let me in."

"Then a state school," Nadira said. "It doesn't have to be some fancy place like Julliard."

"Then what's the point?" I asked. "Then I'd be just one step away from teaching dance in some rundown shack."

Cori gave me a sly grin. "Who said it has to be a shack?"

"Exactly." Des laughed. "Besides, you could always change your major. Or just move to New York and audition until you make it on Broadway." She spanned her hands in a rainbow shape like she could already see me there. At least that made one of us.

"My mom would kill me," I said. "And cut me off so fast you'd think she was an amputation surgeon and not my mother."

Faith frowned. "I get that. I told my mom I wanted to join the Peace Corps, and it was like I'd slapped her in the face or something." She put her hand over her heart and mimicked her mom's voice. "But how are you going to have time for a family?"

"That's so archaic," I said.

"It's so my mom," Faith corrected.

Betty came back with a tray full of drinks and baskets of fries. Most of my friends got milkshakes, which I looked at longingly.

Catching my gaze, Faith said, "Want some?"

"No... just... let me watch you eat it?" I teased. "Slowly?"

Giggling, Faith said, "You're insane."

"Maybe a little," I agreed.

"So," Cori said, "This qualifier... when is it? Can we come watch?"

I fiddled with my straw wrapper, anxiety about messing up on stage sneaking up on me. "The last qualifier's coming up soon, and we have to place in the top three to even get to nationals." My shoulders sagged. "I'm not sure it would be worth showing up to watch."

Des put her hand over the table and said, "Oh, we're not going to watch you. We're going to watch *Carter.*"

Laughing, I shot my straw wrapper at her. "Fine, you can come, but if it goes badly, you must never bring it up again."

"Agreed," Des said, and each of my friends nodded their assent.

I got out my phone and texted them the address of the hotel in LA where it would be taking place. I just hoped, by then, Carter and I would stand a chance. That my dreams weren't already dead.

TWENTY-TWO

ON SATURDAY MORNING, I dressed in workout clothes to go to the gym. I'd thought I was up early, but when I got to the living room, Mom had her entire wardrobe covering each piece of furniture. She stood amidst the chaos, arms folded across her chest, one hand on her chin.

"What's going on?" I asked cautiously, setting my bag on the ground.

She looked over at me as if she'd been expecting me, then back at her clothes. "Is my wardrobe old?"

My eyebrows drew together as I looked from her to all of her clothes. There was everything from matching sweatsuits to pastel summer outfits, jewel-toned winter clothes, richly colored fall outfits, and silk pajamas. "You know you're asking a seventeen-year-old, right?"

She let out a sigh and sat on the floor.

"Mom... are you okay?"

She let out an almost manic laugh. "Do I look okay?"

I picked over the clothes until I could go and sit by her. "What's going on?"

She looked over at me before pushing her perfectly done hair away from her face. "I started that styling class yesterday. I didn't realize how far out of touch I was with today's trends... Skinny jeans are out? Mom jeans are in? And what's the deal with middle parts?"

She started talking faster and faster, and I said, "Whoa, whoa, whoa. What kind of class did Janice tell you to take?"

"It doesn't matter." She looked around. "I was sitting there with all of these young people, realizing how old I really am. Honey, I'm *forty-seven*. I could have given birth to the girl your father's married to. And I never realized how much life I let get away from me." She reached out and grabbed one of her more...sensible bras, holding up the beige satin with supportive cups. "I've had this for seven years,

Adriel. Seven. You hadn't even learned long division yet when I bought this bra."

"So throw it away!" I said. "It's not like it's a set of diamond earrings!"

"But it's *comfortable!*" she moaned, collapsing over her lap and tossing the offending underwear aside.

"Then keep it!" I laughed. "Mom." I nudged her shoulder until she sat back up and looked at me. "You are the most polished person I know. And you're smart. Do you remember how many times you saved Galina's butt on costumes over the years? You can figure this out. Whatever *this* is."

Her eyes watered, and she blinked, sending a tear down her cheek. "What if Ted gets tired of me?" Her voice quivered, making my heart ache right along with hers.

For all the things Ted was—work obsessed, tone deaf, and emotionally unaware, he loved my mom. Dad had never been all that interested in Mom or me, choosing instead to spend time with his business partners and friends, which we eventually learned were affairs. Ted was different. "Have you seen the way he looks at you?" I asked.

She sniffed. "How?"

"Like he can't wait to get you to that beach in Mexico and see you in a swimsuit."

She laughed, shaking her head.

"Seriously," I said. "Have you booked the tickets yet?"

She nodded, wiping at her nose with another sensible bra, then hesitated.

"What?" I asked.

"We're leaving the day you should have been at nationals."

Her words sobered me in a way I didn't understand, and I nodded, standing. "It's fitting. The end of my dance career is the start of your marriage. The real one." The one that involved the new family they would start.

"Honey," she said sadly.

"It's okay," I said through my own tears. "I'll see you tonight. And don't you dare change the part in your hair before I get home, okay?"

She laughed softly. "Yes, ma'am."

I walked out the door and sat in my car for a long moment, the tears falling down my cheeks. I was supposed to be at the gym in half an hour, but I decided to take a detour. As I drove down the highway, I got closer and closer to the gated community Mom and I used to call home.

I pulled up to the wrought iron gate and used the passcode Dad used to use for everything. 3344. It was Mom's and my birthdays—March third and April fourth. He used to say we were his lucky pair. But now, an error code flashed across the screen.

I remembered my half-brother's birthday. With shaking fingers, I typed in the digits, and the gate slid slowly open.

I didn't need to go into the community to know that my dad had moved on. My mom would too, and soon there would just be me.

I backed away from the entrance and started down the road toward the gym. I had a dream of my own to focus on too.

TWENTY-THREE

MONDAY AT SCHOOL, I met my friends by Des's locker. She'd scored big time, getting a spot close to the lunchroom, which meant it was centrally located and in a blind corner from the office.

"How were college apps?" Faith asked as I approached.

"Two hours of torture. I applied to six colleges that have dance majors. But it was still better than my mom's midlife crisis," I answered and told them about my mom's semi-breakdown and my decision to keep nationals a secret.

Cori frowned. "You're not going to tell her?"

"I haven't even told her about dancing with Carter," I said, whispering so no one around would overhear us. Especially not Tatiana or Isabella. I was *not* ready to hear their opinions on me dancing with Carter.

"Why not?" Des asked.

I shrugged. "It just feels like it should be my thing, you know? She's given up so much for me."

Nadira put her arm around my shoulders. "Well, we're here for you."

I smiled at her. "Thanks. Now if you could just be here for me for my chem quiz. I need to go get some studying in before class starts."

I waved goodbye to them and went to my first hour, using the spare few minutes to go over the equations Mr. Cho wanted us to memorize. Every now and then during the first-hour lecture, I'd peek at my chem notes, carefully hidden behind my textbook. I should have been paying attention, but this was really an important lesson in economics. Not failing chemistry was more valuable than paying attention in that moment.

When I got to chem class, I walked back to my seat beside Carter and said, "Are you ready for this quiz?"

He shrugged. "I was pretty busy Saturday, considering my dance partner is about as intense as a drill sergeant. But I got some studying in Sunday."

I laughed. "Your dance partner should have studied more too." I'd spent most of Sunday trying to perfect the choreography while Ted and Mom went shopping. Mom came home with bags upon bags of new clothes, including bras.

The bell rang, and Mr. Cho stood at the front of the room with the quizzes. "I could give you these right now, but..." He dropped them with a thump on his desk. "I'm going to give you fifteen minutes to study instead."

A collective sigh of relief swept across the room, and Mr. Cho gave a small smile. "Now partner up, and don't make me regret it."

Carter turned to me. "Looks like it's our lucky day."

"I was hoping our lucky day would be qualifiers," I returned, getting out my notes. "What do you want to start on?"

"I actually made a study list... if you want to use mine?"

"That would be great." Cute *and* smart? *Why* did he have to be my dance partner?

He got out the first page, which had four equations, and I worked through them on my own sheet of paper while he did the same on his. When we finished, I said, "Want to check answers?"

He nodded. "You read them, and I'll tell you if I got the same thing."

"Okay, the first answer I got was P."

"Same."

"Then R."

"Yep."

"O?"

"Mhmm."

"Then M."

"Yeah." He looked at the paper. "See any patterns?"

I searched the answers, trying to understand, then said, "It just spells prom. That's weird."

He chuckled. "I couldn't exactly get a sheet of equations to spell out winter dance."

My eyes widened, and I looked at him. "Do you mean..."

"Addy, will you go to the winter dance with me?"

My mouth fell open, and I closed it as my words attempted to catch up with the squealing, love-struck girl in my mind, begging me to say yes. "Carter... I told you we couldn't do anything until after qualifiers, maybe even nationals."

"We're not." He shrugged, sitting back in his chair. "See, in my mind, this is just another practice where we can work out some kinks and gain some chemistry."

My lips spread into a slow, annoyed smile. "So, it's not a date?"

"Not at all. Just a practice session. Where I'll be picking you up...and bringing a corsage. Then getting you some food afterward."

"The best practice sessions do involve food," I agreed, grinning despite myself. But then I got serious. "This can't change anything, Carter."

"It won't. I promise." He covered my hand under my desk with his own. "If anything, it will make things better."

I practically sashayed to the lunch table where my friends were sitting.

"What are you so happy about?" Cori asked, struggling to get a packet of string cheese open.

Des, Nadira, and Faith seemed to lean in.

"Nothing," I said lightly. "Nothing except I have a date to the winter dance."

"What?" Des cried so loudly I put a finger to my lips.

"I don't want the whole school to know." Or

Carter to know how excited I was about our not-date.

Faith put her hands together as if praying. "*Please* tell me it's Carter."

"Right?" Nadira said. "Imagine how good he'll look in a suit."

I handed them both a napkin from my pile. "You guys are drooling."

They threw them back at me, and Cori said, "So it is Carter?"

Grinning, I nodded. "But it's not a real date. It's just so we can gain some chemistry. As dance partners."

Des waggled her eyebrows. "I'd say you already have some chemistry."

My cheeks heated because she was absolutely right. Staying away from Carter, or getting my mind to stay off his biceps or incredible smile, would take an act of God.

Cori pointed at me. "You like him!"

"I can't like him!" I said, throwing my hands in the air. "What if it all blows up before nationals and I've lost a chance at my future *and* my first boyfriend?"

Des perked up. "Did he call you his girlfriend?"

"No, no, no," I said. "You are all getting way

ahead of yourselves." My heart pounded. Maybe I was too.

My friends were quiet for a moment until Faith said, "Does that mean we get to help you find a dress?"

My smile returned. "Definitely."

TWENTY-FOUR

MY FRIENDS and I planned to meet up after Carter and I were done training the next day. I only had a week to find a dress for the dance. But as we made plans to find that dress, I realized I'd gotten so caught up in choreography that I hadn't thought of what Carter and I would wear at qualifiers.

Although I could easily order something online for Carter, it wasn't that simple for girls—especially not ones my size. I hoped I could find a dress at a store in Emerson Shoppes. Making a trip to LA may not be that simple.

But first, my focus had to be on the dancing. For the duration of our practices Monday and Tuesday, I drilled the choreography with him over and over so he could get used to the moves and how it felt to dance alongside someone. We wouldn't dance in unison, so he had to know the steps on his own.

"Addy, I have it down!" he said after what had to be his fifteenth time on Tuesday.

"Really?" I lifted my eyebrows. "Because you were behind half a beat on the six-count, and you still aren't pointing on the grand jete."

"Maybe because I'm terrible at leaping," he said, frustration clear in his voice.

"What do you suggest instead?" I asked. "Some kind of side to side head bob?"

He rolled his eyes. "Give me a little credit."

"What do you mean?"

"I've gone to school at the Academy long enough to know how to do my research." He began walking to the speaker. "I've been watching videos of past Dance Dance Nationals, and I think I could do something like this instead."

He pushed play on the speaker and moved more toward the center of the racquetball court. As he caught the beat, he started the choreography like I had planned, but where he was supposed to lead up to the grand jete, he ran and slid over the floor with grace that contrasted his strength. Showing all the emotion that the music called for, he transitioned back to standing where we would do another lift.

As he stood back up, I turned off the music. He eyed me wearily. "What do you think?"

I hated to admit it, but… "I like it."

His lips spread into a slow smile that I was beginning to love almost as much as dancing. "You like it?"

"Yes, I like it, okay? Let's take it from the top."

"Yes, ma'am."

I rolled my eyes and walked to the court where he'd danced moments ago. It was hard to imagine anyone had ever played racquetball here—or ever would in the future.

He started the song we planned to dance to and hustled to me, taking our beginning pose with his arm around my waist and my cheek on his shoulder. I could feel the hard muscles of his arm behind me and the warmth radiating off his skin. I breathed it in, getting lost in the moment, in the movement of our bodies together as the music began to swell.

Every time we danced, it became smoother, more natural. Harder to resist the growing attraction I felt for him—easier to own the part in the dance. A girl looking for love and finding it on stage.

Carter's grand jete replacement worked even better than the leap, and I fell deeper into the world we were building with our bodies and a song. Deeper, deeper until the song notes faded and we were left in our final pose, nose to nose, breathing in each other and the dance we created.

Banging sounded on the door, and I jerked away from Carter to see my friends' faces in the window. Faith and Nadira clapped, Des grinned like a giddy kid on Christmas morning, and Cori had her mouth in a wide, surprised smile.

My cheeks immediately flushed, and I rubbed my arms, feeling bare, like Carter and I had been caught doing something much more than dancing.

Maybe we had been.

They pushed the door open, and Cori said, "Carter, that was amazing!"

He gave her his signature smile and said, "Addy's an amazing teacher. She makes me look good."

"No way," Des said. "You have real talent. You guys are going to *crush* it at qualifiers!"

Carter turned his smile on me, making me melt. "That's the plan."

I lifted my chin, trying to still the butterflies roaming my stomach. "I think we're good for tonight. Be sure to practice that new transition when you get home."

"Yes, boss," he said with a wink and grabbed his bag before walking out the door.

Nadira stared openmouthed between me and the space where Carter had been. "That was intense."

I nodded. That, I could agree with.

Faith came and looped her arm through mine. "We better get you a dress. You know, to help with the chemistry."

Laughing, I said, "Let's go."

TWENTY-FIVE

WHEN I WALKED in the house, the TV was on and Mom and Ted were sitting together on the couch, her head on his shoulder, their hands linked between them. The second they saw me, Mom broke apart from him and stood up.

"Hi, honey! How was shopping?"

Ted turned and looked toward me too, as if he wanted to hear the answer.

"I found the one!" I held up the garment bags, careful that the one with my winter dance dress covered the one I was wearing to qualifiers.

"Let us see it!" She started to walk my way, but I backed up. If she got any closer, she'd see the second dress and start asking questions. Questions that would ruin her honeymoon that was already happening three years too late.

"Why don't I try it on for you?" I asked.

She clapped her hands together excitedly. "Please?"

"Sure." I walked away to my room and tucked my dance dress in the very back of my closet, behind all my other dance costumes. Then I went back to my bed and unzipped the bag to my dress.

The shimmery pink fabric glinted under my bedroom light. I couldn't believe my friends and I had been able to find something so absolutely...perfect.

As I pulled it from the bag, the light fabric fluttered around me, dancing like it couldn't wait for Friday either. I shimmied out of my clothes, then drew the gown over my head. It slipped over my body like it had been made for me, with its bodice that fit my bust and flared over my stomach. I reached behind my back and tied the laces that corseted the top, then looked in the mirror over my dresser.

It was every bit as beautiful as it had been in the dressing room where my friends had burst into applause. I couldn't wait to see it with hair and makeup. Or the corsage Carter had promised.

I spun, watching the dress flare around me, and couldn't help the giddy grin spreading on my face.

"Are you coming?" Mom called from the living room.

I tried to quiet my excitement and left my room. Ted was standing now too, his arm around Mom's shoulders.

I spread my arms out and spun a slow circle. "What do you think?"

"It's perfect!" Mom cried, patting Ted's chest. "Isn't it perfect?"

He cleared his throat in that awkward way step-dads do when asked to compliment a teenage girl's looks and said. "Yes, of course it is. You look great, Adriel."

"Is it Friday yet?" Mom asked. "I can't wait to get pictures of you two together. I bet that boy looks like a snack in a suit."

"Mom!" I said, already blushing. "Did you just call Carter a *snack*?"

Ted looked confused. "What does that mean?"

Mom patted him as if he were so naïve. "Honey, that's what the kids say about boys who are handsome. That they're snack food."

Ted's eyebrows came together. "Like he's a granola bar or something?"

Mom waggled her eyebrows. "Exactly."

I covered my face with my hand. "Please promise me you won't say anything about granola bars when he's here."

She batted her hand at me. "I will not be embarrassing in the least."

Ted and I both gave her a look.

"What?" She blushed, then looked at the couch. "Want to finish the movie with us, *Addy*?"

I rolled my eyes and started back toward my room. "Goodnight, Mom. Ted."

They chuckled behind me, and I couldn't help but smile. Mom seemed happier than she ever had. It made me feel good about keeping my dancing with Carter to myself. Ted deserved her attention now. Their new family did.

After taking off my dress, I put it back on the hanger and went to the bathroom to shower. As I looked in the mirror, I could see small changes happening in my body. Definition in my muscles where there wasn't any before. I turned, wondering if my belly had shrunk as well, but couldn't really tell.

I stepped on my bathroom scale, the one I'd been avoiding since my appointment with Dr. Edmonson, and saw I'd lost five pounds. I wasn't too worried about the number, not anymore, but it felt good to know my body was on the right track. That it was responding to my medication.

As soon as I finished taking a shower, I got out my laptop and lay in bed, finishing up an online assignment. With it officially submitted, I checked my email and saw an e-vite from Brandilynn, my dad's wife.

TOBY'S TURNING THREE!

Join our family in celebrating our pride and joy, Toby Lee Pruitt!

Drinks and food will be provided, along with fun activities for the children!

(Plus, an open bar for us.)

2 p.m. Sunday, December 1

6211 Warbuckle Lane

Hope to see you there!

My finger hovered over the trackpad, putting the cursor between accept and decline. My dad may have been the one who tore our family apart, and Brandilynn may have been insufferable, but Toby was my brother.

I clicked accept and closed my computer, trying

to focus on happier things. Like the fact that Carter was getting better and better at our routine. Or that I was choreographing some amazing little dancers. Or that in less than a week, he'd be at our front door for a night that was just about us.

TWENTY-SIX

MY CHOREOGRAPHY WAS NOT GOING AS WELL as I thought it would. The kids kept confusing moves or getting distracted and missing them altogether.

"Let's take a drink break!" Mrs. Florence called, not fifteen minutes into the class.

As Anna led the line to the drinking fountains, I turned to Mrs. Angeline and said, "What am I doing wrong? They were doing so much better last week!"

She shrugged. "Full moon?"

I shook my head. "I'm not doing anything different than what Galina did with me at that age..." My stomach soured. That was the problem. I was teaching like Galina instead of like myself.

"Are you okay?" Mrs. Angeline asked.

I nodded. "I have an idea. Let's spread the chairs in a big circle."

Most adults would have questioned me, but instead, Mrs. Angeline went to the stacks of chairs lining the room and got to work. I did too, and by the time the second graders came back in, we had twenty chairs in a circle around the room. One for every student.

Anna came up to me and hugged my arm. "What are you doing?"

I smiled down at her and said, "I have a game." Then I raised my voice so the rest of the class could hear me. "Everyone, find a chair!"

The kids made a raucous scramble to sit in a chair of their own, and I said. "Butts on your hands!"

They all giggled, sitting on their hands like I'd asked them to.

"Today, we're playing musical chairs...with a twist!" The students looked at one another, then to me, waiting for the next instruction. I lowered my voice to almost a whisper, so they'd have to listen carefully—a trick I'd seen Mrs. Angeline use before.

"I will give you a jump you have to do, and I

want you to do that jump in a circle until the music stops and you have to find a chair. Any questions?"

Anna raised her hand.

"Yes, Anna?"

"Can we twirl too?"

I smiled, laughing slightly. "Yes, for the final round, we can twirl."

"Yes!" she said, lisping through her half-grown-in front teeth and pumping her fist.

Mrs. Angeline observed from the side as I walked to the CD player and started the song. "Jete!"

I demonstrated, and soon the children were leaping through the air with all the endearment and grace of baby deer. A couple of the boys tried landing on each other, but once we got them settled down, I was pretty pleased with their form, then I clicked pause on the music.

The children scrambled into their seats.

One student was left without a chair, and I had her come stand by Mrs. Florence so she could practice the moves without being in the competition. Then I had them stand, and I pulled a chair before pushing play.

For the rest of the hour, we worked through

assembles, sissones, and sautes until Anna and a boy named Greg were left standing.

"Now," I said pretending I was holding a micro-phone. "We have a showdown between Miss Anna and Mr. Greg! Which twirler will come out on top?"

The girls in the room cheered for Anna, while the boys rooted for Greg. I giggled, then made my face serious, poising my finger over the play button. "Let the twirling BEGIN!"

Anna spun, making her eyes focus on a spot on the wall, while Greg spun like a wrecking ball, always seconds from crashing and toppling. The kids cheered loudly, and inside, I was rooting for Anna to win.

Cringing, I hit the pause button and watched as Greg twirled for the chair. But he'd spun so fast, he lost balance and fell to a heap in the chair, while Anna sat down gracefully, crossing her legs.

I ran to her, lifting her arm in the air. "Anna wins!"

The kids surrounded us like a mob, celebrating Anna and consoling Greg—that was until the door banged open and a hush fell over the room.

Mrs. Bates, the elementary school principal penetrated us with her beady gaze. "What on earth is going on in here?"

Anna grinned. "Only the *best* music class ever."

To which Greg agreed. By throwing up all over my shoes.

TWENTY-SEVEN

I LIFTED the mascara wand through my lashes, applying a second coat. Getting ready for the dance without my friends was much quieter than it had been for homecoming, but with my dance practices with Carter and the event being on a Friday night, we didn't have as much time. As much as I was excited to spend time with Carter, I was looking forward to hanging out with my friends as well.

I capped my mascara wand and picked up my blush, dusting it lightly over my cheeks. I missed doing makeup for performances. If I was still at Galina's studio, I would have been competing tomorrow afternoon in another qualifier.

The thought of Ben dancing with Tatiana again stung, but I shoved the thought down and focused instead on applying a layer of translucent powder over my face to set the makeup. A glance at the clock told me Carter would be arriving any minute, and I still hadn't put on my dress.

I shimmied out of my robe and went to my closet where *the* dress hung up front. I brushed my fingers over the soft fabric before taking it off the silk hanger. It fit just as perfectly as it had when I'd tried it on Monday. And Tuesday. And every day until now. Because no matter how much I didn't want to be excited about going to the dance with Carter, I was.

But wasn't that what being a dancer was all about? Feeling deeply and translating those emotions on the stage? I could hold them in, shape them, so when qualifiers came, I could put on the performance of my lifetime. I had to.

I heard the front door open, and images of my mom referring to Carter as a snack flashed across my mind.

Dear God I needed to hurry.

I quickly put on the dress, tied the back, and slipped into silver dancing heels. If this night was about gaining chemistry, we would get it on the dance floor.

Almost as an afterthought, I slipped in some

dangling diamond earrings and a necklace. With a final look in the mirror, I left my room before my mom could do too much damage.

My heels clacked loudly on the travertine floors, and suddenly I was hyperaware of every part of my body. My fingers with the press-on nails I'd applied moments ago. The necklace, cold and heavy on my bare sternum. My arms, brushing past my side. The clutch in my hand, packed to the brim with necessities for the night.

But Carter seemed to only see my eyes. His golden ones landed on mine, and if that wasn't enough, his smile nearly took my breath away. All of my skin seemed to grow hot under the weight of his gaze, the depth of its meaning.

I managed a smile and said, "You're on time."

You're on time? *You're ON TIME?* What was going on in my mind? Why was my mouth suddenly not working? "You're on time" was the equivalent of "you look clean," and I'd be livid if he said something like that to me.

So, I tried again. "I mean! You look like a snack."

Oh dear lord.

The second I said it, I shut my eyes tightly, like somehow not seeing them would make what I'd said even remotely better. I peeked open an eye to see Carter and Ted stifling laughter and my mom's mouth open in a gotcha smile.

I turned around, resigned to hiding in my room the rest of the night, but Carter caught my hand.

When I turned back to him, his voice was just as mesmerizing as his smile. "You look like a snack too."

I couldn't help the laugh that fell off my lips, and apparently Mom and Ted couldn't either. We were all laughing so hard I could barely breathe, and I was seconds away from crying off my makeup.

First school dance with a boy? Off to a *great* start.

Through tears of laughter, Mom said, "Let me get a picture of you two. By the fireplace?"

Holding my hand, Carter led me to the stone fireplace and put his arms around my waist so we could pose for a picture. It was surprisingly easy, standing with him like this. Just like dancing.

Mom snapped a few pictures with her phone while Ted stood beside her, watching the whole display.

"That was a good one," Ted commented, looking at Mom's phone.

She smiled at us. "I'll send it to you, Addy. So you can share it with Carter."

"Thank you, ma'am," Carter said with a smile.

"Of course," Mom said. "I need to tell your mother thank you for raising such a polite young man."

"My grandma, actually," he said just as kindly.

Mom immediately tried to apologize, but he said, "No worries. Are you ready to go, Addy?"

"I am," I said smiling. "I think it's time to embarrass myself in your car. Or at the dance. So many opportunities, and the night is young."

He chuckled. "Sounds like a fun time."

I waved goodbye to my mom and Ted, and Mom said, "Have fun." Ted added, "Stay safe."

And we walked out the door, into a night full of possibilities.

TWENTY-EIGHT

THE HOTEL BALLROOM had been converted to a winter wonderland despite the fact we rarely saw snow in California. I gazed up at the large, shimmering flakes reflecting strobe lights from the DJ's stand.

"It's stunning," I said.

"I agree," Carter replied, squeezing my hand.

I glanced around, hoping to see my friends amongst the mingling bodies. Or at least three of them. No doubt Des would be fashionably late, as usual.

I caught sight of bright red hair first. Cori wore a plum-colored dress that clung to her curves, and Ryker's arm was wrapped tightly around her waist.

Next to them stood Faith in a soft blue gown and Nadira in a black lacy dress.

"They look beautiful," I breathed.

"Want to say hi?" Carter asked.

"Not without me!" Des said from behind us.

I turned, letting go of Carter's hand, and saw my stunning friend in her signature color: cherry red. The mermaid dress hugged her ample chest and broad hips. She looked like she belonged in a cabaret lounge instead of at a high school dance.

"You look amazing!" I cried, giving her a hug.

"You too," she agreed and pulled back to smile at Carter. "You're lucky to have this girl on your arm."

My cheeks flushed as Carter agreed.

"Let's go say hi to the girls?" I suggested, hoping to take the attention off me and my bright red face.

The three of us walked to our friends. I loved meeting them this way. Even though we'd seen each other during lunch at school before our volunteer period, it was like greeting each other after a long period away.

Because dressing up, wearing makeup and feeling stunning changed you. It made you bolder, more confident.

The song changed to a group dance, and my

friends and I practically ran out to the floor. We did each step in unison, along with Ryker and Carter, who didn't quite know the steps. I couldn't help but feel Carter's eyes on me. And although I had danced in front of hundreds of people before, I'd never felt more nervous than I did now.

As the song faded to a close, the DJ began another fast-paced song that left us all on the dance floor, jumping to the beat. Several feet away, I could see Isabella and Tatiana and their dates, a couple of guys from Brentwood Academy.

I couldn't believe they were here, the night before a qualifier, when they should have been resting. A spark of jealousy flared within me. They could go out and do whatever they wanted, but because of my size, I had been ousted, left on my own to figure out my future.

"Addy!" Carter repeated. I could tell it was his second time saying it just from his tone.

"Sorry, what?" I asked over the slow music playing.

"May I have this dance?"

With a small smile, I took his extended hand and fell into his chest. It was just as easy as breathing. But instead of swaying back and forth like the other couples, Carter moved with me to the beat.

He practiced the waltz steps I'd taught him in preparation for our dance, along with some other contemporary moves.

As he dipped me low, I could hear my friends cheering, but all I could see were his eyes. Carter had the kindest eyes I'd ever seen on a person, and I just wanted to get lost in them. More than I already was.

He pulled me back up with ease and twirled me into a simple two-step. "How do you think it's going?"

"How what is going?" I asked breathlessly. "The dance?"

"Us."

Just the word, those two letters, had me coming undone. I could think of Carter and me as partners, accomplices, teammates. But *us*? The idea of it was too powerful.

"I'm sorry," I said. "I need some air." And I left him on the dance floor, bringing all my fears with me.

But I didn't get far. Tatiana and Isabella stood in the doorway, looking like supermodels with their slim frames and revealing dresses.

Isabella nodded her head toward the dance floor. "What was that?"

"Nothing." I tried to push past them, but Tatiana got in the way.

"Why are you in a rush?" she asked, a mean smile on her face. "Running away from how horrible that was to watch?"

I turned my eyes toward the ceiling. "What do you want from me? Isabella already got my dance partner. You're still in with the studio. You both have another chance to qualify for nationals."

Isabella folded her slender arms over her chest. "We want to know what you and your other fat friends did to Ryker. You ripping your pants in front of an audience—on camera—should have made state news. You could have been on *Tosh.0*. And because of him, crickets! What gives?"

I so didn't want to be here. Tears were building in my eyes, and I didn't want them to see me cry. Not again.

I opened my mouth to argue, but from beside me, Carter said, "No one is picking on Addy for what happened because she's a *nice person* who deserves better." All the strength in his form was in his voice, but Tatiana and Isabella didn't back down. For every ounce of kindness he had, they had two of spite.

Isabella simply clicked her tongue and said, "Carter, you could do so much better."

He narrowed his eyes at her. "So could you."

Seeing my opening, I pushed past Tatianna and Isabella and fled down the hall to the hotel entrance. The wintery air stung my skin, but not as much as the tears did my eyes.

I wiped at them, careful not to ruin my makeup, and heard the front door open behind me.

"Addy," Carter said, "Are you okay?"

A harsh laugh passed my lips. "Yeah, I'm *great*."

His fingertips trailed down my arm, adding to the goosebumps, until both of his warm hands were holding mine. He dipped his head to the side so I had no choice but to look at him. In the floodlights, his eyes looked a pale honey.

"Addy, why did you run away?"

I shook my head. "It's too much."

"What is?"

"All of it! You spend two hours a day practicing with me after you lift weights. You pick me up for the dance and buy me this beautiful corsage. And not only that, you're practically the only reason I'm not failing chemistry at this point."

"So?" he asked.

"So, *why*? Tatiana was right. You could do better. Why would you want to dance with me?"

He took one of my hands and pulled it over his shoulder and then the other so we were close enough to dance. Close enough to kiss.

"Because," he breathed. "Nothing feels better than this."

TWENTY-NINE

CARTER and I went back inside and danced together for the rest of the songs, and I tried to ignore the weight of Isabella and Tatiana's stares. Or the vulnerability of Carter's eyes on me. He was quickly becoming more than a dance partner, and I was having a hard time remembering the reasons why I shouldn't go all in.

Why I *couldn't* go all in.

When the DJ called the last song, I told my friends I would see them later and let Carter hold my hand as we walked to his car. He opened the door for me, then hurried around to the other side.

As soon as he turned on the car, he pushed the button that activated the heated seats. Immediate relief flooded my body as I sagged into the warmth.

"You're my hero," I sighed.

He grinned. "Anything to please." As he pulled out of the parking lot, he asked, "What did you think of tonight? Worth saying yes?"

I rolled my head over on the headrest, and despite the scene the *IT* Girls had made, the aching in my feet, and the dried sweat at the nape of my neck, I smiled. "Totally worth it."

"Good." He gave a satisfied smile in return and turned on the music in his car. Songs from my dance playlist surrounded us.

My eyebrows came together. "You've been listening to our practice playlist? I thought you liked country."

He nodded. "It helps me get in the right headspace."

My heart swelled, even more than earlier, and I reached across the console to hold his hand. "Thank you."

"For what?" he asked, not letting go.

"For taking this as seriously as I do."

His smile melted my resolve almost as much as his words. "I don't know if you've figured this out yet, Addy, but you've got me wrapped around your finger. I've always noticed you, but with weightlifting and school, I didn't want to get distracted."

"What changed?" I asked, needing to know.

"I realized my senior year is almost over, and I might not ever have a chance again. I couldn't waste it."

My cheeks warmed as he squeezed my hand. Was this what I'd been missing out on all through high school? Dating? Having fun? Feeling special in the eyes of a boy? It was nice.

But was it nice enough to make up for all I'd lost? Mom seemed to hope so, but I wasn't so sure.

As if he could feel the tension radiating off me, he asked, "Why has dance always been so important to you?"

I glanced over at him, at the contrast of our skin as we held hands. "Because it was the first place I ever felt like I belonged."

"What do you mean?"

I chewed on the side of my cheek, trying to decide what was enough and what was too much. I didn't like bringing up the past, but he was asking. And for the first time, I wanted to tell him. To lay myself bare, and not just on the dance floor.

"My dad worked a lot," I said, "and it was

always just my mom and me. She used to work as a stylist, and she'd bring me to appointments where I was supposed to be quiet and sit still and not cause a distraction. And then one day, instead of bringing me to a styling appointment, she brought me to a dance class.

"I fell in love," I said, looking at the streetlights and cars passing by. "For once my body wasn't something to control but something to express. Mom stopped taking me to styling appointments so she could be at practice. And as I got better and started competing, my dad would come and watch. And tell me how proud of me he was."

My throat tightened and tears threatened to fall. "But when he left my mom, that all stopped. Mom moved us into an apartment while Dad got the house. And even when I went back to visit him, it never felt like home. The studio was always home for me. It was there, regardless of who my dad was dating or who my mom married. Regardless of where I lived."

My chest ached as I realized how much I had lost in the last month. I hadn't just missed out on a chance to perform in front of dance recruiters, but I'd also lost the one place that had always been home base. My safe place.

Carter squeezed my hand, rubbing the back of it with his thumb. "I understand."

I looked over at him skeptically, trying to judge his expression as he kept his focus on the road. "What do you mean?"

"That's what Grandma's house was for me. *Is* for me. When my parents were out on marches or demonstrations, they would always drop me off at her house. No matter when I got there, if it was the middle of the night or early in the morning, I knew where she kept the milk in the fridge. The cabinet that held the best candy. Which bed was always mine to sleep in." His smile was bittersweet. "It was home before it had to be."

Now I was squeezing his hand as my heart went out to him. It was like my soul was somehow leaving my chest and dancing with his just like our bodies did. The newness and rawness of it left me breathless.

He pulled along the curb in front of my house and said, "Is it okay if I walk you inside?"

My lips quirked. "Why wouldn't it be?"

His eyes sizzled on my skin as he said, "Because, if I walk you to the door, I'm going to want to kiss you."

My heart skittered in my chest, desperate to

both run away and kiss him now in this car with our dance music playing around us. But I simply said, "Thank you, Carter, for a wonderful night." And I opened my door and walked inside on my own.

THIRTY

MY FRIENDS INVITED to me to hang out at Des's house after practicing with Carter Saturday. Des's family had a hot tub, and I wasn't about to turn down some warmth in the winter.

I pulled up to her house, amazed by the view of the ocean, as always. My other friends were already there, so I grabbed my gym bag and walked up to the front door. As soon as I knocked, one of her younger siblings threw open the door.

Upon seeing me, he shouted over his shoulder, *"DES! TUS AMIGA ESTA AQUI!"*

I understood *friend* and *here*.

He walked away from the door, leaving it open, and I took that as my cue to walk inside to the living room. Des came in, wearing her bikini, and said, "You made it! We're all changing in my room!"

I followed her in, and all the girls paused at the sight of me.

"A!" Cori said. "PLEASE tell me you and Carter kissed last night."

My cheeks heated at just how close I'd been to giving into that very urge. "We didn't." Disappointed sounds came from each of my friends, but I lifted my hands. "I told him *and* you guys that nothing can happen until after nationals. I'm not just some love-struck girl who can be swayed by a pretty smile."

Des quirked an eyebrow. "What about the muscles? That would do it for me."

I snorted, tossing my bag on Des's bed. "No amount of muscles or pretty eyes or dance skills could keep my eyes off the prize."

My phone dinged inside my bag, and I checked the notification. Benjamin had just posted online.

I clicked to it just in time to see a live video of everyone at my dance studio cheering and celebrating the fact that they qualified for nationals.

Seeing what was happening over my shoulder, Faith said, "You need a scotcheroo."

I couldn't disagree.

Nadira put her arm around me and said, "That's going to be you in two weeks. Don't give up."

I nodded and set my phone down. It *would* be me. Carter and I had been working too hard for it not to be us. As Faith handed me a scotcheroo, I said, "You guys will come watch us, right? My mom won't be there, and I just want..."

Des smiled softly at me. "To see a familiar face?"

I nodded.

"I'll be there," she promised, and the rest of my friends said they would too.

Feeling much lighter, I changed into my swimsuit and followed the girls out to the hot tub. For a moment, the air hit me like ice, but as soon as I eased into the water and steam rose around us, my shoulders relaxed.

"How's mathletes going?" I asked Nadira, leaning my head back against the side of the hot tub.

"Mathletes is great." She sighed. "My love life on the other hand? Not so hot."

"Same," Faith said.

Des shook her head. "What about your self-love life?"

"What does that mean?" Faith asked at the same time Nadira rolled her eyes and said, "Here we go again."

Des gave Nadira a look before saying, "You attract the kind of love you give yourself. Why do you think there are people out there who get cheated on over and over and over again? Or people who are always single?"

"I don't know," Cori said. "I don't think Ryker really liked himself before we started dating."

"Exactly," Des said, pointing a finger at Cori. "You hated him, remember?"

Cori shrugged. "True."

"So what?" Nadira asked. "I'm just supposed to *magically* love myself and boys at our school will *magically* have their eyes opened to my 'beauty?'"

"Don't finger quote me," Des said. "It's true!"

Faith frowned. "It's fine and dandy to say 'love yourself,' but how are you supposed to do that when everyone's told you you're ugly your whole life?"

Des shrugged. "When you hear the bad voice in your head, or anyone for that matter, that says you're not good enough, you tell it that it's full of crap and think something else instead."

I chuckled. "That easy, right?"

Des raised her eyebrows. "You should know. You have so much confidence."

"How?" I asked.

"Um, maybe because you ripped your pants in front of hundreds of people, caused a human domino pile, and you're still back at it? That's confidence."

"More like insanity," I muttered.

"And getting a guy to look at you like Carter did the night before?" Des continued. "There has to be some self-love there."

I shook my head. "I don't know about self-love. It's more like a love of dance. How could I give that up?"

Cori looked at me. "Isn't there room for all of it? Can't you love yourself and dance and Carter?"

I gave her the honest answer. "I don't know." I hadn't tried having a boyfriend and dancing before, and now wasn't the time to start. There was too much on the line to get my heart involved.

THIRTY-ONE

THE REST of the week passed in a blur of dancing and school. I should have been looking forward to qualifiers, but instead I dreaded Toby's birthday party. What would it be like to be around all Dad's friends? The ones who used to come to *my* parties?

What would it be like to be around Dad?

As Carter and I changed out of our dance shoes and into tennis shoes on Sunday, he asked, "What are you up to after this?"

I rolled my eyes toward the ceiling. "A three-year-old's birthday party with my estranged father and a stepmother young enough to be my sister."

"Ouch." He sucked a breath through his teeth. "Need a wingman?"

I lifted my eyebrows. "More like a bodyguard.

But I wouldn't volunteer for that if I were you."

He shrugged. "It's that or hanging out at my house while Grandma's friends come over to play pinochle."

"That sounds more fun," I said.

He shrugged. "There's just one problem."

"Yeah?"

"You won't be there."

My cheeks heated, and I refocused my gaze on tying my tennis shoes.

"What time is the party?" he asked.

"Two."

"Pick you up at one thirty?"

"Sure," I said as he walked toward the door. "And Carter? Be sure to dress up. Brandilynn likes to keep things formal."

"You just want me to look like a snack again," he teased.

I covered my face. "On second thought, don't come. I should never show my face in public again."

Chuckling, he said, "See you at one thirty."

"Are you sure you're going to be okay?" Mom asked, wringing her hands. "I can go with you if you want."

I took another bite of the salad I was having for a late lunch. "I'll be fine... Carter's going with me."

Her eyebrows raised. "You and Carter sure have been spending a lot of time together lately."

My heart raced, belying my guilty conscience. I wanted to tell her about dance, but I didn't want to take away from this life she was building. For the last week, she'd spent hours in front of her computer, taking the styling class, and had even shown me a new twist I could put in my hair to keep it out of my face at school.

"What with weightlifting and the dance and now the party," she said. "Are you two an item?"

I put my hand over my face. "An item?"

"Yeah, are you going steady?"

Cringe. "We haven't talked about boys enough, have we?"

Laughing, she said, "Definitely not."

"We're not 'going steady,'" I said. "I want to focus on—" I almost slipped and said dance, but instead said, "school."

"That's good," Mom said. "I've been going crazy waiting to hear back from those schools you applied to!"

"Yeah." To be honest, I hadn't even thought of

college. I knew I was running out of time to make a decision, but I could focus on that after qualifiers.

And if I dared to dream... after nationals, I wouldn't have to worry about it at all.

She reached over and rubbed my hand. "I know you had your heart set on dancing with a ballet company, but I'm so proud of how well you're taking the transition. You're making new friends, learning a new skill, and you have your whole life to look forward to. Sometimes the biggest setbacks lead to the best comebacks."

I managed a pained smile. "Thanks, Mom."

A knock sounded on the door, and I stood from the counter, forgetting my salad completely.

"Someone's excited," Mom observed.

"Shh," I said, going to the door. I opened it to see Carter holding flowers, dressed in khakis and a plaid shirt rolled up his muscular forearms.

From behind me, Mom called, "Come in, Carter!"

I stepped back from the door, taking in the flowers in his hands. They were delicate and pink, mixed with various shades of greenery.

"These are for you," he said, handing them my way.

I took them gingerly in my hands. "They're

beautiful," I breathed.

"They smell even better," he said, dipping his head slightly. "Grandma told me when I buy flowers for someone, I should make sure they smell good too."

I smiled, brushing my nose against the petals. A sweet fragrance filled my senses, making me smile just as much as the guy next to me.

When I looked to the kitchen for a vase, Mom had her hand over her chest, blinking quickly.

"Are you crying?" I hissed.

"It's just so sweet." She wiped at her eyes. "Your first boyfriend."

I glanced over my shoulder at Carter, who was stifling laughter. Giving him a pained look, I said, "Let me put these in some water and we can go... Although if we wait long enough, I may not need the sink to fill the vase." I shot Mom a look.

She held her hands up. "Sorry, sorry. Let me get you a vase." She stood from her stool by the island and walked to the cupboards, retrieving a crystal vase. "I'll take those. You two have a good time."

Handing them over, I said, "I'll see you later, Mom."

She waved goodbye, and I picked up my present for Toby before walking down the sidewalk.

"Sorry about that," I said to Carter. "I think she's having a midlife crisis."

He shrugged. "It's kind of sweet, how much she cares."

"And embarrassing," I said.

"You called me a snack." He gently bumped into my shoulder. "I think we're a little past that."

My cheeks were just as red as the wrapping paper on the present in my hands. "I'm never going to live that down."

"Nope." He unlocked the car, and we got in together.

As I gave him the address to type into his phone, I realized I was coming to love the scent of his car, like gym clothes and the new leather fragrance that failed to completely cover it up. As he turned the car on, our dance music played. I smiled at the radio. "I love that you listen to our routine music."

"About the song..." Carter said, pulling onto the road.

I raised an eyebrow. "It's perfect."

"Yes, but I had an idea."

I gripped the present in my lap tighter. I realized I didn't want to have to tell him no.

"What if Desirae sings it for us?" he asked. "No

one else at the competition would have anything like it, and then she could add it to her channel. My friend Griffin could lay down a track for her."

My mouth went slack. "That's...actually a really good idea."

"As though I'm incapable of having those," he teased. "In case you don't remember, I'm the one who suggested we dance together in the first place."

"True."

"And that we go to the dance together."

"That was fun," I agreed, smiling.

"Just like we'll have fun today," he replied.

"You haven't met my father... Or his mistress." I groaned, sitting back in my seat. "This is going to be a nightmare."

"How long has it been since you've seen him?"

I shrugged. "Counting the time I accidently saw him in a café and he had no idea about the dance debacle and my half-brother didn't remember who I was?"

Carter sucked in a sharp breath.

"Yep."

"Okay, so the way I survive these kinds of parties is to come up with an inside joke. Like I count the number of times someone talks about Spain or brings up their private yacht."

I rolled my eyes. "I'm not sure you could count that high in this crowd."

"That's the fun," he said. "So what should we keep track of?"

I tapped my chin. "Every time someone comments to my dad how lucky he is to have Brandilynn."

"Oh my gosh." Carter's mouth was open in a circle. "Her name really is *Brandilynn*."

"Uh huh." I glanced over. "And I'm pretty sure she's already had three surgeries since being with Dad, so..."

"This will be good," Carter said with a smirk.

We pulled up to the gate, and I gave him the pass code...the new birthday. Then we drove down the winding path lined every so often with clusters of balloons. Soon, we reached my former home. My dad's home.

"There's valet?" Carter muttered as a guy in black pants and a red polo approached the car.

"Of course," I muttered. "It's for Toby."

The valet opened the door for me, and Carter got out on his own. After passing the keys over, Carter came and took my hand. Leaning close, he whispered in my ear, "Bodyguard, at your service."

THIRTY-TWO

I HADN'T SPENT the night at my former home since Toby was born. Hadn't spent much time there at all, really, since the divorce. Walking inside felt like entering a parallel universe.

There was still the grand entry with the winding staircase, but now it was covered in a massive cascade of brightly colored balloons. Although Brandilynn had said no gifts were needed, a table towered with extravagantly wrapped presents.

Carter and I added ours to the pile and continued walking to the open concept living room and dining room, which was completely packed with people. Over the fireplace rested a large printed photo of Dad, Brandilynn and Toby. The kind you knew was posed but they laughed so happily it almost convinced you they were thrilled just to be in a field. They were the perfect family. Without me.

Carter squeezed my hand. "You okay?" he whispered.

I nodded, unable to speak.

A few children ran past, maybe six or seven years old, knocking me into Carter. I tried to catch myself, placing my hands firmly on his shoulders. I looked meekly up at him, and he grinned down at me.

"Are you...falling for me, Addy?"

Rolling my eyes, I pushed myself up. "And I thought I was the one who was trippin'."

"You know what they say about bit—"

"There are children here!" I hissed, to which he chuckled.

"Adriel!" Brandilynn crooned in the high-pitched voice only she could manage.

By the time I plastered a smile on my face, she was already wrapping her spindly arms around me. Over her shoulder, I glared at Carter. What happened to him being my bodyguard?

"Hi, honey!" She patted my back. "It is *so* good to see you here! Your dad and Tobster are going to be thrilled!" She stepped back, clapping her hands together. "And who is this handsome slice?"

I would have been embarrassed, but it was Brandilynn. She probably talked with her sorority sisters like that all the time. "Brandilynn, this is Carter, my friend from school."

"Hi, *friend*." She extended her manicured hand for a shake, which Carter did quickly.

"Great party," he said.

"My Toby deserves the best."

Carter squeezed my hand. "Where is he?"

Brandilynn took a sip of her mixed drink and batted her hand at us. "Probably in the bounce castle. It's in the playroom."

My eyebrows came together. "Playroom?" There had never been one of those when I lived here. "Where is it?"

"Upstairs, second door on the left." Someone accosted Brandilynn, greeting her with kisses on the cheek.

I blinked as what she'd said registered. The "playroom" was my old room. I had to see this for myself.

"Come on," I said to Carter, practically dragging him toward the stairs. I climbed them as quickly as I could with all the guests going up and down, then walked to the room with people spilling out the doorway. The room that used to be mine.

I shouldered past the guests until I walked inside, covering my mouth. Where my bed used to be, there was now an inflatable that nearly reached the fourteen-foot ceilings. Instead of the soft pink paint that had covered the walls, it was now a grayish blue. A big sign with Toby's name on it hung on the wall. Where my dresser had been, there was now a massive toy chest. Where my desk had been, a mini trampoline.

Everything that had been mine, any trace of me, had been erased.

"Are you okay?" Carter asked softly, but before I could answer, my dad approached us.

"Adriel! I'm so glad you came!" He leaned in to hug me, but I stepped back.

"What did you do to my room?"

Dad looked around, a crease growing between his eyebrows. "You can't seriously be mad. You haven't stayed here in what…two, two and a half years?"

"Three years." I shook my head, blinking quickly. He didn't even know how long it had been since I'd spent the night with him. He didn't care.

"You and Brandilynn couldn't wait to get rid of me, could you?"

The crease between his eyebrows deepened even more. "Don't blame Brandilynn. I agreed; it didn't make sense to have a room you never used sit empty."

Each of his dismissive words sliced me open, one burning papercut at a time. "I didn't think you'd just forget me like this."

"Brandilynn and I have a son to take care of, Adriel."

I'd thought it couldn't hurt worse, but it did. My breath came out in a shudder as I said, "Forget about your daughter." He already had.

I turned to leave, and Dad put his hand on my shoulder, saying, "Adriel."

I turned toward him, glaring at his hand, but I didn't need to. Carter stepped between my dad and me, cutting off the unwanted contact.

Dad looked from Carter to me, seeming to sag. "We all make our own choices, and I have to be with the family who chose me."

That was a cop-out. I looked him straight in the eye and said, "Don't forget, you chose them first."

I turned and left, and Dad didn't try to stop me. Carter walked alongside me until we were outside and he gave the valet his card. As the guy left to pick up the car, Carter gently directed me to a bench along the driveway.

Still in a daze, I sat beside him. My eyes were glazed with tears as I looked at him. "Why wasn't I good enough for him to want me to stay?"

He brushed his thumb over my cheek, swiping away the moisture. "You're asking the wrong question, Addy."

"What do you mean?"

"You should be asking why he was *stupid* enough to let you leave."

THIRTY-THREE

MOM ASKED me about Toby's birthday party, but I just told her it was fine. I didn't want to bring up Dad and how much he really had moved on from us. From me. Mom had a new husband, Dad had a new wife, and what did that leave me with?

Dance.

Without it, I wouldn't have much left.

I spent the rest of the afternoon in my room, working on choreography for the second graders and then for Carter and myself. Working through the dance moves and seeing them play out in my mind was more fun than I ever thought choreography could be.

I'd always seen myself as a dancer, a performer, but maybe there was more that I could be. After all, teaching the second graders my routine was one of the most fun things I'd ever done, twirling throw up and all.

A small part of me wondered what it would be like to open a competing studio in Emerson, to go head-to-head with Galina. To give dancers a safe place that would be their home like the dance studio had always been for me.

I could practically hear Galina's voice in the back of my head. *Those who can't do, teach. You should only teach* after *a long streak of doing, and doing well.*

I shook away the thought and her voice and got back to work.

On Monday in chemistry, Carter gave me a concerned look as I sat down, but I busied myself getting my notebook out and setting up my pens just so. Taking the hint, he stayed quiet throughout the hour, except to say he'd see me at the gym after school.

Over lunch, Nadira helped me with my math homework so I wouldn't have to worry about it that night, and then I was back at Ted's Gym, lifting weights next to Carter.

As I worked through the routine Raf gave me, I noticed how much more easily the movements came. Like with dancing, my muscles memorized the pattern. If only life, and love, could be ingrained so easily.

In the racquetball court, Carter and I worked through our choreography over and over again until our time was up. There were still a few transitional moves I wanted to smooth out, but I was happy with how it was going. My heart lifted with the crazy hope that maybe we could pull this off. That we could qualify for nationals.

I was already feeling lighter than I had all weekend when Carter picked up his gym bag and said, "Do you have a few minutes?"

Although we'd just spent three hours together, I nodded. "What's up?"

Unzipping a side pocket of his bag, he pulled out a sandwich bag filled with black plastic squares and some black electrical tape.

I tilted my head to the side, examining it. "What's that for?"

The smile that spread across his face was full of mischief. "We're going to find out who's taking those kettlebells, once and for all."

I giggled, walking toward him. "You know I'm in."

After getting my bag, I followed him out of the racquetball court and toward the hallway that led to the gym equipment.

Carter asked, "Is there a size that they usually steal?"

I wracked my brain, but I couldn't remember Ted mentioning a specific size. "Ted just told me they've stolen hundreds of pounds of weights."

"That's okay," Carter said. "My friend gave me quite a few Tracker Tiles. We should be able to get it on one."

"Where did he get them?" I asked, glancing at his bag.

"His dad's patenting a new kind of Tile that's ultra-thin. He wanted some product testers, so I volunteered." Carter said it like it was no big deal, but the fact that he even remembered the kettlebells or cared enough to help me catch the thief meant the world to me.

"That's amazing," I said. "Which friend?" The scary thought that it could be a girlfriend came to mind, but I shoved it down.

"You know Apollo Ashe?"

I nodded, hating how relieved I felt. "He's a sophomore, right? The mayor's son?"

"Yeah," Carter said. "And his dad is an inventor. They have this massive garage filled with tools and wires and everything. It looks like *Dexter's Lab*."

I laughed, remembering that old cartoon. "Incredible."

We drew closer to the rack that held kettlebells and glanced around. There were a few people working out, but they seemed to be using the dumb-bells, not the kettlebells. Surreptitiously, Carter handed me a few of the plastic squares and a strand of tape.

We set to work, glancing around to make sure no one noticed us, and taped all of the Tracker Tiles to the bottom of the kettlebells. Black electrical tape had been a genius move—if you weren't looking closely, you wouldn't notice the small strip of tape along the bottom of the black kettlebells.

Once we finished, Carter offered to walk me to my car. Of course, I accepted. As we exited the gym, I asked, "How will we know if one's been stolen?"

"I have an app on my phone connected to the Tracker Tiles. If one moves more than five hundred feet from the original location, I'll get a notification."

"That's a little creepy, isn't it?" I asked.

He shrugged, causing him to have to readjust the strap of his gym bag. "It's meant to protect expensive merchandise. Like to go on the tags of diamond necklaces and in jewelry boxes. I think Ashe's dad will probably be careful who he sells them to."

"That makes sense." People were so quick to protect precious items. Even quicker to throw away the things that really mattered. We reached my car, and I looked up at Carter. I'd never be able to thank him enough for all he'd done, but I decided to try. "Thank you"—I gestured toward the gym—"for this." I shook my head. "I feel like you're always swooping in to save the day."

A gust of cold wind swept across the parking lot, pulling a strand of hair over my face. Carter carefully pushed it back behind my ear. "I've always wanted to be your Superman."

I lifted a corner of my lips. "I never pictured myself as Lois Lane."

"Me neither," he said, his hand falling away from my cheek. "Addy Pruitt is so much better."

My eyes were on his lips as he said the words. I

wanted to close the gap between us and put my lips on his. Only twelve inches separated us. Twelve inches and my dream for a future in dance.

If my parents had taught me anything, it was that love derailed your dreams. And dreams could derail your love. I wouldn't do that to Carter. Wouldn't open the possibility of him doing that for me.

I looked away from his lips and into his warm honey eyes. "Goodnight, Superman."

As I got into my car, he breathed, "Goodnight, Addy."

THIRTY-FOUR

DES DRUMMED her hands on the lunch table where the five of us sat eating. "I feel like we should have an after-party for qualifiers."

"An after-party?" I asked. "What if we don't qualify? It won't be much of a party."

"Please," Faith said. "If you dance half as well as you two did at homecoming, you're a shoo-in."

I smiled and shook my head. "It's not that simple. They judge us on costumes, chemistry, dancing, emoting... There are so many ways it could go wrong."

Cori stuck her finger in the air. "Or right."

I shook my head.

"So the after-party," Des said. "I'm thinking we

could go to Seaton Pier, have a fire, and plenty of food. You know Mama De will hook us up."

Cori smiled, shaking her head, and mimicked Des's mom's voice. "Empty stomach, empty heart. That's what I always tell you girls. Better to have some meat on your bones and a good head on your shoulders."

I giggled at her spot-on impression, and Des said, "Nailed it."

Nadira said, "So what? We just go to the beach and eat? Sounds like a *great* celebration."

Des put her arm around Nadira's shoulders and drew her in close. "No, we go to the beach and have a toast to our amazing friend Adriel, who *definitely* made it to nationals. We listen to some music, watch the sunset, warm up with a bonfire... maybe kiss some boys." She waggled her eyebrows. "It will be amazing."

She already had me convinced. "I'm in," I said. "Minus the kissing part. Carter and I need to wait until after nationals."

Des giggled. "We can't peer pressure you, huh?"

I rolled my eyes. "Who do you want to invite?"

"Everyone," Des said. "Especially the *IT* Girls. After how they treated you at the dance, I want to rub your win in Isabella and Tatianna's faces."

I smiled, picturing what would surely be shocked expressions. But the expression I really wanted to see was Galina's. She had cast me aside just as easily as my father had. I wanted to show her that had been a mistake. That even a big girl could be an asset on a dance team.

"So, Saturday?" Cori said. "I'll have Ryker spread the word. It'll get to the *IT* Girls."

"Perfect," Des said, smiling.

For the rest of lunch, we made plans to stay at Des's house the night of the party. I just hoped it would be a celebratory event rather than consolatory one.

As soon as I got to the gym and saw Carter in his usual spot, I went to him and said, "Party at Seaton Beach, Saturday night."

He lifted his eyebrows. "Party?"

I nodded. "To celebrate us qualifying for nationals."

"That sounds great," he said. "Except for a minor detail."

"What's that?" I asked.

"We haven't qualified for nationals yet," he said.

From behind me, Ted said, "Nationals? Are you two competing in something?"

My cheeks immediately flushed as I turned to see my mom's husband standing near us at the weights station.

"For school," I stuttered. "What are you doing here? I mean, besides the obvious. I know you own the place but—" God, I was rambling. I sealed my mouth shut.

Ted chuckled. "Just came to see how training was going. Where's Raf?"

"Right here," Raf said from a few feet away. "How's it going, boss?"

Ted said, "Good. Just checking in on these two."

Raf smirked. "They need checking in on. Always running off to play racquetball after weightlifting."

It felt like Raf had dumped ice water over my head. He knew we were going to the racquetball courts?

"Racquetball?" Ted said skeptically. "It is a fun game... private courts."

I nearly choked on my own saliva at what he was insinuating, but Carter laughed, playing it off.

"An alumnus from the Academy said they play intramural racquetball in college, that it's a great way to make friends," Carter said, putting his arm around my shoulders. "Since Addy's nervous for college, we thought we could practice."

Ted's expression seemed to soften, and he said to me, "You'll do great, Adriel, whichever school you get into."

His words softened my heart toward him. A small voice in the back of my head wondered if he cared about more than just my mom. If he cared about *me*.

"Well, I'll let you get back to it," Ted said, then made the I'm-watching-you gesture to Raf and Carter. "Take care of my girl."

Okay, 'my girl' might have been going a little far. I rolled my eyes and turned to Raf. "What are we working on today?"

"That was a close one," I said on the way to the racquetball court. My cheeks were still hot, and the pounding in my heart had less to do with the workout than it did with the near miss. If Ted found out Carter and I were dancing together, he would tell Mom. And if Mom found out, it would be the end of their plans for Cancun. She'd be sucked back into my world—the dance world—and I didn't want to ruin her plans when she had so much to look forward to.

In the last couple weeks, she'd finished her online course and even managed to get a couple of styling clients. Not to mention, her beautician had her on the path to growing out her bangs. I couldn't picture Mom without bangs, but she was excited. I couldn't take that away from her.

Carter said, "It was okay, but I did learn something very important about you."

I raised my eyebrows. "And that would be?"

"That you're a terrible liar." He laughed, and I hit his arm, coming into contact with rock-hard muscle.

He only laughed, but I had to fight down the eager swoop that went through my stomach. Keeping my heart in check when it came to Carter was getting harder every single day.

Carter reached the racquetball court door first and held it open for me. Once we got the speaker set up, I ran Carter through some flexibility drills, but we quickly dove into the routine, working through it again and again. Sweat beaded on my forehead, just as it had when we were lifting, and I felt more at home, more alive, than I had in a long time.

We hit our final pose, our faces inches apart, and I breathed, "Hold. Let it sink in for the judges."

Carters eyes searched mine. We were so close.

The door creaked open, and I jumped apart from Carter, my heart squeezing tight.

Ted stood in the doorway, holding a racket.

My mouth fell open as I took in the scene as Ted did the same. Moments ago, I'd been hot with sweat, but now I was cold. Ice cold.

Ted stepped forward and said, "Adriel, why don't you tell me what's really been going on here?"

THIRTY-FIVE

WHY DID I feel like I'd been doing something wrong? I looked between Carter and Ted and felt *guilty*. Guiltier than if Carter and I had been doing what Ted first assumed we'd been doing.

I wished I could have clammed up. Hidden under the sand at Seaton Pier and never come up for air again if it meant keeping this secret, but Ted was waiting for an answer, and I had to give him one.

"We've been dancing," I said, my voice shaking.

"I can see that," Ted said. "What I want to know is *why?*"

I met Carter's eyes for a moment, and he looked torn. But he gave me a small nod that provided me just enough strength to keep going.

I turned back to Ted, taking a deep breath. "Carter and I are training for the Dance Dance qualifiers on Saturday."

Understanding crossed Ted's expression. "So the reason you've been doing so well is because… you haven't given up yet."

Tears brimmed my eyes as I shook my head. "I couldn't." They were the two truest words I'd ever spoken. "I *can't.*"

Ted scrubbed his hand over his chin and rested his chin in his palm. "Why didn't you tell us? Your mom?"

His eyes settled on mine, and I let out a shaky sigh. "Cancun."

"Cancun?" he asked.

I nodded slowly. "You and Mom have been married for almost three years, and you haven't even taken your honeymoon yet. Because of me."

"What does that have to do with this?" he asked.

A frustrated sigh parted my lips. "Don't you get it? Mom is finally moving on. Having a life of her own. If I told her about this, she would go back into dance mode. You would lose your wife all over again."

"Oh, kiddo," he breathed. "But you would have your mom."

My lips trembled. "I still have my mom." I wasn't sure who I was trying to convince. Him or myself. "But if Carter and I make it to nationals, you wouldn't have her in Cancun."

Ted's lips set into a frown. "They're the same day?"

"Your trip and nationals?" I nodded. "Ted, you can't tell her."

Now he seemed frustrated. "Adriel—"

"No," I said. "My mom has lost so much because of dance. Years of her career... my dad." My voice shook. "I won't let her lose you too."

Carter gripped my fingers, giving me the strength I needed to stick to my plan. What I wanted for my mom, even if it meant going it alone.

"She won't lose me," Ted said, shaking his head.

"Maybe not this time," I said. "But some day, you'll get tired of always coming second. Of sitting on the beach alone. And Mom? She'll resent me. Maybe not now or five years from now, but she will. It's time for both of us to see how we stand on our own. How she stands with you."

Ted pressed his palm to his lips, shaking his

head side to side as if what I said wasn't the truth. He knew it just as well as I did, though, because he let loose a long breath and said, "You know what you're asking me to do, right?"

I nodded.

He sighed.

I chewed on the inside of my cheek, praying he would make the right choice.

For a long moment, he looked between Carter and me, then he said, "I'll keep it between us, for now, but the second we get back from Cancun? You tell her everything."

"I promise," I said.

Then he did something I never expected he would. He crossed the gap and held me to his chest in a tight hug. As he stepped back, he said, "You're an amazing young woman, Adriel. Your mother is so proud of you. And so am I."

My lips quivered as I pulled them into a tearful smile. "Thank you, Ted."

He nodded swiftly and gave Carter a parting glance before leaving us in the racquetball court. Just me, Carter, and all of the secrets we'd somehow managed to keep.

THIRTY-SIX

THE GIRLS and I met in the AV room on Thursday, and I couldn't believe how this place had become one of my favorite places in Emerson Academy. The room looked like a throwback to the eighties, with VHS tapes lining the walls, covering the wood paneling.

Our guidance counselor, Mrs. Bardot, had brought in food catered from La Belle, and all the Italian food on the table looked like heaven. Even the salad, loaded with chopped vegetables and seasoned croutons, made my mouth water.

Nadira came in beside me. "You're early."

"You too, although, that isn't really a surprise." I sat beside her and began helping myself as the others came into the room. "I thought you had a Mathlete competition today?"

She grinned at me, lighting up. "We leave after lunch. Good timing, right?"

I chuckled. "Perfect timing. If math wasn't involved, I might sign up myself."

She snorted and took a bite of a breadstick. I took in her features, thinking Nadira really was beautiful. Even though she was insecure about her vitiligo, a skin condition that took pigments from her dark skin, I thought it made her that much prettier. She was one of a kind—there was no one like her.

From behind me, Cori said, "Oh my gosh, Italian. Yes, I was *starving!*"

I giggled, turning to see her making a beeline to the chicken alfredo. Faith came in soon after, sitting on my other side, and then Des arrived, fashionably late as usual. How she managed to look so glam in plaid and navy blue, I had *no* idea.

Soon, we all had plates full of rich Italian food, and even though most of mine was covered in salad, I did take small portions of fattier foods. My thyroid medicine was helping me finally slim down a bit. Even though I was still bigger than most dancers, I felt more like myself. Less sluggish. Less sad. More...me.

Des looked across the table at me. "Getting pumped for this weekend?"

"The party or the competition?" I teased.

"Both," she said easily.

I frowned. "Pumped, yes, but I'm just starting to worry that our costumes aren't good enough. Usually my mom helps add extra beading to my outfits, but since she doesn't know..."

Faith perked up. "I can sew."

"What?" I asked, staring at her like she'd grown a second head.

She smiled shyly. "My grandma brings me along to her quilting club meetings. I know it's not the same thing, but I can sew beads onto your costumes?"

My eyes widened. "That would be amazing! But are you sure? I'd need them by noon Saturday, and that doesn't leave a lot of time."

"Definitely," Faith said as if she wasn't totally saving my life. "I can bring them over to Grandma's after school Friday, and we can work on them together."

I put my arms around her shoulders and gave

her a sideways hug. "You're the best! I'll bring the costumes to you tomorrow?"

Smiling, she nodded. "Sounds great."

Tension eased from my shoulders, and I felt like I could enjoy the meal even better now.

Cori looked up and said, "Do you guys ever wonder who the anonymous sponsor is?"

Des swallowed her bite and said, "What do you mean?"

"I don't know." Cori twirled her fork in her fingers. "Someone pays for this meal every week... Who do you think it is?"

My eyebrows came together as I thought about it. I did remember Mrs. Bardot telling us someone sponsored these meals, but Cori had a good point. Why?

Nadira said, "Do you think it could be a parent of the last Curvy Girl Club?"

Cori snorted. "I know it's not my parents. And Mrs. Hutton would never pay for us to eat such fatty food. Zara Bhatta's dad is a movie producer... maybe him?"

I shrugged. "Maybe. But isn't Jordan dating a billionaire? Do you think he could be paying for it?"

"No idea," Faith said. "I'm just thankful for the blessing. Try not to question it too much."

Cori seemed to ponder on it a moment longer but shrugged. We ate and talked until the bell rang and it was time to get to class. Although I had a test coming up, most of my nerves revolved around qualifiers.

Would Carter and I do well enough to place in the top three?

I never remembered feeling this nervous when dancing with Benjamin. We'd practiced the routine so many times and put in so many collective hours at the studio, placing was a given. Galina was the best, and she prepared us to be the best as well.

Would my years of training be enough? I hoped so.

THIRTY-SEVEN

SATURDAY MORNING, I was in my room, packing my bag for qualifiers and the after-party when Mom came in. Thankfully, Faith had my dance costume, so Mom didn't have a sightline to anything other than my toiletry kit and an extra outfit.

"What are you doing?" she asked, seeming confused.

"I'm staying at Des's tonight. Remember?"

"Oh." She seemed disappointed. "I must have missed it with all my new client work." She came and sat on the edge of my bed. "I was hoping to spend some time with you and Ted. Maybe go to the apple orchard and have some cider."

My heart wrenched. That actually sounded like

fun—doing something with Mom that didn't involve dance or school. "Rain check?"

Sadly, she nodded.

"Maybe you can go with Ted?" I suggested. "Have some fun together just the two of you?"

She seemed to brighten slightly at the idea, but then said, "It won't be the same without you."

"Maybe that's a good thing," I replied. At her confused look, I finished zipping my bag and went to sit by her, resting my head on her shoulder. "Do you think...maybe if you wouldn't have been so preoccupied with dance that Dad wouldn't have..." I couldn't finish the sentence. Not over the lump forming in my throat.

The guilty feeling I always carried with me seemed larger than ever.

"Oh honey." She stroked the loose tresses away from my face. "You know as a parent, you're always trying to protect your kids." She let out a heavy sigh. "Sometimes you even try to protect them from the truth."

I frowned. "What do you mean?"

"Your father's...infidelity started well before our marriage. Before you were born."

Her words doused me like ice water, and I jerked away from her shoulder, stunned. As I tried to take in exactly what she was saying, my mouth fell open and closed. Was she really telling me that in their *fifteen years* of marriage, he'd never once been faithful? And that she'd stayed through it all?

Mom scooted forward on the bed as if to come closer, but I shook my head. How could she have stayed with a cheater? And if she'd known this all along, why had she let me be so surprised by the divorce?

"Why?" I demanded. "Why would you stay with someone who cheated on you?"

Her features steeped in compassion. For me. For herself. "Honey, when you don't feel good about yourself, you'll accept a lot of things you shouldn't."

Her words echoed Des's from the hot tub, but I still didn't understand. "Why wouldn't you feel good about yourself?" My mom was the kind of beautiful I hoped to be at her age. Curvaceous, always well put together, and a devoted mom. How had I never known she struggled with self-esteem?

She smiled tearfully and shook her head. "My mom was a beautiful woman. I was always in her shadow, and she knew it. I was a burden to her, never living up to her expectations. I always promised myself I would do anything for my child, be there for her like my mom never was for me."

My heart ached at her words, because she'd done the exact opposite of what her mother had done. She'd become a martyr to my needs, suffering through a loveless marriage and endangering the marriage she had with Ted. If it was better. Was it better?

"But things are different now?" I asked, slowly coming closer to her again. "Ted wouldn't cheat on you...right?"

"Of course not," Mom said. "Why would I put myself and you through that again?"

With a sad smile, I mirrored what she'd said earlier. "When you don't feel good about yourself, you accept a lot of things you shouldn't."

Shaking her head, she said, "How did I raise such an incredible daughter? I hope you know how proud I am of you. Of how well you bounced back after what Galina did. And you're letting yourself have adventures I never had, a great group of friends"—she nudged my shoulders—"dating a *snack* of a guy."

My cheeks warmed despite the ice in my stomach. Was I really letting myself have more than Mom had when she was younger? Or was I diminishing my life to only include one thing I lifted above all else?

After all, hadn't I turned down Carter, time after time, because I didn't want to risk dance?

She put her arm around my shoulders. "Promise me you'll have fun with your friends this weekend and that you'll always accept the things you deserve. Nothing less."

I leaned closer into her hug. "I promise."

THIRTY-EIGHT

QUALIFIERS TOOK place in a giant convention center in LA. I'd planned to meet Carter at his house and ride together, but he texted me that he would come and get me instead. He pulled up outside my house at noon.

And he wasn't the only one in the car.

I tried to see through the window who was with him, hoping it wasn't another girl. That I hadn't lost my chance.

My talk with my mom this morning had my heart, and mind, on Carter, even though I should have been putting all my focus on qualifiers. I closed my eyes, taking a deep breath like Galina's meditative training had taught me. The fact that it helped only irritated me a little.

Feeling more centered, I picked up my bag and opened the door just as he made it to the front steps.

He seemed surprised, but his features quickly relaxed into a smile. "Addy. You're ready?"

I lifted my duffel bag, which held all of my stage makeup and hair products, as well as clothes for tomorrow. "I have what I need, and Faith is meeting us with our costumes!"

"Great," he said, then, noticing me peering at his car, he said, "Don't hate me, but my grandma wanted to come watch."

His grandma? My lips spread into a seriously massive grin. "Of course I don't hate you!" Maybe that came off a little too eager...

He seemed relieved. "Good." He took my duffel bag from me and started toward the car. "She's been so excited about us dancing, and when she found out qualifiers were today, there was no talking her out of it."

I smiled at the wrinkled but beautiful woman through the car window and waved. "It's fine. Really."

He put my bag in the trunk, and before I could open the back door to get in, he took my hand, pulling me closer. It was stunningly easy to fall into him. To relax into his presence.

"How are you feeling about today?" he asked, searching my eyes.

I was so caught in his own honey eyes it took me a moment to register his question and another yet to think it through. "I'm scared," I said honestly. So much of what I'd been working toward the last several years rested on how today went.

He nodded, pulling me into a hug that was much too short. "You can do this."

"What about you?" I asked. "How are you feeling?"

He chuckled and bit his lip. "I'm fine. You're the one carrying the team, remember?" He teasingly nudged my arm. "Look at those guns."

I rolled my eyes and reached for the handle, feeling better already. Something about Carter's presence both sent my heart racing and soothed me at the same time. I'd never been around anyone who made me feel that way. Anyone except Carter.

As I got in the car, his grandma turned toward me and extended her beautifully manicured hand with long, bright red nails. "I'm Dorothea. Nice to meet you, Addy."

I smiled and shook her hand, feeling the warmth of her strong grip and the chill of her multiple rings. "Nice to meet you."

Carter got into the car and put on his seat belt. "Ready to go?"

Dorothea buckled her seat belt again. "Absolutely."

He turned toward me, a spark of excitement in his eyes. "Addy?"

I nodded, smiling. Today was going to be one heck of a ride.

As he took off, my phone vibrated, and I checked it to see a picture from Des. She'd taken a selfie with Faith, Nadira, and Cori in the car. My phone vibrated again as a new message came across the screen.

Des: On our way!

Adriel: See you soon. <3

I clicked my lock screen and sat back in the seat, trying to distract myself from all the adrenaline already rushing through my body. Thankfully, Dorothea turned and said, "How long have you been dancing, Addy?"

I smiled softly at her question. "All my life. Have you ever danced before?"

"Carter's grandfather and I used to cut a rug or two. Carter grew up dancing in the kitchen." On the side of her face I could see, her wrinkles deepened with an easy smile. Now I knew where Carter got it from. The smile and his dance moves.

"Has he practiced for you yet?" I asked.

Carter cleared his throat as Dorothea chuckled.

"Only every night," she said. "I can't tell you how much fun we've been having since this started."

I smiled, already feeling better, more relaxed. Maybe Dorothea would be our good luck charm.

She let out a happy sigh. "It reminds me of dating Rutherford."

"My grandpa," Carter added over his shoulder.

Outside the car, the city quickly passed by as Carter drove us toward LA. I kept my eyes on Dorothea and asked, "What do you mean?"

She smiled, and in the rearview mirror, I saw Carter's kind eyes on me. He was happy, and that made my heart swell.

"Back in those days," she said, "they had barn dances. We'd go out to the country, to a friend's barn, once a month, and dance the night away. There would usually be a band, just a group of friends playing together, but we didn't care much about the music. The company was more important." She put a hand on Carter's shoulder. "Your grandpa was fine company. Always a gentleman." She turned back toward me and winked. "Rutherford always made sure to bring me flowers and to get me home ten minutes before curfew so Daddy wouldn't be mad."

I chuckled, picturing this beautiful woman as a teen my age. "How old were you when you married him?"

"Eighteen," she answered. "We went to the church right after graduation. Didn't even change outfits... Things were different then."

I couldn't imagine getting married at eighteen. Much less twenty. But I wouldn't have minded going to another dance with Carter. Spending time with him.

Carter said, "If someone in my class got married after graduation, I'd think they were crazy."

"You'd be right," she chuckled. "But sometimes it's just as crazy to deny what's right in front of you."

I glanced into the rearview mirror and saw Carter's honey eyes on mine. They gripped my heart just as surely as his hands gripped my waist in our dance. What would it be like to go all in and follow my heart?

I glanced down, blinking away the thought. Right now, we needed to focus on qualifiers. And afterward? One way or another, I would make my move because I knew I had something incredible in front of me.

THIRTY-NINE

WHILE CARTER WENT to help his grandma find a seat, I met my friends to get the costumes. They stood near the entrance of the convention center, Faith holding two garment bags. They were also wearing bright yellow shirts...

As I drew nearer, they spread out their jackets so I could see the words on the front.

JETE ALL DAY

My mouth fell open. "Those are adorable!"

They greeted me, and Cori said, "It was all Faith! She made them!"

My mouth fell open. "You're crazy. The costumes *and* this?"

She smiled abashedly, handing me the garment

bags. "Don't be too thankful until you see them." She scratched her arm. "I hope you like them."

I unzipped the bag to my dress, and I covered my mouth. She'd delicately beaded the front so it had gone from a simple black tulle dress to a complete masterpiece. I didn't have words, so I hugged her instead.

She giggled. "This means you like it, right? You're not just really bad at murder?"

Laughing, I wiped at my eyes. Why was I so tearful? "It's perfect, Faith." I sniffled. "Thank you."

"Of course," she said. "Grandma and I had a great time. Stayed up all night eating candied nuts and watching the shopping network."

"Sounds like a heck of a time." I giggled, then caught sight of Des looking over my shoulder. I followed her eyes, finding Carter walking toward us. Today, he'd worn fitted sweatpants and a jacket that hugged his shoulders. Even though I'd seen him in less, my mouth still wanted to water.

Because I was *that* much of a creep.

I made sure my jaw wasn't hanging on the floor and waved him over. "Look what Faith made!" I gestured at their shirts.

He read them, grinning. "You'll have to make one for my grandma for nationals."

"Actually..." Faith said, reaching into her big purse. "I have an extra for you and Adriel."

"She can have mine," I offered.

Carter looked at the smartwatch on his wrist. "Do we have time? We still have to check in and get ready."

I gently touched his arm, angling the watch toward me. Excited tingles lifted from his skin to my fingers, and I dropped my hand, hoping he didn't see how much the simple touch had affected me. I needed to get it together because we'd be touching even more on stage. The thought sent a small shiver up my spine that I tried to ignore as I said, "You're right. We need to get ready..."

Des said, "We can bring it to her. What does she look like?"

Carter opened his mouth to answer, but I said, "She's beautiful. Red scarf, bright red nails, silver hair."

Des grinned. "My kind of woman. You two go get ready. We've got this."

I thanked her, and as they walked toward the ballroom, I turned to Carter. "Are you ready for this?"

He slipped his fingers through mine. "I do have a great teacher."

My cheeks flushed as I smiled. "Come on. Let's get checked in."

We walked back toward the middle of the large entrance hall where a registration table was set up. My hands shook as I signed our names and took the packet containing the information for the event and our dressing room.

The directions on the photocopied map led us to a small room with a mirror lit up with a line of glaring bulbs.

I pushed the door open, taking it in. There didn't appear to be a bathroom. Or a closet. Or anything that would give us privacy, let alone breathing room.

Carter didn't seem to mind as his shoulders brushed against mine. "Do I get to see the costume finally?"

"I told you it wasn't a big deal," I said, unzipping the bag. But as soon as I saw his costume inside, I ate my words. Adriel and her grandmother had beaded the black vest and even added strips of pink satin fabric, transforming the outfit into something that would hold attention on its own.

Carter's lips tugged into a smirk. "If Griffin or Ashe saw me in this…"

"They'd say your dance partner has incredible taste," I finished, teasing.

"Of course." He took the hanger and glanced around, realizing the same thing I had earlier. "I can go find a bathroom?" he offered.

I shook my head. "I'll turn around." I faced toward the corner and stood there like I used to when I'd gotten into trouble as a kid. Mom didn't believe in spanking, so I'd spent plenty of time with my nose in a corner.

The soft shuffle of clothing moving against Carter's body reached my ears, and my pulse quickened. My mouth dried. Only feet from me, Carter was undressing, revealing what were surely perfect muscles. It took all my strength not to turn around. To keep my balance.

Finally, he said, "I'm dressed."

I turned to take him in and couldn't help but giggle. Carter's muscles were so much larger than the typical dancer's, and he looked way more in place in his workout clothes than he did in this gaudy dance outfit.

"Hey." He caught my hand. "Don't make fun."

It made me laugh more. "I'm not. You look great."

He lifted an eyebrow.

"Okay, it's a little flamboyant, but hey"—I ran my hand over the ridges of his bare shoulder—"no one will be looking at you with me on the stage."

I'd meant it as a joke, but his eyes heated as he looked me over from head to toe and back again. "That's the truth."

My stomach somersaulted, and I bit my lip.

His eyes flicked to my lip caught between my teeth, and I knew if I wanted to, I could kiss him. That it would be incredible. But I couldn't throw him that curveball this close to our performance.

"I, um," I breathed. "I need to get dressed."

Clearing his throat, he nodded and stepped back, breaking the spell. Slowly, he turned around, taking the same stance I had earlier.

I walked to my garment bag resting over the lone chair in the room and unzipped it. The rough of the zipper seemed so loud that it echoed in the room. Each second revealed more of *the* dress, and I gingerly pulled it from the velvet hanger. One of my best friends had spent hours on this dress...for me.

I ran my fingers over the beads before reaching for the hem of my shirt and pulling it over my head.

As I exposed my skin, I became acutely aware of who was in the room mere feet from me.

What would he think if he saw my body? My stretch marks? The small ridges where muscles were beginning to form under the softer flesh? Would he still be as interested as he'd been moments ago?

I took a deep breath, shaking the thought, and lifted the dress over my head. The fabric stretched over my chest and stomach, and the tulle skirt ballooned over my legs, landing mid-calf. I pulled on a pair of dance bloomers and straightened my skirt, then looked in the mirror.

A gasp fell over my lips that had Carter turning around, his molten honey eyes widening.

"Addy, it's perfect," he breathed. I looked to him and back into the mirror, watching the reflection as he stepped beside me, forming the other half of our partnership.

Where he'd looked gaudy before, he appeared strong next to me, capable. My white skin contrasted his dark complexion in the most beautiful way. We almost looked like a painting, standing next to each other in the mirror.

He reached and tipped my chin up with his index finger, so I had no choice but to look into his eyes. "You are stunning, Adriel Pruitt." His voice was soft, but rough, husky.

My heart stuttered its next beat as I smiled up at him. "I can't believe I'm here."

"I can't believe I was ever anywhere else."

Three hard taps sounded on the door. "Pruitt and McCormac?"

Carter cleared his throat. "That's us."

Us.

"You're on the docket. You'll be performing in an hour."

I nodded, although the woman couldn't see me.

"Thank you," Carter called, then looked at me. "What's left to do?"

I rifled through my bag for my makeup kit. "I'll touch up my makeup. Why don't you start stretching?"

For the next hour, we remained fairly silent as I touched up my hair and makeup, then joined him in warming up. We went through our routine at a quarter intensity. There was nothing more to do. We were as ready as we were ever going to be.

Three knocks sounded on the door.

"That's us," Carter said.

All I could think was no, that's *destiny*.

FORTY

WE FOLLOWED the woman with a clipboard as she took off at a quick clip down the hall. Passing door after dressing room door, we saw dancers at all stages—slick with sweat after a performance, just arriving, and everywhere in between. But I kept my focus on Carter and his hand firm in mine.

His hands were rough from lifting weights, and I found it comforting to have someone so strong to hold on to. I squeezed his hand, and he sent me a small, excited smile, squeezing my hand back.

We approached the backstage area, seeing rows of curtains and people running AV. The woman positioned us by the stage so we could see the couple being announced.

As they began their routine, my mouth fell open. It was Benjamin and Tatiana dancing our old routine.

"What?" Carter whispered, following my gaze.

"They didn't even change the routine," I muttered, trying not to be jealous of how seamlessly the two seemed to move together. Why were they here? They'd already made it to nationals, and Galina never sent dancers to a meet after they'd qualified to prevent injury.

That only meant one thing: Galina was trying to keep a spot away from someone else. Someone like me.

Carter put his arm around me, trying to steady me, but I just felt sick. Carter and I had been working hard, but would it be good enough to rank against this?

I glanced at the crowd, nerves threatening to overtake me, and my eyes caught sight of a row of yellow shirts. All of my friends and Carter's grandma were here to cheer us on. To support us. I needed to focus on that.

The song faded to a close, and Benjamin and Tatian struck their final pose, looking like royalty on the stage.

The crowd erupted into cheers, but Carter took my shoulders, making me see him. Only him.

"Addy, you are the best dancer I've seen. Head and shoulders above that. You just have to believe in yourself. In us."

I bit my lip, looking from him to Benjamin and Tatiana walking off the stage.

The announcer called, "Our next performance is from Emerson as well. Please welcome Carter McCormac and Adriel Pruitt to the stage!"

A polite smattering of applause sounded, but Carter took my attention again. "Tell me we can do this."

Was he asking for me or him? Either way, I let the words fall off my lips. "We can do this."

Smiling, he took my hand and led us onto the stage.

The spotlights were hot on my eyes, but I focused on Carter. As soon as the opening notes drifted through the speakers, I knew I was exactly where I was meant to be. My body moved with the music, going to a place between memorization and instinct.

Carter worked through the moves, nailing each one. But he didn't just do that. His face emoted each feeling. He was every bit as into the dance as I was, and there was a moment, as he spun me through the air, that nothing existed except for him and me.

Could he feel it too?

We went through the final counts of the song and into the grand spin, where in the story of our dance, I fell in love. My fingertips trailed down his cheek, and he gazed into my eyes, and a feeling so strong overcame me, I couldn't hold it back.

Carter had been here for me like no one ever had before. He'd put in hours of practice; he'd been patient, kind. Even made an attempt to catch the thief at Ted's Gym.

All of the emotions I'd been suppressing struck me as the notes faded, and I pressed my lips to his, continuing the dance of him and me. I was *exactly* where I was meant to be.

The strong sound of applause hit my ears, reminding me of where I was. And that I needed to breathe.

Carter's eyes were bright as he took me in, then he raised my hand, and we bowed together before waltzing off the stage.

The second we were out of sight, he picked me

up and spun me in a circle. "That was amazing, Addy!" He set me down gently. "*You* were amazing."

But I didn't want to talk; I wanted to kiss him again. To explore the electricity that had flowed so freely through my veins when my lips were on his.

I closed the distance between us and did just that, slower this time, and his body molded to mine, forming into the cocoon where I could emerge and be *me*. I moved my hands over his shoulders, hooking my fingertips behind his neck as he deepened the kiss.

His tongue slid across my lips, and I opened my mouth, welcoming him in. Welcoming the feeling of excitement and need and passion that flowed unimpeded between us. He nibbled softly on my bottom lip, and I gasped as my stomach swooped at the sensation.

It was like all this holding back had built up a desire so intense there was no hiding from it anymore. There was no hiding from the way I felt about Carter.

Our lips parted, and we were both breathless, from the dance, from the kiss, from this new world we'd entered into where maybe, just maybe, there could be more than one love in my life. More than just dance.

His hand cupped my cheek, and his honey eyes held mine as he asked, "What does this mean?"

I smiled as I kissed him again. "It means you're mine."

FORTY-ONE

MY FRIENDS RUSHED up to us in the main lobby, hugging me and congratulating Carter.

"That was amazing!" Nadira cried. "I've never seen anything like it."

Des nodded emphatically. "I can't wait to have you dance to my song at nationals!"

Still smiling, I shook my head. "We haven't qualified yet. There's still a few dancers left."

Cori shook her head. "There's no way you could dance like that and not win. You were even better than Isabella. You should have seen her after she watched your performance. She was *pissed*."

My eyebrows rose as a satisfied feeling welled within me. "Seriously?"

Cori nodded and gave me another hug. "That

was incredible! You too, Carter," she added, stepping back. "I'd never guess you hadn't been dancing all your life."

I winked at him. "Maybe it was all those kitchen dancing sessions with your grandma?"

With an embarrassed smile, he said, "I do have the best teachers."

Plural? My heart melted as I took his hand. I noticed my friends looking at the connection, and I couldn't wait to tell them later about what I'd decided. That I'd been brave with my heart, just like Cori had been with Ryker. My mom would be thrilled when she found out Carter and I were together. He was a snack, after all.

"What happens now?" Faith asked. "Will they email you the results?"

I shook my head. "I mean, yes, they'll send me feedback, but we have to wait until the awards ceremony."

Carter squeezed my hand. "Want to go watch with Grandma?"

I nodded, leaning my head on his shoulder. I wanted to be anywhere he was.

My friends, Carter, and I went to back to the ballroom and slipped in the back while a dance team performed a tap routine on stage. Technically, nationals only had three categories. Solo, Pairs, and Team. It didn't matter which style you performed, as long as it was exceptional.

I spotted Dorothea in her bright yellow shirt and pointed her out to Carter. The six of us traveled down the row to sit by her, and she beamed at Carter and me. She reached out a wrinkled hand and squeezed his cheek. "You never told me you could dance like that!"

Carter chuckled softly. "I told you it had to be good."

"And that kiss?" She folded her hands at her cheek and let out a dreamy sigh. "That was beautiful choreography." At the pallor in my expression, she said, "Unless it wasn't," and winked.

I couldn't help the smile that spread on my face. Carter seemed just as happy as me.

We settled in our seats and watched as team after team performed their routines. To most people, the dancers probably looked incredible. And they were. But Galina had taught me to pick out the flaws so I never committed them. I noticed when someone's foot wasn't pointed or when they weren't emoting or if they got off the beat.

I hadn't been able to watch most of the couples perform, but I thought Carter and I were up there with these teams. It would be close, but we had a chance.

I laced my fingers through his and squeezed.

He smiled over at me and squeezed back. I tried to tell myself it was okay. That I would be alright even if I didn't make it to the Dance Dance Nationals, but I didn't know if that was the truth.

As the final dance came to a close, the announcer stepped to center stage. He was a middle-aged man with apple cheeks and dressed even more gaudily than Carter. He held the glittering microphone to his mouth and began announcing the solo qualifiers from notes in an envelope.

Each time he announced someone, I cheered, hoping my name would be called when the time came.

As he began announcing the couples, Carter squeezed my hand tightly again, and Nadira took my other hand. I smiled at her, and she nodded encouragingly. I missed my mom, but it felt good to know my family had grown. That my friends were family now too.

"In third place, earning a spot on the Dance Dance National Stage are Courtney Chambers and Franklin Benedict!" the announcer said excitedly.

My heart sank, knowing third place was our best bet. Tears stung my eyes as the pair walked to the stage. They were the quintessential dance pair. Thin, graceful, and beautiful. Suddenly, I felt big in my dance costume. Clumsy. Out of place. How could I have ever hoped to compete against them? Why had I let Carter, or myself, get our hopes up?

The couple sashayed off the stage with their small trophy, and I whispered to Carter that we should just go.

But he held my hand firm. "Don't give up yet," he whispered.

"And in second place," the announcer called. "Carter McCormac and Adriel Pruitt!"

Blood rushed through my ears, silencing everything around me. I couldn't have heard him right. Couldn't have heard him say our names.

Carter stood, taking my hand, and Nadira pushed on my back, but I still couldn't believe it. As we walked to the aisle formed from a gap in the chairs, I turned to Carter. "Us? Really?"

Grinning, he pointed toward the stage. "Let's get our trophy. You've earned it."

I could hardly feel my legs as they carried me to the stage where the announcer waited with a big silver trophy. As we crested the stairs, I looked between the announcer and Carter.

Was this real? Was I crazy to hope?

Carter nodded encouragingly, and I wrapped my fingers around a column of cool metal. This was ours.

Tears streamed down my cheeks as I turned to Carter and whispered, "We're going to nationals?"

He tucked me close against his chest and walked with me off the stage, saying four words I never thought I'd hear. "We're going to nationals."

FORTY-TWO

THE SUN PLAYED with the horizon, fracturing into sunset streaks of orange, pinks, yellows and purples. I stared over the ocean at a remote spot of the beach, hardly able to believe this party was our celebration. That Carter and I had done the impossible, and I was one step closer to making my dreams come true.

Faith walked up to me and extended a red cup my way.

I eyed it skeptically, and without having to hear my question, she said, "It's Sprite. Not the healthiest, but better than beer, right?"

I couldn't argue. I took a sugary sip and said, "Thank you. You've been a lifesaver today."

Faith shrugged, taking a drink. "That's what friends are for."

She was right, but I was starting to realize that before this year, I hadn't had any friends. Not really. I had people I spent time with at the studio. I had my parents. I had classmates. But no friends.

No one to stay the night with or wear ridiculous shirts at my dance competitions. This was new, and it was worth celebrating just as much as qualifying for nationals.

I leaned my head on her shoulder. "Still, thank you. It means a lot to me."

"Of course." She took another sip. "So, the kiss. Are you and Carter... official?"

My heart skipped a beat at the mere mention of his name. "We haven't put any labels on it." I bit my lip. "Should I be worried?"

"With the way he was looking at you? No way."

I smiled despite my initial worry. "Now, we need to find you a guy." I glanced around the party. Des had followed through on her promise, as it looked like half the kids in our school were here and even some people I didn't know or recognize. "Have a crush on anyone here?"

"Not at all," she said. "Everyone's either taken

or so far out of my league they may as well live in another country."

I rolled my eyes. "Out of your league? You're the nicest girl in school."

"Which means everyone sees me as a friend. Not as girlfriend potential."

I frowned. She had a point. Being a big girl in high school meant you were the approachable one. The one the guys always asked about your friend and whether or not she was single. But that was a boy's game, and there were real men out there. I'd met one. Kissed one. "It'll happen," I told her with confidence. "If you've seen the thirsty comments Des gets on her YouTube channel, you'd know there are plenty of guys who want girls like us."

Smiling, she shook her head. "How does she have ten thousand followers already?"

"Her voice is good," I said simply.

"True," Faith agreed. "Her latest cover of that Jude Santiago song." She did a chef's kiss. "Perfection."

"I agree," I said, taking another sip of soda.

A muscled arm wrapped around my waist, and I looked over to see Carter next to me with his friend Ashe.

Ashe was tall and thin, with a pile of curly hair

atop his head and a smile that told you he was either going to be the next Bill Gates or the next evil genius. There would be no in between.

"Hey," I said, leaning my head on Carter's shoulder.

He kissed my temple just as easily as breathing, and I wondered why I'd resisted this so much. Now that I knew how amazing it was to feel my feelings for him, I couldn't believe I'd ever held back.

Ashe sipped from a red cup. "Guess we have to get used to this, huh?"

I rolled my eyes as Carter smirked and said, "Definitely." He planted a kiss on my lips that left me breathless.

As he broke the connection, I blinked quickly and took a breath to still my frantically beating heart. How were Carter and I supposed to practice for nationals when kissing felt this good?

The sun sank even lower over the horizon, replacing orange with faded hues of blue and purple.

"It's beautiful," Carter said, kissing my cheek.

"It is," I agreed. "I've lived here my whole life, and I don't think I'll ever get tired of a California sunset."

"Sure, it's great," he said, turning toward me, "but have you ever seen it reflected in your eyes?"

My heart melted, practically dripping from my body and pooling at his feet. Carter was one in a million. That was for sure.

He slipped his fingers through mine and said, "Want to sit by the fire?"

"Sure," I agreed.

Ashe extended his arms at his sides. "What are Faith and I? Chopped liver?"

My cheeks heated as I realized I'd completely forgotten about them. But Faith grinned and pushed on our shoulders. "Go, you lovebirds, have fun."

Carter led me to thick tree trunks that had been placed around a bonfire growing taller by the second. Some guys from the baseball team were piling pieces of driftwood atop the flames, making the fire spark different colors.

I sat beside Carter, looking at the flames and thinking of the sunset he'd seen in my eyes.

If I was being honest, it was probably more like a sunrise. My whole life had been about dance, but now that I opened the door, all the things I wanted but denied myself came flooding back. I realized that I wanted love and romance and parties and the things that high school had to offer, and I only had a few months left to get them.

"What are you thinking about?" Carter asked.

I turned back to him. The fire reflected in his eyes, making them dance like the flames.

"Possibilities," I said.

"Like what?"

I shrugged, leaning closer to the warmth of the fire. "Did you know I had my first sleepover this year?"

His eyebrows drew together. "Like a slumber party?"

I nodded. "And the dance you took me to? That was my first school dance."

"But you're a dancer!" he replied incredulously.

"I am. But not for fun." I shook my head. "Dancing has never been about fun. I've enjoyed it, needed it, but never truly had fun doing it... until I met you."

His eyes shone. "I'm happy to be of service."

"But why were you?" I asked. I still didn't understand why he'd committed so much of his time to me and something that had such a minis-cule chance of succeeding. Even now, he wouldn't gain anything out of making it to nationals. Most college application deadlines had already passed—it wasn't like he could add *national qualifier* to his resume.

He reached up with his thumb. In the glow from the fire, I saw an eyelash on his finger. He held it out for me, and I softly blew, my breath carrying the strand away.

His eyes held mine, keeping me captive in his gaze. "If it's not clear yet that I like you, I haven't been doing a very good job."

A soft laugh slipped through my lips. "I guess I'm not used to someone taking an interest in me. It's always been about dance."

He nodded slowly, resting his elbows on his knees. Then he cast me a sideways glance, asking, "What if it could be about more?"

A small smile hit my lips. It already was.

"Addy, will you be my girlfriend?" he asked.

I grinned and gave him the easiest yes of my life.

"Really?" he asked like he couldn't believe it, so I kissed him to make it real. This feeling of newness and adventure was intoxicating. I wanted to experience everything I'd missed out on during high school. Everything I would want to remember.

When we broke apart, he grinned and sat back, taking a sip of his drink.

I glanced at Carter's cup. "Are you drinking?"

He shook his head. "It's just soda. But I can get you something if you want?"

"I want a beer," I said quietly. "Just to try it."

"Sure," he said, standing. I followed him to the keg. He poured my cup a quarter full, and I took a drink, tasting the disgusting, bitter liquid on my lips just as I saw the flash of blue lights.

FORTY-THREE

"IT'S THE COPS!" Carter hissed.

Their spotlight shined on us, pinning us to the spot. My eyes darted around, but as the law enforcement pickup pulled over the sand, I realized there was no way out. Despite everyone scattering, I couldn't run fast enough through sand to escape a cop. Especially not as I saw a second and third car cresting the hill. What had started out as a fantasy had quickly become a nightmare.

Two cops jumped out of the first truck, running toward us so fast I hardly knew what was happening. In seconds, they'd checked my cup, clasped handcuffs around my wrist and were saying my Miranda Rights.

"I wasn't even drinking!" I argued, trying to

fight loose. Panic was rising in my chest so quickly I felt like I could puke.

"That's not what I smelled in your cup," the cop said, gripping me so tightly the cuffs dug into my skin. "I watched you drain your cup, and your boyfriend here poured you another." He roughly pushed my shoulder, getting me into the back of the pickup. "Looks like you just got an MIP."

On the other side, the cop shoved Carter in too, although Carter wasn't fighting. Not at all.

My eyebrows came together as I turned toward the cop. "What's an MIP? Don't you have to take a blood test or something? I can prove I wasn't drinking!" He shut the door on me, mid-sentence, and I let out a frustrated groan.

"Minor in possession," Carter answered for me dejectedly. At my questioning look, he added, "Means you had possession of alcohol before you were twenty-one. It doesn't matter that you weren't drinking it."

I frowned. "So being good doesn't matter."

He lifted his eyebrow, smirking slightly. "I thought you were about to be bad."

I bumped his shoulder with my own. "Don't make me laugh! I'm getting arrested!"

"It's no big deal now that we're in the car,"

Carter said. "If it's your first MIP, they can write it off your record."

I eyed him suspiciously. "How do you know so much about this?"

"My cousin goes to Seaton High, and he got like three MIPs last year." He closed his eyes. "Maybe if we behave, they'll let us off with a warning."

"Yeah," I muttered. "These handcuffs really feel like a warning."

I turned, looking through the back glass, and saw the cops cuffing other teens. Were my friends okay? I would be so upset if they'd gotten in trouble at my party too.

"My parents are going to be so mad." I sagged. "This is horrible."

"I'm here for you," he said, scooting closer to me.

And somehow, that made it just a little bit better.

He twisted in his seat, and I glanced down to see his wiggling fingers. I turned and brushed my fingers with his.

"Hey, Addy?" he said.

"Yeah?"

"There's no one else I'd rather be in a cop car with."

I couldn't help but laugh. "Same. Let's just make sure it doesn't happen again."

"Deal."

After a while, the cop got back in, shoving another kid I recognized as a freshman in the back seat with us. The kid looked terrified, and even though Carter tried to comfort him, big tears rolled down his cheeks.

Maybe I should be crying too, but it was hard with Carter's calming presence right next to me.

That was, until we got to the jail. Then the crying started. They separated the guys and the girls, and I looked around the holding cell to see half the girls from my school, but none of my friends. At least they'd managed to make it out okay.

But I felt lonelier realizing I'd gone to school with these girls for the last three and a half years and yet I barely knew any of them. Not well enough to talk with them while an officer came to get us one at a time to call our parents.

When he finally reached me, I scrambled from the cement floor to my feet and followed him to the pay phone. My heart skittered as I typed in my mom's phone number. It rang and rang until it hit voicemail. "She didn't answer," I said disappointedly. "Is that it for my call?"

The officer rolled her eyes. "That's only in the movies. And for adults. Call your daddy."

I sighed. The last person on earth I wanted to call was my dad. So, I called Ted instead.

No answer.

Feeling dejected, I turned to the cop, and she said, "Do either your parents have a different phone you could try?"

Closing my eyes, I nodded.

I picked up the phone and dialed my dad's number. I hated that I knew it by heart.

After several rings, he answered. "Adriel? Are you calling from jail?"

I glanced at the officer before muttering, "I need you to come get me."

I could hear something in the background, a party maybe, but not as loudly as his sigh. "I'll be right there." The line clicked off. He'd hung up on me. As I walked back to the cell, part of me regretted calling him at all.

I sat down on an open spot on the floor and leaned my head back against the wall. How could a day that had started out so perfectly go so wrong?

My mind wandered to Carter. Had he gotten ahold of his grandma? Was he home already? My fingers itched to text him and make sure he was alright.

One by one, the girls' parents came to get them. I wasn't sure how long I waited—a half hour, an hour—until the cop said, "Adriel, your dad's here."

He was wearing a suit and tie like he'd been at a party, but his worst accessory was the annoyed frown on his face. He wasn't worried or concerned. He was inconvenienced.

I didn't meet his eyes, following the officer instead as she returned my phone in a Ziplock bag. I walked behind Dad, out of the station, looking at my messages from earlier in the day.

Mom: Since you're staying at Desirae's, Ted and I decided to stay in a cabin near the orchard! Service is spotty, so we're turning off our phones. Here's the landline if you need it.

She sent a picture of a business card that looked like it was made in the '80s. I wished I had known this earlier.

There were texts from my friends too, checking in on me, but none yet from Carter.

The locks on Dad's car snapped up as he unlocked it, and he said with a tight jaw, "Get in."

Bristling, I said, "I can get an Uber."

"Clearly you're not responsible enough to do that. Get in the car."

I glared at him but followed his direction. "Interesting time for you to decide to be a parent," I muttered, buckling in.

"I get a call from my daughter at jail in the middle of a work function. Not my finest moment as a father."

"No, you save all those moments for Toby, don't you," I bit back.

He was quiet as he pulled the car on the road and began driving.

"Where are you taking me?"

"Your house."

Good. I stared out the window, at the orange streetlights and cars passing by. I couldn't wait to get away from him. We rode in dead silence until he pulled up to the house I shared with Mom and Ted. I reached for the handle, but he said, "Adriel."

I glared back at him. "What?"

He let out a heavy sigh. "I'm going to have to tell your mother about this."

"Tell her." I got out of the car, then walked to the front door. I pushed myself inside, shut the door, and collapsed against it in a pile of tears.

FORTY-FOUR

I PROBABLY WOULD HAVE STAYED THERE all night, just sitting numbly, if my phone hadn't gone off. It was a video call from Carter.

I hurriedly answered it and breathed a sigh of relief at his face in what looked like a car.

"Hey," he said.

"Are you okay?" I rushed out. "Did your grandma get you?"

From off screen, I heard her say, "Mhmm."

He turned the phone to her, and I saw her driving in her shower cap. "Next time you win something, you're celebrating at my house," she said.

I let out a tearful laugh. "That's fine by me."

A look of concern crossed Carter's face. "Are you okay, Addy?"

Surely I looked a mess, with my puffy eyes and ruined makeup and frizzing hair. "It's been a long night."

"You can say that again," he agreed. "Were your parents mad?"

"You mean my sperm donor?" I muttered. "He was disappointed. Not that it matters. I'm more worried about what my mom and Ted will think when they get home."

He cringed. "You think they'll be mad?"

"Oh yeah," I said. My stomach growled, and I pushed up from the ground, walking mechanically toward the kitchen.

"Are you okay?" he asked again, looking concerned.

"I think so?"

He chuckled, but I wasn't really joking. I'd had a perfect record, had never done anything wrong, and just a few months without the structure of Galina's studio had left me rethinking everything I'd been so sure about before. From my avoidance of relationships to my strict no-partying rule, so much had changed.

Was it a change for the good or would it just

lead to more heartbreak? With drinking, definitely. With Carter, I'd have to wait to see.

"I need to get some food," I said. "See you for practice tomorrow?"

"See you," he said, and his grandma said, "Goodnight, Adriel."

"Goodnight," I replied with a soft smile and set my phone on the counter.

The refrigerator was full of prepped food, from cut vegetables to precooked meat. I had my pick. I settled on some Greek yogurt with berries and went to the couch. Turning on a movie, I quickly fell asleep.

FORTY-FIVE

THE HARSH SOUND of the doorbell woke me, and I sat straight up on the couch, making my fuzzy throw blanket slip to the floor. I looked down at myself, still wearing my clothes from the party yesterday.

I rubbed my eyes, wishing Mom were here to answer it instead.

The bell rang again. No chance of them going away long enough for me to clean up my empty plates from the night before and get dressed in something new. I surely looked a wreck.

Instead, I rubbed at my eyes as I walked to the door, hoping whatever mascara had bled down my face would look more like an early morning smoky eye. As if.

I pulled open the door and stopped in my tracks. Galina stood on our front doormat dressed like she'd just been at church, with her hair pinned back in a bun and pear earrings dangling from her ears.

"Galina?"

Her lips pursed. "I'm not a ghost. Are you going to let me in?"

Deftly, I stepped back, giving just enough room for her to sidestep me. Her nose crinkled as though I smelled bad, and I almost checked my armpits for BO. Almost. Instead, I stared at her, wondering *why* she was at my house. Why she was willing to stand so close to me after I'd allegedly ruined her reputation.

She stepped forward, glancing around at the décor my mother had so carefully arranged. "Dance is about passion. Letting your body move from your heart and not from your mind."

I knew that. I'd heard it from her a thousand times. Felt it as my body moved across the dance floor without my head telling it what to do. So why was she repeating facts?

"Your dance yesterday was filled with passion like I've never seen before."

My lips parted as I recognized the look on her face. She was impressed.

Finally, she met my gaze with her cold green eyes. "If you had been dancing with Benjamin, you would have placed first. Even over him and Tatiana."

A pang went through my heart. "Is that why you came here?" I demanded. "To tell me that without you I'll always be second best? To remind me that you cast me away from your studio like I was worth less than a retired pair of ballet shoes?" I walked to the door, swinging it back open. "No, thank you."

To my surprise, her lips lifted in the slightest smirk. "Actually, the reason I came here was to offer you your spot back, at my studio."

There was no hiding my surprise now. My mouth fell open as I slowly registered her words. "You want me back?"

"Yes. But of course, you'll have to say goodbye to your partner."

"To Carter?" My chest constricted, and I instinctively shook my head. "I can't."

With a small shrug, she said, "I suppose that is your decision." Her heels echoed against the tile floor as she strode to the door. But as she walked through, something stopped me from letting her leave.

"Galina, wait," I said, following her onto the porch. The cold winter air immediately enveloped me, and I hugged my arms to my chest.

She turned toward me, a knowing smile in her eyes. "Yes, Adriel?"

"Can I... have a little bit to think about it?"

After a long breath, she said, "I'm afraid I need an answer by Monday night." She turned and walked away to her car waiting alongside the curb.

Despite the cold, I watched until she drove away. Nothing could feel as cold as the dread washing over me at the decision I had to make.

FORTY-SIX

GALINA'S OFFER had me so off-kilter, I couldn't remember whether I'd washed my hair or not. So, I started over again using the special soap Mom had gotten me to help prevent hair loss due to my new medicine.

Mom was always doing little things like that. Her car always had healthy snacks for me to eat between school and dance. She made sure I had enough bobby pins since they always seemed to grow legs and walk off. When my uniform tights got a snag, there was always another pair waiting for me within a day, without me having to remind her or sometimes even ask.

I realized I hadn't appreciated her enough over the years. How many little sacrifices had she made for me that had gone unnoticed? If I didn't take Galina's offer, did that mean Mom's work had gone to waste?

I'd been thinking about it so long, the water coming out of the showerhead was getting cold. I let out a sigh and turned off the water. Maybe I should talk to Mom about this.

But I knew what would happen if I did. She would be so thrilled for me that any thoughts of her stylist career or adopting or Ted or Cancun would be completely off her mind. Was it selfish of me to tell her?

Or was it selfish of me not to?

I pondered the idea as I rubbed a towel over my body and sprayed on leave-in conditioner.

I wanted to tell Carter about the offer, but something about it seemed like a betrayal. After all the hours he'd put in, would it be fair to leave him hanging?

But then again, didn't he say he'd done it for my benefit? Objectively speaking, going back with Galina would be for my benefit. She was the best— had the best training, the best connections to popular dance companies...

I let out a groan. If it was such a great offer,

why did it feel like I had a rock on one side and a hard place on the other?

I didn't like being pressured, and this Monday deadline was getting to me.

Trying to push it out of my mind, I reached through my dresser and picked out some leggings and a long-sleeved workout top. Either way, I'd agreed to meet Carter at the gym, so I might as well get ready.

As I pulled mascara through my lashes, a soft knock sounded on the door. I glanced at the doorway, seeing my mom standing there, a smile on her face. She looked so happy; she was practically glowing. She dropped her bags and gave me a tight hug. "My little convict."

I raised my eyebrows, pulling back. "Dad told you what happened, right?" I was braced for a lecture, a grounding, something. I'd never gotten into trouble like this before, hardly gotten into trouble at all.

She waved her hand. "He told me what happened."

"And you're not...mad?" I finished lamely.

Ted came through the door behind her, carrying three bags, and chuckled. "Honestly, I think she was a little happy you were being a teenager and not a mini adult for once."

I lowered my chin, gazing between him and Mom. This wasn't how it was supposed to go. "But I got arrested. I have to go to court."

Mom nodded. "And you will go. And you will work at Ted's Gym on the weekends next semester to make money to pay to have it expunged from your record."

"That's it?" I asked.

"Well, did you drive home?"

I shook my head.

"Did you stay within a reasonable limit?"

"I only had a sip, just to try it."

"And you won't do it again?" she asked.

Emphatically, I shook my head. "So not worth the risk."

"Good." She grinned. "Then I think you've learned your lesson." She turned back at me. "Just don't let it happen again, okay?"

Taken off guard, I launched in to hug her. My dad had been so cold, so cruel, had never taken my side into account, and here was my mom, giving me grace when it would have been just as easy to write me off as a delinquent. "I love you so much, Mom."

"Oh, honey." She chuckled slightly, then

brushed back my messy hair and kissed the top of my head. "I love you too."

"Now," I said, stepping back. "I want to hear all about the orchard."

"I'd love to tell you... but your breath kind of stinks." She laughed.

I covered my mouth. "Meet you in the living room once I've brushed my teeth."

"Sure," she said, leaving with a wave over her shoulder.

I went to my bathroom and shut the door, but soon after, a soft knock sounded. Wondering if Mom had changed her mind about my non-punishment after all, I pulled the door open with trepidation. But instead of my mom, Ted stood there.

He glanced back at the hall and said, "Your mom went to look for something in the car. How did yesterday go?"

My lips spread into a smile. "We qualified for nationals!"

Grinning, he said, "That's amazing, Adriel!"

He seemed genuinely excited. Genuinely proud. "Thank you. We couldn't have done it without you and the gym space."

"Of course," he said. "And you're sure you don't want your mom and me to come watch?"

I shook my head. It would have been nice to have them there, but knowing we were all getting our happily ever after was better. "You two have fun in Cancun. We'll be alright here."

The front door opened, and Ted glanced down the hall. "I better get back, but good job."

I thanked him one last time before shutting my door and going to the bathroom. I was in a better mood than I thought I could be this morning as I brushed my teeth. When I was done, I called Mom in.

Coming to sit on the bench at the foot of my bed, she said, "The orchard was...amazing." Her voice had the happy, breathy air of a lovestruck teenager. Just like when she'd met Ted for the first time. "There was this big window in the bedroom, and we had a perfect view of the sunrise through the forest."

"That sounds incredible," I said.

"It was. How was Des's?"

I smiled, thinking of *Des's*. "I had a great day." Even if it was marred by this morning's events. "I'm actually getting ready to see Carter at the gym."

She smiled. "Ted said he found out you two are playing racquetball together after your training sessions." Her eyes narrowed playfully. "Told you that you'd like the gym."

My cheeks burned, but there was also a part of me in awe that Ted had really kept our secret, even if he'd told Mom about the time Carter and I were spending together.

"You like him, huh?" she asked.

Something in me was laid bare in those words. It made my throat feel tight and my eyes sting. I could only nod with the tears threatening to spill.

"Oh, honey." She covered her mouth. "Did I say something wrong? Is everything okay with him?"

I shook my head, blinking quickly and tried to smile. "We had our first kiss yesterday."

An excited look crossed her face, immediately followed by confusion. "Am I missing something? Why are you crying?"

I laughed, sending tears down my cheeks. God, I was a mess. "I don't know. It's just... maybe I'm realizing how much I was missing out on all those years with Galina."

She nodded solemnly. "If I would have thought for a second it was hurting you—"

"It wasn't," I said. "Honestly, if she'd never

have kicked me out, I probably wouldn't have given Carter a second glance."

"I get it," she said. "It's funny how things like that work out, you know? Even though a door closed, another one opened."

I nodded, looking back at myself and my mostly finished makeup in the mirror. "That's true." A door had opened. But was it the one I wanted to walk through?

I still didn't know.

FORTY-SEVEN

ON MY WAY to the gym, my phone pinged with a new email. At a red light, I checked it and saw I'd gotten an email from the qualifier judges detailing their feedback, along with a recording of our performance. Hopefully we could watch it together for some insight.

His car was already in the parking lot when I arrived, and when I reached the racquetball court, I looked through the window to find him walking on his hands. I giggled as he walked to the wall and did a pushup, his muscles bulging.

As if sensing me, he gracefully put his legs on the floor and stood up to glance my way. I grinned at him and pushed inside. "Look at you, Mr. Gymnast."

"The three years of lessons Grandma forced me through didn't hurt," he muttered, coming to me and putting his hands on my hips. They were large, and warmth immediately flooded me from our contact.

How easy it was to slip into a new relationship with Carter, into a new way of life. I'd never dreamed of dancing and relationships before now, but I had them both. Was it too good to be true?

His hands slipped up to the narrowest part of my waist, and his fingers linked behind my back, pulling me closer. My hands flattened against the hard muscles of his chest, and I looked up at him, at the smooth skin of his face and the gentle curve of his lips.

He was beautiful.

My eyes flicked to his and back again to his lips, and I got lost in his kiss. In the give and take of our bodies and our hands and our breaths and heartbeats. Kissing Carter was like nothing I'd ever experienced. Heaven and fire at the same time.

Our kiss left my breathing ragged and my chest heaving just as much as any dance. His eyes were hazy, hot on mine as our lips broke apart and he placed a gentle kiss on my forehead that sent chills down my spine.

As he ran his palms down my arms and linked his fingers with mine, he asked, "Should we get to practicing?"

My eyes snapped open. How had his kiss made me completely forget the reason we were here in the first place? The realization stunned me, scared me. We needed to focus on nationals. It was my chance.

"Right," I said. "I thought we could watch the judges' feedback and go over the routine? See if there are some spots where we might want to tweak it?"

Galina's visit was on the tip of my tongue, but I couldn't bring myself to tell him. Not before I figured out if I needed to break bad news or push us harder than ever.

So instead, I sat along the wall, getting my phone from the pocket of my leggings. He sat beside me, watching as I pulled up the email and opened the first video file attached. Two men and a woman looked into the camera, a woman speaking first.

"You both had an electric performance today! Not only did you manage to captivate us, but the audience was enthralled as well. We do have a few pointers for you as you move forward in the competition."

"Right," the balding guy on her right said. "The reason you didn't place first today was twofold. Form and difficulty. Carter, my guess is you're a newer dancer, and although you manage well, you'll need to focus on the details like straight legs and pointed toes. Every move counts on the national stage. Plus, if you want to gain some points in the scoring system, we expect you to try more acrobatics and combinations. What you did was great, but we want you to be extraordinary. Without that, I think you'll have a hard time being competitive at nationals."

The guy on the left nodded. "And Adriel. You're a beautiful dancer, but if you want to really wow those judges, be sure you're strong in your core and holding good posture through your neck. While you did great with Carter, be sure to engage the audience more. A few simple changes can make your performance a homerun."

The woman smiled. "Great job, you two! We can't wait to see what you do next month!"

The recording reached the end, and Carter eyed me with his eyebrows raised. "That's good, right?"

"Good?" I asked, my stomach sinking. "They

basically said I need to teach you advanced skills that take years to learn in less than a month."

Carter frowned. "How hard can it be?"

My eyebrows rose. "How hard can it be? Hard enough that I spent every waking hour at Galina's studio or practicing before school." I stood, frustrated, and began pacing the floor. I hated when people acted like dance wasn't a sport. I could dance circles around any of the football players at Emerson Academy, literally.

Carter stood as well, taking my hands despite my hesitation. "Hey," he said softly. "I know it's not going to be easy, but things that are worthwhile take time."

My heart softened slightly, and he drew me closer.

"Besides," he added. "I have the best teacher in a hundred-mile radius."

My heart ached. He was right. But who was *my* teacher if I kept dancing with Carter? How would I get to the next level?

"We can do this," Carter said, gently touching my chin so I'd have no choice but to look into his eyes. They were warm, convincing. "And I've never seen my grandma as happy as she was this morning talking about our performance. It's more than just a contest to me."

My heart lurched. "Really? Even after the MIP?"

He nodded. "She was whistling our routine's song while she cooked. And then she told me she'd never been prouder of me as she was watching us on stage."

His words had me parting my lips, in shock, in surprise, in...guilt at was I was thinking about doing. "That's...incredible," I managed.

"Yeah." He rubbed the back of his neck bashfully. "She's practically raised me. Even before my parents died, and now for ten years after. It means a lot, you know, that she's proud of me."

My hand settled gently on his shoulder. "I understand."

He smiled. "Good. So, what about the recording of our performance? I want to see how amazing you were."

I giggled, heat rising on my cheeks. "Okay." I went back to the email and tapped the second document to open it.

Whoever'd taken the recording had been right behind the judges' stand with a phenomenal camera. I could see us clearly, see the beads Faith had sewn on our costumes shimmering in the spotlight.

For the next few minutes, I watched our performance in awe. Although we'd practiced the routine for hours, I could hardly believe it was us. Carter did miss a few points, and he could have done better at keeping his base leg straight, but overall, his performance was solid. And I could see where the judges were coming from on my posture and connection to the audience.

It felt good, watching the two of us and knowing that I had taught Carter. That in only two hours a day he was good enough to place at a qualifying meet. Teaching him had been almost as fun as performing the dance myself.

But was our dance good enough to place at nationals? To get the attention of a top recruiter? I wasn't sure, and I had to be, or else Mom would have me on the road to college faster than a *bourrée*.

"That was amazing," Carter said. Our shoulders had been touching, but Carter put his arms around me, pulling me into his lap. My stomach somersaulted as my shoulders brushed against his chest muscles, as my forearms felt the strength in his abdomen.

My breath sped as I felt him under me, and all I

could think about was the feel of his lips earlier. How his breath tasted like mint and something sweet. Maybe syrup from breakfast?

It didn't matter because his eyes were on mine, making my stomach heat and my cheeks flame. His eyelashes curled away from his eyes, framing the molten honey irises. He was a masterpiece, and I wanted to thank the painter personally.

"You're beautiful," Carter breathed, his voice husky as he moved his hands over my arms. "The way your body moves."

Goosebumps rose on my skin despite the fiery trail his touch left behind. I barely repressed a shiver.

His lips were mere inches from mine. Millimeters. And I closed the distance, knowing in my soul which choice I had to make when it came to Galina. I hoped beyond hope that I had the courage to make it.

FORTY-EIGHT

MONDAY MORNING IN CHEMISTRY, Mr. Cho had us doing an experiment with acids and bases. But first we had to work the equation, and then we had to carry it out. Carter sat next to me, working on his own paper. We were so close to each other our knees touched under the desk, but my body ached for more. To feel his lips on mine.

Even though Carter was my first kiss, it felt like we'd been kissing forever and for no time at all. I constantly felt the ghost of his lips on mine and the hunger for more.

His eyes met mine, and I realized I'd been staring at him.

I smiled abashedly and turned back toward my page.

I was sure my answer to the problem would be wrong. Yet another reason not to go to a traditional college. I could keep up with schoolwork, but it drained me, didn't ignite me like dance did. I just had to hope that dancing with Carter would be enough. That whether or not we placed at nationals the right eyes would see me.

Mr. Cho told us to compare answers, and I looked guiltily at Carter.

"What?" he asked.

I glanced down at my page, showing him the blank spaces.

"That's okay," he said gently. "Here." He walked me through his equations, showing me how he came to each answer, and I copied the process in my own notebook. Chemistry seemed to make way more sense when he explained it.

Knowing what I had to do that night didn't help. I needed to go to Galina's studio and tell her in no uncertain terms that I would not be rejoining her dance studio. Not only would moving there hurt Carter and his grandma, but she'd humiliated me in front of all my dance mates. Dismissed years of hard work. If she didn't want me at my worst, she certainly didn't deserve me at my best.

Somehow, no matter how slowly, the day passed.

From school to weights to teaching Carter how to arabesque, it was finally time to face Galina.

My hands shook as I got in my car and drove the familiar path across town. Her studio was near the Emerson-Brentwood border, and the sign, Emerson Dance Studio, flashed at me as if a big warning sign of the storm inside.

Although it was later in the evening, nearly half past seven, the parking lot was still full. She worked her dancers to the bone. It was how she made stars. But I wasn't going to implode just to shine.

I walked up to the front door, feeling like a completely different person than I had been just a handful of weeks ago. No, I was stronger. My life didn't revolve around fitting into a dance costume anymore. Not for Galina. Not for an audience. Not for anyone.

I tried to keep all that in mind as I walked into the studio where I knew she'd be.

At the sound of the door opening, her cold brown eyes landed on me, and she whispered something to her assistant before stepping toward me.

I felt the eyes of every dancer in the studio narrowing in on me like lasers. I could only imagine the thoughts going through their minds, especially of Benjamin or the dancer who'd replaced me in the group routine.

With a confident smile, she led me to the empty reception area and said, "Is this it? You're joining us?"

I took her in, the bun tight atop her head, the graceful way she held her shoulders even years after she'd stopped dancing. But then I saw her mouth and the fine wrinkles around her lips that had spoken so harshly to me all those weeks ago.

"I'm not," I said, my voice shaking. "I'm not," I repeated, more firmly this time, growing more confident in my own decision.

Her eyebrows rose slightly as though she hadn't heard me. "Excuse me?"

"I won't be coming back to the studio, Galina. Not now, not in a million years."

Now her eyebrows furrowed, and the lines around her lips deepened. "Is this because of that boy?"

"No," I said, telling only half the truth. "It's because of me. I want to dance somewhere I belong, somewhere I won't be shamed for looking a little different."

She barked out a bitter laugh. "I don't shame dancers. I push them to be better. I get them outside of their limitations so they can be the best in the world. My dancers have performed in Moscow, Prague, London, New York City, Madrid. The most prestigious shows and companies in the world. And you're telling me you'd rather go it on your own."

Her words had me doubting myself, but I nodded. "I can do it on my own."

This time she scoffed. "I've heard these words before. But you know what always happens?" Without waiting for my answer, she continued. "A boy comes along. And instead of dancing, there's kissing. Instead of practice, there are dates. Instead of a future on the stage, there's a future in the kitchen. Is that what you want for yourself?"

I shook my head. "No." She seemed to settle a bit, but I added, "I don't want this either."

Her lips pursed. "Once you leave, Adriel, there will be no second chances."

"I understand."

Seeming disappointed, she turned and walked toward the studio. With a sigh, she said, "You could have been great."

As the door shut behind her, I whispered, "I still will be."

FORTY-NINE

MY ENTIRE BODY seemed to vibrate as I walked to the parking lot, as though I'd just shifted the earth off its axis and now it wasn't sure how to exist. Or maybe that was just me.

In a state of shock, I got in my car and turned it on.

A warning signal flashed across the dash, and I looked at it closer. Low tire.

"Great," I muttered, opening my door to get out and check it. Hopefully it would make it until I drove home. Instead, I found the rear driver's side tire completely flat.

All of the adrenaline I'd been operating on fled my body. I couldn't call Mom and ask her to come get me. She would immediately ask what I'd been doing, and there was no racquetballing this away.

Calling Triple A to come and get me would take just as much explaining.

I would have called my friends, but they were probably just as clueless to car maintenance as I was. I needed someone to help me change this tire and get me out of here.

That only left me one choice. I let out a sigh and got my phone from the center console.

Carter answered his phone, and I said, "I have a huge favor to ask."

"What's up?" he replied.

"I need you to help me change my tire... I don't know how. I know it's a lot, but I'm desperate."

He chuckled. "Didn't I tell you it feels good to be a knight in shining armor? Let me call my grandma to tell her I'll be late, and then I'll head that way. Where are you?"

I gritted my teeth and said the three words I didn't want to say. "Emerson Dance Studio."

Carter was quiet for a long moment, and then he said, "I'll see you there," and hung up the phone.

I lowered my cell and pressed against the head-rest, feeling like the world's biggest idiot. A few people walked in and out of the studio, and I just prayed they didn't recognize me. At least my car blended in at this parking lot filled with perfect cars that shuttled perfect people.

I used to feel so at home here, but now I realized I didn't belong. I didn't want to. Seeing Galina, watching the other dancers, it made me miss dancing with a group, but I didn't like who I'd been at the studio. I'd been solely devoted to one thing, not realizing everything I'd been missing out on.

Carter came to mind. Him and his smile and his perfectly full lips.

His tone had completely changed when I'd told him where I was. What was he thinking? How could I explain?

My chest felt tight as I waited for him to arrive.

Headlights panned over the building in front of me, and I glanced over to see Carter driving up. My heart immediately eased, as though simply beating was harder without Carter around.

I got out of my car and walked to him. There was a guarded air in his stance as he looked from me to the building to my car. But instead of asking the obvious, he said, "Does your car have a spare?"

"A spare what?" I asked, trying to read his eyes

in the darkness. Then I remembered why he was here in the first place. "A tire. I don't know."

"Do you have the manual?" he asked.

Silently, I nodded and went back to my car, reaching for the glove compartment. Any relief that had come with Carter's arrival was gone now. My fingers fumbled over the thick book, and I gripped it again, handing it to him.

Using the light cast from my open door, he went to the index, then flipped to another page. "The donut's under the car," he said. "Unlock the trunk?"

I unlocked it and followed him to the back of the car. He opened the trunk, which was cluttered with some beach stuff and extra dance shoes. Pushing them aside, he opened a compartment I didn't even know existed. Inside were tools and metal pieces I didn't recognize.

Glancing from the book to the tools, he picked one out and dropped it to the ground. The asphalt was clear of debris, but I cringed as he got his sweats dirty sliding under the car. The tool he'd selected clanged against metal, and he said, "Come here."

My eyebrows drew together. "Here?"

"Under the car," he gritted out.

Apparently, my clothes were getting dirty now

too. That would be easier to explain than a tow truck, though. I lowered myself to the asphalt and slid under the car with him. He had his phone face down on the ground, the flashlight shining under the car.

"The tire's here," he said, pointing at it, "and you need to use the tire iron to let it loose."

He handed me the tool, and I raised my eyebrows.

"You need to learn to do it," he said, letting go. "You never know when you won't have someone around to help you."

His words hit my heart. Was he trying to say I wouldn't have him around?

My hands shook as I put the tire iron on the nut and tried to turn it. As it came free, I realized Carter could have been speaking about his own experience. He'd lost his parents, his grandpa. For all intents and purposes, he was the man of his family.

He held on to the tire as I loosened the last bolt and gently put it on the ground between us. I scooted out of the way first, getting out from under my car. He came next, dragging the tire with him, and walked to the flat tire at the back of my car.

After steadying the tire so it stood still, Carter said, "Loosen the bolts."

I looked at him, confused. I'd watched enough movies to know you were supposed to jack it up somehow.

"If you don't loosen them now, you won't be able to get the bolts off once the tire's in the air. Here, take the locking nut." He handed me a small heavy nut, and I gripped it tightly.

I followed his directions, using all my strength to get the nuts started turning. In the back of my mind, I thought I'd have to tell Raf the weights had helped. While I worked on the bolts, Carter went back to the trunk and got more tools.

Holding one out, he said, "This is the jack." He handed me another long piece. "You connect this to that and turn to lift up the car."

Not quite meeting his eyes, I knelt and looked under the car, trying to figure out where the groove on top of the jack went. I couldn't see an obvious spot, and my eyes stung with frustrated tears. I felt so helpless, embarrassed in front of Carter. "Why don't they teach this at the Academy?" I muttered.

He scoffed. "You think those guys are going to get their hands dirty? They'd just call Triple A."

My cheeks flushed. It had been my first thought too.

He knelt beside me, his warm shoulder brushing mine as he guided the jack into place. "Start turning."

Following his directions, I turned the handle one way and then the other until it began rising and eventually hit the frame of my car. Slowly, I turned it enough times for the back tire to snap back into the right shape and lift slightly off the ground.

"Get the rest of the nuts," he said.

My chest tightened as I began unscrewing them. Carter was being so short with me. Why wasn't he talking? Deciding enough was enough, I handed him the first nut and said, "Why aren't you talking to me?"

"I am," he said, but I didn't miss the tick in his jaw.

"What's going on?" I asked, giving up on the nuts entirely. "Why do you seem so upset?"

Instead of answering, Carter took the tire iron and began loosening the other nuts—much more quickly than I had. Then he pulled the tire off the exposed bolts. It bounced on the ground until he steadied it under his hand. Then he reached for the spare, pushing it in its place.

"Carter," I said.

"I'm trying to change a tire here," he gritted out.

My shoulders tensed, and I stepped back.

"You need to put the nuts on in a star pattern," he said, "to make sure your tire stays balanced."

He screwed them on quickly with his fingers, then gave them another turn with the tire iron. Getting to his knees, he lowered the jack. "Tighten them again when it's down to make sure they're on good."

He let out a puff of breath with each final turn, his muscles flexing with the effort. Then he began picking up the tools, rolling the flat tire to the trunk. "You'll need to get this to a shop to get it fixed."

"Carter," I said again, putting a hand on his arm.

He flinched away.

I stepped back, surprised at his retreat. "You're not even going to ask me why I'm here? You're just going to assume I was doing something wrong?"

He pressed his lips together, looking over his shoulder, then met my gaze. His eyes were dark in the glow of the streetlights. "What were you doing here, Addy?"

I let out a sigh. Guilty before proven innocent. "Galina came to my house on Sunday."

His face screwed up in confusion. "The dance teacher who kicked you off the team?"

I nodded, pain of the rejection forming a dull ache in the pit of my stomach. It wasn't a fresh wound, but it hadn't completely healed either. "She wanted me back at the studio."

"And what?" Carter asked, hurt clear in his guarded tone. "You're quitting me?"

"I told her *no*," I said, desperation leaching into my voice.

Carter looked from my hand to my eyes. "But you wanted to say yes."

I held my arms out at my sides. "Of course I wanted to say yes! I've been dancing at that studio since I was five years old! And we were just dancing together to get to nationals, right?" I asked. "I'm taking up so much of your time!"

His mouth fell open, but he quickly scrubbed his face with his hand, clearing the emotion there. He began walking toward his car, but I touched his arm, feeling the strength underneath his sweater. "But I chose you, Carter."

His eyes were hooded, not revealing any emotion, any hint of a thought swirling under the surface. "You didn't even tell me you were coming here. That she offered to take you back."

"I didn't think it mattered, since I was choosing to dance with you."

"It didn't matter?" he scoffed. "Of course it matters, Addy. Loyalty matters. *Honesty* matters."

"I'm telling you the truth," I said. "I've always been honest with you."

He opened his mouth to reply, but his phone rang out loudly in his pocket. He swore under his breath and reached for it.

"What is it?" I asked. It didn't sound like his ringtone.

He held it out. "Someone's taking the kettlebells."

My eyes were wide. "What do we do?"

"Get in the car," he said, walking to the driver's side of his vehicle. "Let's finish what we started."

FIFTY

MY HEART RACED as I reached for my purse and phone from my car, then locked it up. Both at the potential of catching who had been stealing the kettlebells and at the finality in Carter's tone.

I got in the car next to him, breathing in his familiar scent and bathing myself in the soft country music he'd been playing before he arrived.

Now, he had his phone out, the blue light washing out his dark skin as he tapped on the screen. As he set it in the display holder on the dash, I recognized map directions to somewhere near the gym. There was a red flashing dot on the road.

"Where are they going?" I asked.

"Looks like they're getting on the highway." He

pulled out of the studio parking lot and began driving to the highway that connected Emerson and Seaton.

With so much heaviness between us, I felt like I needed to clear the air. "Carter, I was never going to dance at nationals without you."

Carter shook his head. "I don't want to talk about it right now. I need to think about it."

My heart ached. Carter had always been so kind, so open, but it was like he'd put up a sky-high wall between us. I missed our closeness. The easiness of his smile and the softness of his laugh.

Trying to distract myself, I got out my phone to text Mom. It was already later than when I usually got home.

Adriel: Mom, I'm out with Carter. I think we figured out who's stealing Ted's kettlebells.

Mom texted back almost instantly.

Mom: What? Are you at the gym???

Adriel: No, they're heading toward Seaton.

She didn't reply right away, but an incoming call flashed across my screen. With a glance at Carter, I held the phone to my ear, saying, "Hello?"

"Adriel," Ted said, "You mom just texted me. What's going on?"

I filled him in on Carter's idea to track the

kettlebells and then told him we had a tracker going toward Seaton.

"Don't follow them," Ted said. "It could be dangerous. I'll call the cops."

We were already en route, getting closer to the highway. I could see the flashing dot on the screen showing the car entering the Seaton city limits. "We can call them," I said. "We already know where they're going."

Ted was silent for a moment and said, "Okay, but the second you know where they stop, you call and let me know. And wait for me somewhere safe in Seaton, okay? I'll come get you the second you tell me where."

"Sure," I answered, then said, "I'll let you know when we know more." I ended the call and set the phone in my lap.

Carter glanced at me, asking, "What did Ted say?"

I filled him in, and Carter nodded. "It looks like they're slowing down anyway. They must live in Seaton."

I shook my head. "Why would they be stealing kettlebells anyway? I still don't get it."

Carter shrugged. "To sell for cash?"

That was a good point. I got out my phone

again, going to the local marketplace apps I knew of, and my mouth fell open. There at the top of the page were the kettlebells from Ted's Gym listed for sale. I didn't know what was more offensive—that they'd so blatantly list stolen items to sell or that they had only listed them for ten dollars apiece. According to Ted, they were worth way more than that.

"What?" Carter asked.

"I found him." I clicked through to the seller's profile. "Some guy named Brent Hamby."

"You got him," Carter said. "And it looks like he stopped at the corner of Hidalgo and Dublin."

I tapped out of the app and called the cops. I'd never called the police before, so my voice shook as I told the dispatcher I had information on items reported stolen. They asked me questions about the location and the stolen items and then asked for Ted's contact information. I gave it to them, realizing I knew his number by heart, and then hung up.

A giddy feeling of relief swept over me. We'd done it. We'd found the guy stealing from Ted's Gym.

"Let's go to Seaton Bakery?" I asked. "To wait for Ted. And celebrate."

"Sure," Carter said, not sounding excited in the least. He pulled off the highway and took us down city streets. His expression seemed more relaxed than earlier, but he still didn't seem happy. Why wasn't he happy?

He pulled into the parking lot at Seaton bakery and I reached to open my door, but I realized he wasn't opening his.

"Aren't you coming in?" I asked tentatively.

He bit his bottom lip, looking out the window, then turned my way. "You gave up the studio for me?"

The question seemed to hit me out of nowhere. My voice was shaky as I said, "Of course I did. You're my dance partner now. My boyfriend."

But instead of looking relieved, Carter's frown only deepened. "But dance is everything to you."

My lips pressed together as if even they knew there wasn't a good way to reply. A perfect word to say. "It was."

His eyes met mine, and I wished there was an answer I could give that would take the pain out of them. I didn't understand what had put the hurt there.

"What did I do wrong?" I asked. I thought I'd done right be turning down Galina's offer.

"Maybe... maybe you were right," he said. "You never would have given up a chance to dance at the studio before me."

If I'd thought my chest was tight earlier, it was wrung in knots now. I didn't know what I would have said before Carter. But I couldn't guess at it now. He was in my life in more ways than just dance. "What are you trying to say?" I choked out.

"I mean, I don't want to be the reason you give up on your dreams," he said. "I was always holding my parents back, you know? That's the reason they were at that march where they were killed. They wanted to go to DC, but they stuck to LA since I was here. In Emerson. It *killed* them."

I covered my mouth at the horror in his words, the pain in his voice. Then I reached for his hand, trying to tell him through my touch that this wasn't the same thing. "Carter, I *want* to dance with you."

His lips trembled as he took my hand and kissed it. "I think you were right." He let out a shaky breath. "We should focus on dance. Make sure we're performing our best at nationals."

"Carter, no, I—"

He sniffed and nodded toward the bakery. "I don't know if you've tried out this place yet, but they have really good cupcakes. I bet you and Ted can celebrate with some desserts."

"Celebrate?" I managed. What could I possibly be happy about right now?

"Catching the kettlebell bandit." He gave me a halfhearted smile that nearly tore my heart in two. "And learning how to change a tire."

My lips quivered as I took in his words. He was *ending* us before we even really began.

I wanted to stay, to fight, to tell him that I never felt more like myself than when I was with him. That I'd said no to Galina because she'd humiliated me—that he'd treated me with more dignity in months than she had in years.

But the way he waited with his eyes forward, both hands on the steering wheel, told me he wasn't listening. Not anymore.

So, I picked up my purse, and the pieces of my broken heart, and walked into Seaton Bakery.

FIFTY-ONE

INSTEAD OF WALKING to the ordering counter, I went straight back to the bathroom. I pulled on the door handle, but it was locked. Inside, an older woman said, "Occupied."

I stepped back, folding my arms across my waist as if that was enough to keep me together. I'd only felt like this a few times before. When my parents divorced... when my grandpa died... when Galina was kicking me off the team. The only difference now was that I had nothing left. No chance of going back or moving forward.

I was stuck. Stuck in this miserable moment.

The door opened, and the woman gave me a red-lipped smile. "It's all yours."

Averting my eyes, I walked past her and into the

sanctuary of the bathroom. The light flickered overhead, and the tile was a dingy white that would never look perfectly clean. It didn't matter. It had all I needed to fall apart.

I sobbed over the sink, tears slipping down my cheeks and leaking into the corner of my lips, dripping down my chin.

How had I been so stupid to fall for Carter? Hadn't my parents taught me that this was how relationships ended? With tears? With regret? No matter how cautious I'd been with my heart, this was still how it went.

Carter had agreed to dance with me, but how would I be able to perform so close to him knowing he could never be mine? That I'd let myself fall so hard only to be dropped when I should have been caught?

Didn't he see that my dreams had changed since we met? My eyes had been opened to so many new things. Who even knew if I would dance professionally? Maybe I'd open my own studio, choreograph. Now I wanted so much more. I wanted to live, on *and* off the dance floor.

I wiped at my eyes and looked at myself in the mirror. Yeah, this was living—mascara streaked down my red face, huddled up in a public restroom where the toilet seat was probably still warm.

I ran cold water and splashed it over my face, trying to wash away the mascara and quell the puffiness at the same time. Of course, it only worked half as well as I wished it would. I waved my hand in front of the paper towel dispenser, and brown towels whirred down. It felt like sandpaper over my skin, especially with the raw sting of salty tears.

My phone dinged from inside my purse, and I reached for it, hoping it was Carter. Instead I saw a message from Ted.

Ted: I'm at the bakery. Where are you?

I let out a sigh, disappointment washing over me.

Adriel: In the bathroom. I'll be right out.

Facing myself in the mirror, I smiled wide. It looked more like a grimace. But it would have to do.

I walked out of the stall and found Ted waiting at the counter, gazing up at the handwritten menu. As soon as he caught sight of me, his lips spread in a huge grin. "It's our hero!"

Despite myself, I managed a smile.

He gave me a hug that quickly turned awkward

when he realized what he was doing. He disengaged with a pat on my back and looked back at the menu. "What are you thinking?"

With a twinge in my heart, I said, "I heard the cupcakes were good."

A woman came out of the kitchen, tying an apron around her waist. Her smile was so friendly it practically lit up the room. "Hi, you two. What can I get you?"

Ted didn't seem to notice her, instead looking at the desserts showcased in the front counter. "How about an Oreo cupcake for me and an unsweet tea. Adriel?"

I asked for a peach flavored one and a lemonade.

"Great choice," the woman said with a wink. "That's my favorite."

Maybe it was just the presence of another female, but I found myself wishing my mom had come too. I wanted to hug her, to cuddle up on the couch like we had the night Dad moved out.

"Thanks," I said.

As she rang us up, she said, "Is this your first time here?"

We both nodded, and she smiled even wider.

"I'm throwing in an extra cupcake for you. On the house."

"That's nice of you," Ted said.

She shrugged. "I'm the owner. I need to make sure you come back."

Ted chuckled and I managed half a smile before we went back to a booth and sat down with our cupcakes and drinks. The extra sat in a folded white bag between us, sealed with a Seaton Bakery sticker. It was like the universe knew we were missing Carter from the celebration.

"I heard from the cops as I pulled up," Ted said. "They have a warrant to search his home, and I should know more about the investigation tomorrow."

"That's amazing." I tried to sound happy, but I'd never been more miserable.

He took a long sip of his tea, studying me. Seeing too much. "Everything okay, Adriel? Did Carter have to go home?"

I let out a sigh, not wanting to relive the last few hours. "No," I answered. "On both accounts."

He swirled his straw around his drink, making the ice bump and crackle. "Want to talk about it?"

Lifting a corner of my lips, I shook my head. We were surrounded by couples and families enjoying dessert or a light supper, and all I could do was feel sorry for myself.

Ted let out a sigh, then leaned forward. "Adriel, I know I'm not your father, and I would never mean to replace him, but I want you to know that I'm here for you. If you ever just wanted to talk to someone."

His words hit me, hard, but in the opposite way Carter's had. Ted was right; he was here. He'd been in my life for more years now, consistently home at night, supporting my mom, and by proxy, me. He'd even kept my secret, for my mom's happiness just as much as mine.

I couldn't speak, so instead, I stood and went to his side of the booth and fell into his hug. It was exactly what I needed.

FIFTY-TWO

I KEPT HOPING I'd wake up and all of it would be a nightmare. Galina coming over, the flat tire, and Carter calling it quits—but I couldn't have been that lucky. No, I woke up the first morning of Thanksgiving break feeling completely empty inside.

Carter and I were supposed to practice on Friday, but how could I bring myself to be so close to someone who'd retreated so far away?

But no matter what, I had to dance. If I didn't have Carter, if I didn't have a chance back at the studio, what did I have left? The thought was a bitter one, and I clung to it. Dance required emotion—not happiness. I could make this work. I had to.

After I got dressed for the day, I went to the dining room to get breakfast. Instead, I found Mom and Ted sitting at the table with three place settings and a full-on spread of brunch food.

Any other day, I would have been thrilled, but today it made my heart sink. My unhappiness didn't belong in their bubble. But Mom waved me over like it did.

"Morning, honey! I was just about to come get you."

My eyebrows came together. Why would she need to get me for breakfast? We usually did our own things on the weekend anyway. We definitely didn't eat this fancily at home. "What's going on?"

She glanced at Ted, and my heart sank. This was it.

He nodded, and I saw his arm move as he gripped her hand.

My pulse rushed between my ears, and it was like the world was moving in slow motion. I wanted to tell them to stop, that I couldn't hear their good news. But instead I stood, frozen to the spot.

"Sit down," Ted said, gesturing at the empty plate meant for me. I had a feeling it would stay empty once I heard what they had to say.

My legs moved like cement as I went to the

table. "What is it?" I aimed for neutral but probably missed, judging by the way Mom looked to Ted, as if for reassurance.

Mom reached across the table, and it took me a moment to realize she was hoping for my hand. I put my fingers in her open palm, and she squeezed.

"Honey," she said, practically vibrating with excitement. "You know I'm too old to have any more children, but Ted and I are thinking of adopting." She quelled her elation just enough to ask, "What do you think?"

The problem was, I couldn't think. Not with both of them looking so hopefully at me. All I wanted to do was cry. Before they said something about the adoption, it was always in the future, a distant possibility. But now? The possibility was more than that. It was real.

Mom spoke quickly, the eagerness clear in her voice. "We're going to start classes to become a certified home. We were thinking an older child. Obviously, we're too old to start over with a baby or have one of our own, but an older child could be wonderful. Hopefully a girl. I so love being a girl mom. I think I have you to thank for that. It would just be so wonderful to raise a family with a man who cares for me like Ted does." She seemed to realize she hadn't taken a breath yet and filled her lungs. "What do you think?"

Her words hit me like slams from a wrecking ball.

Adoption.

Older child.

Girl.

Family.

I took a breath too, the oxygen scratching my throat like it was sand instead. "Great," I choked out. My eyes darted around the room, desperate for an escape, and my gaze landed on my purse. It sat on the counter like a beacon in a stormy sea.

I reached for it, and Mom said, "Are you going somewhere, honey?"

"I, uh, yeah. Meeting Carter. I'll be back soon." I walked out the door before there was time for follow-up questions, because truth be told, I had no idea where I would actually go. It was the day before Thanksgiving. My friends had plans with their families. It was cold outside, and I had only grabbed a jacket.

I hurried to my car and got inside. Although my mind had gone self-preservingly numb, my body had not.

I shivered as I started the car and tugged on the

sleeves of my fleece-lined jacket. Without waiting for the heater to warm up, I backed out of the driveway and started down the road.

My arms drove me to the gym without letting my mind in on the plan. It was closed today, the parking lot empty save for a couple of cars that clearly hadn't been moved in a while. Absently, I wondered if Ted would call to have them towed.

Somewhere under the numbness, I realized Carter wouldn't be here. And he probably wouldn't want me to call him, not about this. He wouldn't understand anyone choosing another family anyway.

No, my dad was the only one who would understand that.

I put my car into gear and started down the road. I had questions, and I knew my dad had the answers.

FIFTY-THREE

MANSIONS HIDDEN AWAY behind the wrought iron community gate came into view. I typed the numbers of Toby's birthday into the pad, and it slid open with the slick sound of lubricated metal sliding on metal.

I rolled the window up as I entered the community, feeling the security cameras watching me. Every time I came back here, it felt less and less like the spot I used to call home. Or maybe I just felt more and more out of place.

Either way, I pressed forward, following the turns that were just as much a part of my memory as an arabesque or grand *jete*. Eventually, I reached the circular driveway of my father's house.

The festive balloons from Toby's party were

gone, replaced with a large Thanksgiving wreath over the door. It was filled with fake leaves in fall colors and a giant P inside. Brandilynn had claimed the family name, just as she'd claimed my father.

With a sigh, I turned off my car and got out, not bothering to lock the door. The stones under my feet were level, but my steps were anything but steady as I walked to the front door. Suddenly, I wondered what I was doing here. I'd come for answers, but what if they weren't what I wanted to hear.

Mom and Dad had left each other, but they were both reaching for the same future—one with a child other than me. What if Dad said I wasn't enough for him to want to stay?

I steeled my resolve and reached from the button, my finger shaking. I needed to know not just why Mom would want another child, but why Dad had wanted an entirely different family.

There wasn't any noise behind the door before the handle clicked open and Brandilynn answered, looking like a model for a holiday magazine. She wore a deep maroon dress that wrapped around her perfect body. Her platinum blond curls framed her face, and her false eyelashes enhanced her wide blue eyes.

"Adriel! We weren't expecting you." She stepped back, the stiletto heels of her leather boots clacking on the marble floors. "We're having a few of your dad's colleagues over later for an early Thanksgiving meal. I'll make sure you get an extra place setting at the table!"

For the first time, I realized, she was being nice. Maybe she was just a nice person. Was that why Dad had left?

"Actually..." I paused. "I was wondering if I could talk to my dad?"

"Oh, sure," she said. "He's trying to turn Toby into a football fan. They're in the media room."

A pang of jealousy came and left. "Thanks."

I went to the room where I used to watch countless dance movies like *Dirty Dancing*, *Step Up*, and *Save the Last Dance*. My favorites were always the ones where the dance partners fell in love.

A new ache spread in my chest, but this time it didn't go away.

I missed Carter, and I'd only been away from him for a day. What would happen to us when nationals were over? Would he ever understand that he held a place in my heart along with dance? Or had I lost him too?

If I dwelled on it for too long, I wouldn't make

it to the media room. I would only collapse into a ball. It was taking all my strength to get up the grand staircase. To pass the door that used to be my room. To just keep going toward answers that could build me up or tear me down.

Through the door, I heard music playing, and I leaned my ear against the crack. When I was younger, Dad gave up on football and watched movies with me instead. I could hear music playing and Dad telling Toby, "That girl's a ballerina, just like your sister!"

My heart melted and froze at the same time. I had been replaced, but maybe not completely.

"Adabelle?" Toby asked loudly.

"Adriel," Dad corrected.

I let out a sigh and pushed open the door.

Dad glanced at me and then did a double take like he'd been expecting Brandilynn instead. "Adriel?"

"Sister?" Toby said, confused.

"Hey," I said, then cleared my throat. "Hey, can we talk, Dad?"

He nodded, then looked at Toby. "Want to watch the movie in here or go find Mommy?"

Just the word Mommy drew up emotions I didn't know how to handle. But that wasn't the point. My feelings could wait to tear me apart until I was at home in my room. I had to stay strong, for just a little bit longer.

Toby said he wanted to watch TV, and Dad told him, "I'll be back in five." As though his daughter arriving on the day before Thanksgiving were just a minor inconvenience.

Toby's eyes were already trained on the big screen as Dad walked toward me. Like Brandilynn, he was dressed well, in navy slacks and a crisp white shirt. The top button was down though, revealing some of the hair creeping up his chest.

"Adriel." He almost put his arm around me but seemed to think better of it, rubbing his wrist instead. "Let's go to the landing?"

He was talking about the space at the top of the stairs. There were a couple of small armchairs and an end table there, but I couldn't remember ever sitting on them before. When we reached them, they felt stiff, uncomfortable, and in the back of my mind, I thought I wouldn't sit on them again. If I ever came back to the house at all.

"What's going on?" Dad asked. He seemed confused, and maybe... maybe I was too, because now that I was here, what did I say?

Only one word left my mouth. "Why?"

His thick brows came together, and he leaned forward, confused. "Why what?"

My jaw shook. "Why, Dad? Why did you leave us?" My voice trembled right along with my bottom lip, and tears stung my eyes. I gestured to the entrance below in the home he'd taken from Mom and me and made his own with Brandilynn. "Why did you need to have a new wife and a new kid? Why wasn't I enough?"

He let out a sigh and rubbed his brow. "Adriel..."

His reaction just infuriated and hurt me more. He couldn't even do me the service of looking at me? His daughter? Or would he rather I stay permanently in his past? In a long-distant memory?

"*Why*, Dad?" My voice rose, echoing off the vaulted ceilings and marble floors below.

His eyes darted around as though he were looking for Brandilynn.

"What? Are you afraid your perfect wife or your perfect son will see me?" Tears rolled down my cheeks. "Is that it, *Daniel*?" Saying Dad didn't feel right. Not anymore. Why had I given him a title that he'd tossed aside as though it were garbage?

"Adriel, what did you expect me to do? You had your mom. What about Toby? Who did he have?"

My mouth fell open, breaking the sobs. "So, you chose to be a dad to Toby instead of me. Your mistress mattered to you more than your family."

"Adriel." He ground his teeth. "They *are* my family."

"And me?" I asked, standing up. I couldn't tolerate sitting here any longer. Being so close to him. "What am I?"

He leaned forward, his elbows on his knees, hands rubbing his temples. "My daughter. You'll always be my daughter." But instead of fighting for me, the words came out resigned, like even he knew it was a lie.

A fresh well of tears spilled from my eyes. "You and I both know I haven't been your daughter since the day you decided Mom and I were worth risking." A sense of freedom and loss I'd never felt before flooded my body.

This man, the one sitting before me, he wasn't my father. He didn't show up like a father. He didn't love like a father. He didn't protect like a father.

No, the man who had was at my home. My real home. And that was exactly where I needed to be.

FIFTY-FOUR

WHEN I PULLED into the driveway, I could see Mom and Ted sitting on the couch in the living room through the big bay window. She had her head resting on his shoulder and her feet tucked underneath her. Instead of a perfectly trendy dress, she wore a sweatsuit (that matched, of course). Ted had on jeans and a Brentwood Badgers T-shirt. They looked comfortable. They looked in love.

Mom told me that she had met my dad while working as a stylist. That a rich and hopeless man had come into the store looking for suits and had found his future wife instead. I used to think it was adorable, the fact that love could find you anywhere.

But maybe the truth was that real love was harder to find. Discovering something true took missteps and heartbreaks and false starts and years of discovering what you didn't want to find something you did.

Before getting out my car, I checked my phone. There wasn't a message from Carter, so I began typing one of my own.

Adriel: I miss you already.

I couldn't send it, though. I began deleting the characters, searching for one that felt right.

None did.

My cursor blinked in the messaging box, reminding me of all the space between us only silence could seem to fill.

I started another message and sent it before I could back out.

Adriel: Hope you're having a great Thanksgiving. I'll see you for practice on Monday.

Without waiting for text bubbles that might never appear, I put my phone back in my purse and walked inside.

Mom sat up, looking at me and opening her mouth, but before she could speak, I went to sit between her and Ted on the couch, hugging them both tight and crying thick tears.

"Your new daughter is going to be so lucky to have you as parents." I didn't say more, because I couldn't. Mom just held me like I was a child again and Ted patted my back, and my family, my real one, spent the moment together, just as we were.

FIFTY-FIVE

THE NEXT DAY, I called Faith to ask if she wanted to go shopping with me. Mom hated Black Friday shopping because she said pressure while picking out clothes was never a good idea. For me, that was part of the fun. Besides, she was going to the gym with Ted to help him handle their own Black Friday crowd.

She answered quickly, and I gave her my plan—hit a few stores, then raid the dessert cart at La Belle.

"Thank God," Faith said. "I need to get out of this house. Let me go ask my mom."

I sat on my bed as I waited, hoping she would be available. I didn't just need a shopping partner; I needed her advice.

After a few moments, she came back on the line and said, "Are you still there?"

"Yeah," I said.

"Mom said I can come! Do you want to meet me at the store?"

"And have both of us deal with parking? I'll come pick you up."

"Awesome," she said.

"I'll see you in half an hour?"

"That works," she said. "Hopefully I haven't murdered one of my brothers by the time you get here. Apparently, Thanksgiving is the weekend where guys get to sit on the couch and watch football while women clean everything up."

"Ew," I said.

"I know. Hurry."

Usually, I lived in gym clothes, but I hurriedly slipped on a pair of jeans and was surprised to find the waistband was loose.

I looked down at it, almost in disbelief. Only a couple of months ago, these had been so tight they left indentations in my skin. I glanced at the bottle of thyroid medicine that sat on my nightstand as a reminder to take it first thing in the morning and shook my head.

Galina had shamed me for gaining weight. I'd

been on the best diet and still gained. It wasn't until we fixed the underlying issue that my health took care of itself. I breathed a sigh of relief and reached for a belt that hung from a hanger in my closet. I slipped the black leather through the loops and clasped it shut.

I listened to music on the way to Faith's house and texted her when I was outside. I didn't want to intrude on the rest of her family's plans. She came outside almost immediately, looking amazing in a sweater dress and brown riding boots.

As she opened the door, I wolf-whistled. "Look at you!"

Her cheeks flushed red as she said, "You're so embarrassing."

I laughed, putting the car in drive. "That dress is really pretty."

"Thanks," she said. "Grandma and I made it."

"Wait, what?" I asked, doing a doubletake. That dress could have come off any rack at the store.

She nodded shyly. "What do you think?"

"It's amazing. You have so much talent, Faith."

With a small smile, she thanked me and said, "But where do you want to shop today? I heard Vestito might have a sale on prom dresses?"

"I'm up for whatever," I said. "Honestly, I kind of wanted to talk to you about something…"

"What's up?" she asked.

I stalled at a stop light and glanced over at her. Faith was one of the nicest people I knew. She was also the only person I knew who had been adopted. "I don't want to sound rude… Are you comfortable talking about your adoption?" The word came out almost like a whisper as if saying it quietly could quell any pain the word brought up for Faith.

"Sure," she said with a gentle smile. "What do you want to know?"

A car behind me honked, and I realized the light was green. My foot pressed on the gas pedal, and I eased into the flow of traffic again.

"My mom and Ted said they might want to adopt," I confided in her. "But don't tell anyone. I don't know if it's official or anything."

"Wow," she breathed. "Did they say when?"

I shook my head. "They just said they wanted an older kid. But I don't know how old. Maybe five. It sounds like they're at the very beginning of the process."

"Wow," she said again.

Her surprise was already making me feel better. Like maybe I wasn't so crazy for how I'd reacted.

"Yeah," I said, turning the corner to go to Emerson Shoppes. "It kind of took me off guard."

"I bet," she said. "How are you feeling now?"

"I don't know…. You know that I have a little brother, right? From my dad's second marriage?"

She shook her head. "I'm sorry, I didn't."

"Nothing to be sorry about. He doesn't even know my name," I muttered, pulling into one of the few open spots far away from the mall. So many people were out and about, loaded with shopping bags. It was crazy how we could all coexist without seeing the small hurts buried inside.

Faith was quiet as she waited for me to continue.

"I don't know." I leaned my head back against the seat, feeling bad for dragging all this up. "I guess I'm worried."

"About what?" Faith asked gently.

"Everything?" I let out half a laugh. "Nothing. I don't know. I just…I thought I was worried about my mom replacing me, but now I'm worried about something else too. What if I'm a bad sister? After everything this potential girl has lost, what if I just add to the list?"

With a small smile, she reached for my hand, squeezing lightly. "The fact that you even asked that means you'd be an amazing big sister. And as a sister to *four* siblings, I'm an expert on the matter."

I laughed softly. "That's a good point."

"Of course it is." She grinned. "And until then, I'll be your sister from another mister."

I snorted. "You so did not say that."

"Oh yeah." She waggled her eyebrows. Then her tone shifted. "Lots of people don't make it through the process to become adoptive parents anyway. They change their minds or decide to go another route. So even if your parents are thinking it over, it's not set in stone. But I'll be here for you when it happens. If it happens, okay?"

I reached across the console and hugged her. "You're the best."

She hugged me back, and as we pulled apart, she said, "What do you say? Ready to fight some people for a good deal?"

Laughing, I said, "I am so ready."

Faith and I explored the stores, talking about nothing and everything. I even told her about what happened between Carter and me, and of course she treated me to cookie dough at this place in the mall I didn't even know existed. I made a promise that if Carter and I ever got together, I would take him there too.

When we'd been through so many stores my feet were hurting, we decided to call it a day. I dropped Faith off, and as I drove home, my heart felt heavy, but not as heavy as it had before. Maybe that was the power of a good friend.

FIFTY-SIX

CARTER and I had two weeks to practice before nationals. We also had two weeks of school left in the semester. With Thanksgiving break over, our teachers had doubled down on instruction and homework. Which would have been fine if not for the fact that in one of my hardest classes, I sat next to Carter.

Before I even reached the door to Mr. Cho's classroom, my chest tightened as if to remind me that I'd be distracted from science for the next hour. Some of my classmates were there already, sitting in their seats, chatting freely like it was just another day. But the moment my eyes landed on my usual seat, I knew today would be anything but normal.

While Carter would have typically been talking

to those around him, he had his eyes trained on his notebook. His face was expressionless.

Any hope I'd held that Thanksgiving break could have mended things went away, and my shoulders sagged.

Someone bumped into me from behind, and I turned to see Tatiana.

"Clumsy much?" she said, pushing past me.

"Great," I muttered, readjusting my bag, which had slipped down my shoulder. My feet worked like they were stuck in quicksand as I walked to the desk. To the empty space that didn't feel like mine anymore.

As I sat down, Carter didn't even look at me. Maybe that was what hurt the most. Not being able to see his honey eyes on mine with all the warmth and vulnerability in the world focused in that single point.

No. Instead, his hand tightened on his pencil, although it wasn't moving over the page. He froze like an animal caught in a trap, as though I were the one causing him harm.

What pieces were left of my heart disintegrated.

How could we recover from this? I didn't know, but if anyone could help, it was my friends. I promised myself to ask them for advice at lunch.

I approached our table with my tray, and as I sat down, Des said, "So I was thinking that Carter should start sitting with us."

Ryker perked up. "Another guy? Please?"

Cori rolled her eyes. "You sit with your friends on Thursday."

"But I sit with five girls every other day of the week," he retorted and took a big bite of his sandwich. How guys managed to take such massive bites, I had no idea.

Nadira said, "I'm fine with it. Maybe being in proximity of relationships will bring someone to me."

Faith laughed. "If it works like that, you should invite him over today."

"Exactly," Des said with a grin. Although, judging by the way her phone was constantly lighting up on the table, she didn't need any help getting guys. She stretched her neck as if she needed the extra inch to look around the lunchroom. "Where is he?"

"About that..." I flipped my fork in the to-go box that held my lunch. Cold Vietnamese noodles with chicken and plenty of fresh vegetables. But it all tasted like cardboard.

"What?" Cori asked apprehensively. "Is everything okay between you two?"

"Something happened…" I blinked my eyes toward the ceiling, trying to stem the tears. After last night, I told myself I didn't want to cry about him. Not anymore. I needed to focus on dance like I'd meant to do all along.

Faith rubbed my shoulder gently. Just knowing she was there for me gave me the comfort I needed to tell them every ugly detail of my falling-out with Carter.

A crease formed between Des's eyebrows. "But he's still dancing with you?"

I nodded. "He said he wants to focus on winning at nationals."

Nadira groaned. "Half of what made your performance so amazing was the chemistry between you two."

"I know. The judges said just as much." I frowned. "He doesn't want to distract me."

Faith said, "You have to feel for him, though, right?"

"What do you mean?" Cori asked. "I don't feel

anything for him other than anger, and it's not even my heart he broke."

Faith shook her head. "Yeah but it's not that simple. I was just thinking... When you grow up without your birth parents, there's always this hole in your heart like something's missing, and you do anything you can to keep that hole from getting bigger."

A moment of silence swept across the table as we took in Faith's words. Took in the fact that our friend had been suffering so deeply for most of her life.

Ryker shook his head. "He's just scared."

"Of what?" I said. "We made it to nationals feeling what we do. Why would that hold him back?"

Ryker glanced at Cori before looking back at me. "Relationships are different for guys. We grow up our whole lives being told dating is for a good time and serious relationships are for the future."

"No one brought up marriage!" I said.

"No," he agreed, "but those feelings he's having for you? They're real. Realer than what most guys are ever prepared for. And when you feel that way about a girl..." He reached over and squeezed Cori's hand. "You'd do anything to make her happy, even if it means making yourself miserable. Even if it means embarrassing yourself in front of the entire school at the biggest game of the year."

A small smile touched my lips. Ryker had confessed his mistakes, and his feelings, for Cori in front of the entire school and community at the homecoming game. But I had a feeling my happy ending wouldn't come like that. It hadn't for my parents. Why would I deserve any better?

Ryker continued, "He wants you to be happy, and dance makes you happy, so he flipped. If anything, it shows how much he cares for you that he would sacrifice his own happiness for your dreams. All you have to do now is show him that you can go further with him than you could without."

"And how would I do that?" I asked, my heart raw. I'd do anything.

My friends were quiet, pondering my dilemma right along with me. Cori slowly lifted her head. "Wait... you have to have a video display to go with the dance, right?"

I nodded.

A grin grew across her face. "Ginger can help."

"But what does that have to do with Carter?" I asked.

Cori shook her head. "You don't understand. This is the girl who changed our parents' mind about traditional agriculture with a *video*. If she could do that, she could do anything."

My heart turned over in my chest, a flutter of hope making it beat again.

"And the song!" Des said. "He asked me to do a cover of your song, but what if I did something better?"

Cori nodded eagerly. "With the video? Genius!"

Nadira grinned. "With Cori on your side, you know you can't lose."

Faith agreed. "And I can help with shirts. Maybe we can have a special message?"

Hope flared within me, brighter than a sparkler on a starless night. "You think this could work?"

"Oh yeah," Des said.

Cori reached across the table. "By the time we're done, he'll forget why he ever let you walk away."

Ryker's gaze pinballed between us, and he sat back. "You girls are going to rule the world someday."

I couldn't help but agree.

FIFTY-SEVEN

WHEN I REACHED the gym parking lot, I stared up at the Ted's Gym sign, and it struck me how familiar this place had become. Almost like a second home with its smell of sweat and disinfectant. With Raf's steady guidance. With the echoing silence of the racquetball court.

Ted had created a great place, and a strange feeling spread through me. Pride. I was proud of Ted. With a small smile, I got my gym bag from the back seat and walked through the winter cold to the warmth of the gym.

I went to swipe my card and check in but did a doubletake. Was that my mom standing by the front desk in workout gear?

"Mom?" I said.

She turned and grinned wide. "Adriel!"

"What are you doing here?" I asked, trying to keep my voice light and happy. What if she stayed so long Carter and I couldn't practice? We'd already taken Thanksgiving break off.

"I have something to show you." She took my hand and began pulling me toward the juice bar.

"I'm not in the mood for a smoothie," I said, remembering the last time I'd had one infused with wheat grass. Gross.

She giggled. "No, I'm taking you to the store!"

"Shopping?" I said. "This close to Black Friday?"

"Ha ha," she said, still leading me toward the small section of the gym that sold fitness clothing and equipment.

I almost protested that I already had enough workout clothing, but that was before I saw the sign above the door. *Styled by A.*

Through the glass walls, I could see more people than normal milling within the store and bouquets of balloons spread around the entrance.

"What's this?" I asked. Something felt special, electric, but I wasn't sure what.

She rubbed my arm. "I have a clothing line!"

My mouth fell open. "What?"

Nodding excitedly, she turned to me, tears in her eyes, and said, "You inspired me. I hope it's okay I took your first initial."

I wrapped my arms around her, hugging her tight. "Mom, I'm so happy for you! This is amazing!" We rocked in a hug, celebrating what felt like a new beginning for her.

Stepping back, she sniffed. "You have to see the clothes before you tell me good job." She laughed, wiping tears.

"I know I'll love them," I said. "There better be one of everything in my size."

"Already set aside." She winked and led me into the store where I saw Ted and most of the personal trainers. Even Carter was in the store, holding a plastic cup of what looked like lemonade.

Ted approached us, grinning. "You've already had three purchases!"

Mom's mouth fell open. "No way!"

He nodded and hugged her on the other side of me. "I'm so proud of my girls."

I smiled at the look of pride and pure love on his face. It looked like happily ever after. "I'm going to look at the clothes," I said, giving them a moment, and went to the display with the big *Styled By A* sign.

There was a poster too of a photo of Mom in athleisure clothing and writing underneath.

Styled by A was designed by Glenda and inspired by her daughter, Adriel. After being a full-time mom for seventeen years, Glenda was in awe of how her daughter so passionately chased her dreams and picked herself up after setbacks. Her hope is anyone wearing Styled by A clothing will feel confident and powerful exactly as they are.

I covered my mouth, feeling the tears brimming in my eyes. They blurred my vision, and I blinked them away to take in the adorable clothes—leggings with scalloped hems, skirts with cute ties and dance inspired tops.

I ran my fingers over the butter-soft fabric of a top and shook my head. These were incredible. I would wear something exactly like this.

Next to me, Carter said, "See? You need to chase your dreams. It's not just you that would benefit."

My heart constricted. He'd meant the words to be kind, but they just hurt more. "What if I have more than one dream?" I asked, looking at him. Wishing I could kiss away his fears.

His smile was bittersweet. "Tell your mom congratulations for me. I'll see you at practice."

My heart sank as he walked away, but I put on a smile for my mom. This was her moment to shine, not my moment to cry. I had to hope that someday soon Carter would see just how much further I could go with him than without.

FIFTY-EIGHT

IF DANCING with Galina had taught me anything, it was to keep my eyes on the prize. So, I did what I did best. I focused on dance and school and dance again. I was especially excited to work with the second graders one last time before their winter showcase, where they'd be dancing to my choreography.

On Friday, I walked from Emerson Academy to the elementary school with Cori and Ryker.

"Are you excited for the showcase?" Cori asked. "Anna told us about it in gym class. She's so excited."

I grinned. "Did she also tell you about Greg throwing up on my shoes last week?"

Ryker shook his head. "That kid needs to wear a puke bucket around his neck."

"Yeah?" I said.

Cori nodded quickly. "Three weeks back, we were playing with those little scooters—you know the squares with the wheels on them—and Bailey spun him so fast he threw up on the gym teacher's shoes."

I rolled my eyes. "Maybe you guys could work on basketball or archery next so he can get some aim."

They chuckled, and Cori pushed the buzzer to let us into the elementary school. This way was longer for me, but I liked walking with them. Avoid my broken heart strategy number one: never have a quiet moment to yourself.

But when we made it to the gym and I waved goodbye to them, that's exactly what I was. Alone.

My mind instantly went to Carter, but I shoved my thoughts back to dance.

Mrs. Florence greeted me in the classroom before our first class arrived. "I think you'll be impressed when you see the second graders. They've been working so hard this week."

I grinned at her. "Really? I've been nervous for them," I admitted.

"No need to be. They're just as excited to show you what they've been doing at the showcase as they are their families."

"Me?" I asked.

She nodded. "You're coming, right?"

My mouth opened and closed. Why had I never thought about going to watch the actual winter showcase? Teachers watched their students at competitions. This was a performance just like any other. "I'd love to go watch. Is that allowed?"

She chuckled. "Of course it is. You should bring your parents too. Show them how talented you are as a teacher!"

Before I had a chance to thank her or reply, the start of the kindergarten line came into the room, and they sprinted to hug me. As I bent to greet them, Mrs. Angeline said, "See? You're a natural."

Maybe, just maybe, I was.

We had fun teaching the kindergarteners and first graders the basics of country line dancing, and then it was time for the second graders to come in. After I greeted them, Mrs. Angeline clapped her hands and said, "Positions, please! I'd like you to practice for Ms. Adriel so she can give her feedback before tomorrow night!"

They ran into a line, and I giggled at the sight

of Greg, thinking about what he would look like with a puke bucket around his neck.

Mrs. Angeline started the music, and the students went through their steps. In each of their moves, you could see their personalities. Anna with her carefully sequenced steps. Greg crashing through each pose like a wrecking ball. Bailey with all the sass in the world.

Just seeing them shine in their own unique way nearly brought tears to my eyes.

As the music came to a close, I clapped loudly. "Bravo!"

The kids grinned at each other, and Anna said, "You liked it?"

I shook my head. "I loved it."

After my practice with Carter on Friday, where he treated me like a business partner instead of the girlfriend I was for about two seconds, my friends agreed to meet up at Des's house to hang out before our last week of school for the semester. At the Academy, we had a full week of finals coming up, and this would be the one night we'd give ourselves to relax.

I took advantage of the twenty-minute drive there to call my mom and tell her about the show-case. She couldn't come to nationals, but I wanted her to be a part of something. To see that all the sacrifices she made were paying off for more than just me.

After a few rings, she picked up and said, "Hey, honey, what's up?"

"So, you know how I've been volunteering with Mrs. Angeline's music class at the elementary school?"

"Yeah?"

"Well, Mrs. Angeline asked me to choreograph a dance for the second graders' winter showcase."

"What?" Mom asked, sounding surprised. "Isn't that coming up soon? Will you have enough time with all your studying?"

I bit my lip, realizing I hadn't told her about the choreographing at all. It hadn't been on purpose, not really, I'd just been so wrapped up in everything that it slipped. "She actually asked me to do it a while back. I think I just forgot to tell you. But the dance is tomorrow night, and I was hoping you and Ted could come? I know it's last minute, but..."

"Of course!" Mom cried. "Of course we'll be there. I can't believe you didn't tell me though. I always thought you would be a natural dance teacher."

I raised my eyebrows as I steered my car down another turn. "What? You never told me that."

"You've always been so focused on performing that I didn't want to push it. So, tell me all about it. How has it been?"

I smiled. With the sun shining through the windshield and their rehearsal fresh in my mind, everything seemed happier. "It's been incredible, Mom. They're so good."

"They've had a good teacher," she said. "What time is the showcase?"

"Six," I answered. Des's house came into view, so I said, "I'm almost to Des's, but I'll see you later?"

"Sure thing," she said. "And Adriel?"

"Yeah?"

"No MIPs while you're staying at Des's."

My cheeks heated, and I said, "Bye, Mom."

"See you soon, honey. Love you."

I pulled into the driveway and set my phone in my lap. For once, it felt like something was going right.

Feeling lighter than I had since Thanksgiving

break, I got out of the car and walked up to Des's front door.

Des's parents had a Mexican food line that stocked the shelves of almost every store, so it was no surprise that their entire home had the enticing smell of Mexican food when I walked inside. The main room opened up to a living room where Des's family had a movie playing on the TV in Spanish, but my friends hung out around the kitchen island holding fondue sticks.

The girls turned to me and welcomed me to come sit with them.

My mouth fell open. The cheese dripping from a piece of bread on Des's stick looked amazing. "We're eating that?"

"And *tres leches*," Des said. As I was about to protest, she said, "You can have one small piece. Besides, we're celebrating."

"What are we celebrating?" I asked, sliding into a bar stool beside Cori.

"I just got shared by Jude Santiago," she said with a face-splitting grin.

"What!" I shouted. "Doesn't he have like a million subscribers on Youtube?" I asked.

Des nodded so quickly her hair shook in front of her face. "He said it was the best cover of one of his songs that he's ever heard! And he's about to get a record deal! I'm practically feet from the stage. I can feel it."

I clapped my hands together excitedly. "Please tell us you won't forget the little people when you make it big."

"Girl you know you're going to be the first one dancing in my music video," she replied and bit the cheesy piece of bread.

I reached for my own skewer. "I'm holding you to that."

Faith pointed at the bowl of items to dip in the cheese. "You have to try one of those tortillas in cheese. Mama De made them from scratch."

I skewered a piece, dipped it in the cheese, and the spice of the sauce with the softness of the tortilla made my mouth instantly water. It tasted like heaven. After being on a carb-restrictive diet for so long, I swore carbs were the stuff of gods.

Cori said, "My sister finishes her finals at UCLA on Wednesday, so she's going to come home to start working on the video on Thursday. That should give her plenty of time to get it done before next Saturday."

My smile faltered. Cori's sister Ginger had always been the video girl at our school, but I hoped her talents and a handful of days would be enough. "I don't want to talk about dance tonight," I said. It had been my life for so many years, I could take a night off. "Tonight is about us."

Nadira lifted her skewer with a dripping cheesy pepper. "Cheers to that."

We almost touched our food together, saying cheers and enjoying our time together. There would be plenty of time to focus on finals and nationals, but tonight? Tonight was ours.

I got home around eleven so I could wake up and make it to an early practice session with Carter. With the pressure of finals and nationals, we had to make the most of every minute we had.

I'd expected Mom and Ted to be asleep, but when I got home, Ted was sitting at the counter, flipping through a stack of photos. When he heard me walk in, he smiled and said, "Hey, Addy."

Carter's nickname for me took me off guard, but I realized I liked it. If it wasn't just Carter's it didn't hurt so much. "Hey," I replied, going to the fridge for a fresh bottle of water. I'd eaten way too much at Des's and wanted to flush it out of my system so I wouldn't feel so heavy in the morning. "What are you working on?"

He held up a photo of Mom and me hugging. "The photographer from your mom's release got some proofs to me. I thought I could surprise her with an album."

I noticed the photo album sitting on the counter. It was soft pink and in scrolling black text said *It's never too late to dream a new dream.*

It was perfect for Mom. "She's going to love it."

"I hope so," he said. "Do you want to help me pick some out?"

I nodded, sitting next to him at the counter. He handed me half of the two-inch thick stack, and I began flipping through them.

There were some of her first customers checking out at the register. One of her standing proudly beside the poster of herself.

"This one has to go in," I said, handing that one to Ted.

He held it gently in his hands, smiling softly at the photo. "That is a good one."

"How did she get all of this together?" I asked. "I haven't seen her working on it."

"You've been pretty busy dancing with Carter.

And you know your mother is a force of nature in heels."

That much was true. "Good point."

"How has it been going, by the way?" he asked. "You two didn't seem as friendly the other day."

I shrugged, flipping through a few more photos. "Can I ask you a question?"

"Sure," he said. "What's up?"

"Why did you keep our secret?" I looked at him, trying to judge his expression.

He lifted a corner of his lips, setting down a photo. "I know it might be hard to believe, but I love both of you... I've always thought of you like a daughter."

I bit my lip, my worries rising to the surface. "You didn't just want to go to Cancun?"

He laughed softly. "If I cared that much about Cancun, we would have gone by now." He shifted in his seat, looking me in the eyes. "When I married your mother, I didn't just marry a single woman. I married a mom. That's always been her most important job."

My heart softened. "Why did I hate you for so long?" I hadn't meant to say it, but now that the words were in the air, I couldn't take them back.

"Because you'd already lost enough. You didn't want to lose your best friend too."

The truth in his words hit me, and I blinked back tears as I flipped to another picture of my mom. She was holding the mannequin arm, pretending it was picking its nose. I let out a tearful laugh. "This one too."

"Oh yeah." He took it from me, grinning at the photo. "Pure gold." He studied me for a second. "Are you sure you don't want to tell your mom about nationals? You know she'd love to support you."

I shook my head, smiling. "She's doing way too well without dance. She should have her honeymoon. And so should you."

I slipped off the bar stool. "I'll see you tomorrow."

He nodded, lifting his finger in a wave. "Night, Addy."

"Goodnight," I said, and as I walked away, I thought, it really, really was.

FIFTY-NINE

"AGAIN," I said to Carter at our practice Saturday morning. "You have to get this lift down."

He nodded determinedly, but that almost made me more frustrated. We'd been practicing for three hours already, and he still hadn't gotten mad or given up. Hadn't once given less than his full effort.

Dancing so closely with him hurt, but I held on to hope that nationals would give him the peace of mind to know he wasn't holding me back. Not in the slightest. Especially with how hard he was working to help us win.

He nodded and went back to his spot on the side of the racquetball court. I took a few steps back and began the count. I took long strides forward before leaping into his arms and tightening all of my muscles to become stiff as a board. His arms shook underneath me as he gained balance, and finally, we hit the pose.

He gently lowered me down into the slow spin that came after, but he wouldn't meet my eyes.

I let out a frustrated groan, stepping back from him.

"What?" he asked, a sliver of tension easing into his voice.

"You know what," I snapped, the heat of my sweat and exhaustion getting the best of me. "You decided to pull back, and now all our chemistry is gone."

He extended his hands at his sides. "Maybe this wouldn't have happened if you'd gone back to your studio like you'd wanted to all along."

His words hit me straight in the heart. "Don't you get it? I didn't want to go back there! She humiliated me in front of the entire studio—dancers, parents, everyone. Because of my size! *Why* would I want to dance with someone I couldn't feel safe with?"

"Because sometimes the end justifies the means," he said.

I folded my arms across my chest and glowered at him. "People say that all the time to justify horrible things. I'm not one of them, Carter."

He bit his lip and looked down. "I feel like we need help, Addy. I want to do well for you, but I'm out of my depth here."

His vulnerability hit me straight in the heart. Because it reminded me of the old Carter. And because he was right.

I was fine teaching Carter the simpler moves, but I was too close to the routine to be any more help. I rubbed my temples, pacing back and forth. There had to be a solution here.

My first go-to would have been my mom. She'd spent enough hours in the studio to be a great critic. Even if it had gotten on my nerves sometimes over the years, she'd only tried to make me better.

Then it hit me. Benjamin.

He hadn't wanted me off the team. Had even texted me a few times after I'd gotten kicked off. Had we built enough chemistry over the months we'd danced together for him to do me a favor so large? Helping me would mean betraying Galina, and ultimately, creating stiffer competition for himself and Isabella.

"I have an idea," I told Carter. "But I'm not sure it's going to work. Until then, I think we should film the move so I can give you some better pointers."

"We only have a week left," Carter told me, as though I didn't already know.

"Let's just get it filmed," I said, going to my phone and propping it up against the wall. Once I was sure it would capture our full bodies, I hit record and counted down again.

I tried to put all of my emotions into my movements as I ran toward him—the pain of holding back, the changing of my dreams, and finally my desperation to be noticed at nationals.

Carter met me with strong hands, and as I lifted into the air, I could feel the move getting stronger. I could only hope that Benjamin would help take us the rest of the way.

SIXTY

BEFORE LEAVING the gym parking lot, I almost sent Benjamin a text but then thought better of it. He was probably practicing with Galina, which meant his phone was in the locker room. If he'd left it screen up or unlocked somehow, that would be the end of my favor.

Instead, I called him, and it went to voicemail. I left a quick message asking him to call me back and then drove home, taking deep breaths.

Our situation was looking more and more dire, and I just needed something, a divine intervention to get Carter and me on the right path again.

I tried to clear my mind because I needed to focus on finals now. My grades weren't the best, and I was teetering between Bs and Cs in several of my classes. I needed to make the most of my study time.

I'd planned to go to my room, change, and get my backpack to study at a coffee shop until the showcase, but Mom was waiting for me in the living room.

The second I walked through the door, she popped up, holding an envelope.

"You got a letter from Penn State!" she said.

My eyes widened, and I dropped my gym bag on the floor. In all of the commotion, I'd nearly forgotten I'd even applied to colleges. But here she was, holding out the envelope like it was made of gold.

"Open it!" she said. "I've been waiting for hours for you to get home so we could see what it says!"

My heart thrummed in my chest. Why did I feel so nervous? I'd applied to major in dance, and they had a pretty respectable program with a competition team. But now that it was staring me in the face, I realized, I actually cared.

What if nationals didn't work out? What if I didn't get recruited to a dance company? Knowing I would have somewhere to land besides my bedroom meant more to me than I'd realized. From a degree program I could go on to perform professionally, or even open a studio of my own...

My hand shook as I reached for the envelope, and instinctively, I shook the letter so its contents wouldn't be damaged as I ripped it open.

There were a few folded pages inside, and I took them out, not quite sure what to look for. In the movies, the first line always said "congratulations" or "I regret to inform you."

Which would I see? How would it feel?

I took a deep breath and scanned the first page.

Dear Ms. Pruitt,

Congratulations!

I didn't read any further than that because I was too busy looking between the letter and my mom, trying to register what it said.

"I got in," I whispered.

"You got in?" Mom cried.

A wave of relief and joy washed over me, and my next words came in a shout. "I got in!"

Her mouth fell open in a silent squeal. "You got in!" She took the letter, reading it for herself, and this time she screamed out loud. "You got in!"

My grin was so big it hurt, but I couldn't stop smiling. After so many roadblocks, I'd gotten a yes. It didn't even matter if I would eventually go to

Penn State or not. Someone had said yes to me, and that meant the world right now.

Mom insisted we go to lunch with Ted, and I couldn't argue. I went to my room, sprayed on some dry shampoo, put on extra deodorant, and changed into one of the dressier athleisure outfits my mom had designed.

Her clothes fit me perfectly, and I couldn't help but feel like they were made for me. Like this moment was made for me.

As soon as I walked into the living room, she covered her mouth with her hands and burst into tears.

A small laugh escaped my lips, and I said, "Mom."

She shook her head quickly. "These are happy tears. I'm just so proud of you. And I'm proud of me."

I smiled and hugged her. "You should be proud of you. These are incredible. I'm going to tell every single person I know to buy Style by A."

"Did I tell you I have the best daughter ever?"

With a shrug, I said, "Maybe a time or two."

We picked up our purses and went to the car to go to lunch. Since Ted was working at the gym, he met us at La Belle, and we went inside.

I'd had this food catered at school a few times before, but it had been a while since I'd had time to eat inside. It was just as fancy as I remembered it, and I was glad I'd gone for the dressier athleisure wear. With my structured coat, I fit right in with all the couples and businesspeople.

As soon as Ted arrived, the celebration started all over again. He gave me a big hug and ordered a round of sparkling cider. It felt silly holding my non-alcoholic beverage and toasting like an adult, but I loved the moment. It was like dancing on stage and nailing a move for the first time after practicing over and over.

We stuffed ourselves on delicious Italian food and ordered way too much off the dessert tray. And when our stomachs were full, but our plates were empty, it was time to move on. Ted had work to do, and I needed to study for a couple of hours before the showcase.

Mom dropped me off outside of Halfway Café so I could study for the rest of the afternoon.

I went inside the fancy shop, wondering if I would see Ryde Alexander or any other local celebrities. Instead, it looked to be a low-key afternoon, with couples drinking coffee or singles staring at their computer screens between sips of lattes.

I ordered a black coffee with some honey and went to sit at a small table by a window. Although it was cold outside, the sky was a bright blue, and I could see people walking past, going in and out of nearby shops.

My phone rang loudly, contrasting the quiet ambiance of the coffee shop. Sending an apologetic look to the person nearest me, I reached for my phone and answered it.

"Hello?"

"Hey, you called?"

I nearly dropped my phone at the sound of Benjamin's voice on the line. "Oh my gosh, you called me back."

He chuckled, and just the sound reminded me how much I missed him. Benjamin hadn't been the one to hurt my feelings or cast me aside; Galina had.

"What's going on?" he asked.

"I have a huge favor to ask you," I said.

With a bit of hesitation, he said, "Yeah?"

"I know this is crazy, but I was hoping you could help me teach Carter to do the star lift? If you don't want to, say so, but I'm desperate here. I taught him everything for qualifiers on my own, but if we want to get noticed..."

"You have to do better," Benjamin finished.

"And I know it's dumb to help your competition, but I just hoped, I don't know, that you'd do this for me?" My words came so fast, I almost forgot to breathe. I clutched the phone to my ear with both hands, praying Benjamin would find it in his heart.

"If Galina found out, she'd kill me," he said.

I bit my lip. "So, she doesn't have to find out?"

He let out a sigh, and I could hear the exasperated smile in his voice. "I only have an hour tomorrow. And it has to be somewhere my parents won't find out."

"Come to my stepdad's gym. We've been practicing there."

"Okay. I'll see you at ten.... and Adriel?"

"Yeah?" I said, waiting for the catch.

"I've missed having you around. But I'm glad you told Galina no. It was about time someone did."

I smiled. "Thank you. That means more than you know."

SIXTY-ONE

MOM AND TED picked me up at Halfway Café after a couple of hours so we could head to the showcase. As I walked to the car, I felt just as jittery as I would before a performance of my own. These kids weren't performing some random dance off the internet—they were performing choreography I'd created especially for them, in front of all their families and friends.

I tried to stay calm as I got in the car where Mom and Ted waited. I slid in the back seat and noticed Mom and Ted were dressed up.

"How was studying?" Ted asked as I buckled in.

"Great," I answered. "At least, I hope it was great."

"I'm sure it was," Mom said. "You've always been good at keeping up with your grades."

"I guess." I sat back in my seat, looking out the window as Ted backed into the road.

"Is Carter coming to the showcase too?" Mom asked.

Just hearing his name caught me off guard. "Not tonight. He's busy."

I didn't know why I felt the need to lie. It wasn't like I'd ever told Mom that Carter and I were "official", but it still felt bad that he couldn't come. That he wouldn't be there to support me.

I looked down at my hands, the polish-free nails and the callouses forming from weightlifting. My hands still looked better with his fingers linked through mine. I hoped we would get back there, and soon.

As we drew nearer to the school, Ted said. "Man, it's crowded."

Mom nodded. "Tons of people always come to the showcase. It's a big deal that they trusted Adriel with choreography."

"Thanks for the extra dose of nerves," I said, rolling my eyes.

Ted chuckled. "Hey, if anything goes wrong, you can blame the eight-year-olds. At least you don't have to show your face on stage." He looked over his shoulder to parallel park along the road.

"Gee," I retorted. "You two are great confidence boosters."

Mom laughed. "He makes a good point."

"Sure." I waited until the car was in park to slip my coat back on and get out. Formally dressed families were walking into the school as well, and I was glad Mom had suggested I wear my nice coat earlier. It went perfectly with my outfit.

We walked into the building and found a few seats together just a couple of rows back from the front. Of course, that led to plenty of time waiting. That was always the problem at things like this. You could get there early and be bored out of your skull or arrive on time and have nowhere to sit.

Mom and Ted talked about clothing sales at the gym while I occupied myself by playing a game on my phone. Soon, the lights lowered, and the elementary school principal stepped onto the stage to announce the showcase, starting with the youngest children and ending with the fifth graders.

Of course the kindergartners and first graders were adorable. They sang songs and danced and waved big at their parents in the crowd. But when it came time for the second graders, my heart beat quickly.

Mrs. Angeline stood in front the microphone and all the students on stage and said, "This year, we have a special treat from our second graders! As you know, the high school started a volunteer program, and your students have been benefiting from the leadership of our fine high schoolers! I was lucky enough to be paired with Ms. Adriel Pruitt. Adriel, will you stand up please?"

My heart stopped, and I probably would have stayed frozen to the spot if Mom hadn't patted my arm.

I stood, and the spotlight landed on me.

"Adriel has been a huge asset to our class this year, using all her years of dance to expose our students to a different aspect of the arts! Our second graders took to dance, and tonight they are performing to Adriel's original choreography."

A smattering of polite applause surrounded me.

"Give everyone a wave, Adriel." Feeling hot under the spotlight, I turned and wave, but caught sight of someone I wasn't expecting.

Carter sat next to his grandma, and when he saw me looking, he nodded at me. The expression in his eyes was hidden in the shadows, but I wanted to know what he was doing here. Had he come to see me?

I sat down, and Mrs. Angeline walked off stage. Just as we'd practiced in class, the music started, and the students began dancing through the routine. My eyes stayed glued to them as they nailed the choreography and shined on stage like the stars they were.

Mom covered her mouth with one hand and gripped my hand with the other. "They're so good, Adriel!"

I nodded proudly. "They're incredible."

They finished the routine, and the entire auditorium flooded with applause. As my students beamed on stage, I thought maybe Galina had been wrong when she said those who couldn't do taught. Maybe, those who loved their students, who loved investing in others and seeing progress, maybe they were the ones who belonged in a teacher's shoes.

SIXTY-TWO

I WAITED outside the gym for Benjamin to arrive. The breeze was cold, but in the sun, it wasn't so bad.

I watched as his Prius pulled into the parking lot and smiled at him as he got out. He waved and walked my way, and I worried about the right way to greet him. Should I just say hello? Hug him? Would we only walk in together?

He solved the problem for me, wrapping me in a hug.

I hadn't realized how much I missed him until that moment. My arms went around his narrow waist, and I held tight. "I missed you," I admitted.

"Same," he agreed, pulling back. "Isabella is *way* less fun to dance with."

I laughed, leading him toward the front door. "Imagine how fun she and Tatiana are to go to school with."

He let out a groan. "I don't even want to think about it. I'm so glad I'm homeschooled."

"You are lucky," I agreed and led him to the front desk. I told the girl there that he was with me, and she let us through the gates.

"How is it going with Carter?" Benjamin asked. "How are you feeling about nationals?"

A corner of my lips tugged down. "It used to come so naturally between us, but it feels forced now." I hadn't even been able to talk to him after the showcase the night before. I still didn't know why he'd been there, or if maybe things weren't quite as bleak as I'd thought.

Benjamin nodded, his dark eyes deep in thought. "Do you think it's just the pressure of the competition? If he's not used to it, it can be a lot."

I shook my head. "He's a competitive weightlifter, so it's not that." I knew what it was, but it was too embarrassing to admit. The truth was that I'd made Carter think dance was my life. And it had been, but it wasn't anymore. There was so much more I wanted now, in addition to a career in dance.

"You've taught him well," Benjamin said as I led him down the hallway to the racquetball courts. "Have you thought about having your own students someday?"

I bit my lip. "Would it be crazy if I said yes?" I hadn't even come close to getting paid for my talent, yet Carter and the second graders had really grown as dancers under my tutelage.

"Is crazy a bad thing?"

I didn't have time to think about it though as I reached the racquetball court I'd come to think of as ours. With my fingers on the handle, I told Benjamin, "It's not much, but it's an open space."

He nodded, following me into the court where Carter was on the floor stretching. As soon as Carter saw us, he stood and extended his hand to Benjamin. "Hey, man. Thank you so much for coming."

Benjamin's stance immediately relaxed. Carter had that effect on people—setting them at ease.

"No problem," Benjamin said. "I don't have a lot of time, so let's see what we're working with."

I began taking off my winter boots and coat. "We can just run the routine from the top?"

Benjamin nodded. "That works."

I set my phone and speaker up, then went to

stand by Carter in the middle of the court. We'd spent so much time practicing in private, it seemed strange to have Benjamin watching, but I breathed deeply and focused on the task at hand, already losing myself to the opening notes.

Carter and I slipped into our routine, practicing the steps that had been etched into our muscles and minds. Dancing with him didn't feel as charged as it had at qualifiers, but then again, having a crowd and spotlights added something hard to recreate.

We reached the end of the dance, our chests rising and falling with the force of our breaths, and turned to Benjamin.

He leaned back against the concrete wall, his hand on his chin, thinking. I almost couldn't handle the anticipation of what he would say. Or what he wouldn't.

I gripped my first two fingers with the opposite hand, trying to keep from fidgeting. Carter took a few steps away from me, and I felt alone as I waited for Benjamin's reply.

Finally, he pushed up and began pacing. "There are a few things you can fix. Carter, you need to keep an internal rotation on your arms when you lift her up. When you're spinning, you need to keep a single point on the wall, not change it as you go. And Adriel, you're letting your toes get sloppy. When you're on your leg, be on your leg.

"But," Benjamin sighed. "None of that matters if there's no passion to the dance. You two are like robots with a dance routine programmed in." He shook his head. "What happened after qualifiers?"

Carter and I gave each other a look, but neither of us spoke.

"Martha Graham said, 'Dance is the hidden language of the soul.' People watch dance to see your soul reflected in the movements. But when you're hiding the truest parts of yourselves from each other, you're hiding them from the world."

Benjamin gave me a sad look and put his hand on my shoulder. "Good luck at nationals, A."

I put my hand atop his. "Same to you."

As Benjamin walked out the door, tears stung my eyes. Carter and I had come so far. Was this the best we could do now?

Carter said, "Put your shoes on. I have an idea."

My eyebrows came together as I turned to him. "What do you mean?"

"There's something I want to show you."

"Where?" I asked.

"LA."

I glanced at my fitness tracker watch. "But we have finals coming up."

He gave me a look. "Addy, we have *nationals* coming up."

And because I couldn't argue, I put on my shoes and followed him to see what I hoped would be our saving grace.

SIXTY-THREE

CARTER INSISTED we ride in his car, so I sat in the passenger seat, breathing in his familiar scent. He drove with one hand on the wheel and one arm resting on the center console. His fingertips were so close to mine. I wanted to hold them, to feel the scratchy surface of his palms, but I held back.

Instead, I sat beside him, quietly listening to the country music on the radio as he drove out of town.

Finally, I asked, "Are you going to tell me where we're going?"

He nodded. "When we get there."

I snorted. "Then what would be the point in telling me?"

"You tell me."

I rolled my eyes. "That's what you're supposed to be doing."

He laughed softly, and the sound was like a balm to my heart. "Sometimes," he said, "when I'm coming up on a bodybuilding competition, I get close to burnout, and when that happens, my coach tells me to get Ashe and go have a day at the beach. Just for fun."

"Why?" I asked. "When you're that close to the finish line, that's when you're supposed to push the hardest."

He shook his head. "Without the joy, it's not really worth doing, you know? You won't stay as late, you won't work as hard, and ultimately, you won't win as much."

"So, you're taking me to LA for a ditch day?"

His smile lit up the car. "Technically we already had practice, so we're not exactly ditching."

"We are on studying though." Part of me wished I had brought my notebook just to look through on the drive. "I'm pretty sure I'm going to fail chem."

Okay, that wasn't exactly true, but I wasn't quite in the comfort zone with my seventy-two percent in the class.

"We can study together tonight if you need some extra help," he offered.

My heart twitched hopefully. "Yeah?"

He nodded. "Grandma is making fish for dinner. She says it's brain food."

I couldn't help but smile. "Your grandma's amazing."

"She is," he agreed.

"Why did you two come to the showcase yesterday?" I asked before I lost my courage.

Carter kept his eyes on the road as he shrugged. "Ted told Raf, then Raf told me, and I... I couldn't not go."

So, he'd come for me? Without me even having to ask? His words made my heart twitch with hope. I didn't ask any more questions, though, because I didn't want to lose this tenuous closeness we'd gained on the ride.

The blue mountains of LA came into view, fuzzy outlines in the distance, and I wondered where Carter could be taking me. We had a perfectly good beach in Seaton and a marina in Brentwood if we wanted to do something in the water. Or we could have watched TV or gone for a walk at Emerson Trails. What did LA have that was so special?

He took an exit off the freeway and followed streets until a megamall came into view.

"What?" I asked. "We drove an hour to see a mall?" We had one in Emerson that was just fine.

He nodded though, seeming unphased. After parking, he unclicked his seatbelt, moved his wallet from the cupholder to his pocket and got out of the car. I followed him, more than a little frustrated. By the time we got home, it was very possible we could have spent three or more hours on this trip. It better be miraculous to take up that kind of time.

We walked through the revolving front door and into the crowded world of shoppers and children and couples enjoying a Sunday at the mall. It was all fine, except I had so much to do.

"Come on," Carter said, inclining his head to the left. The signs said this was the way to the food court, and I swear, if he brought me here just to eat...

The closer we got to the food court, the better I could see. The dining area extended four levels from the basement to the sky, and it was all open to this massive gathering area on the ground floor.

Hundreds of people congregated in one place, dancing although there was no music. It was the strangest thing I'd ever seen. "What are they doing?" I asked.

"Dancing," he explained, stepping onto the escalator.

"I can see that," I muttered.

As we drew nearer, I recognized white head-phones over their ears. There was music after all. We just couldn't hear it.

He grinned over at me, and I couldn't help my own slow smile.

I followed him to the head of the impromptu dance floor, and he purchased two disinfected head-sets for us. The guy handing them out said, "The music will stop playing in an hour."

I held the set in my hands, pushing on the pads meant to go around the ears. Carter slipped his headphones on and began nodding to the rhythm as he walked to an open space on the dance floor. A mom and her kids made room for us, and we stepped into place.

The whole thing seemed strange to me, but the second I put on my headphones, it became magical.

Electronic dance music played loud in the speakers that wrapped around my ears to block out all other sound. Now, instead of being an outsider looking in, I was on the inside looking out.

Everyone went about their day, eating, shopping, talking, not noticing the fun that could be had just a few feet away.

Just like it always did, the music led my body and I began dancing. No routine. No choreography. Just dancing like I did when I was a little girl, spinning in my most twirly dresses.

I closed my eyes, breathing in the moment. It was the first time in weeks I'd felt at ease, and I wanted to etch every bit of that feeling into my memory so I could always access it when I wanted.

I felt Carter's eyes on me. He was looking at me, smiling while biting his bottom lip. The warmth in his gaze sent a shiver down my spine.

He extended his hands to me, and I laced my fingers through his, letting the music take me where my heart was afraid to go.

We danced together, letting our bodies say all the things our words couldn't. I felt his fears while he discovered my wants. And slowly, the tension eased out of my chest and was replaced with one thing: hope.

SIXTY-FOUR

CARTER and I studied at his house, eating the delicious crab cakes his grandma had made and going over and over chemistry. He was better at schoolwork than me, but I finally got to a place where I didn't feel completely helpless.

When I looked at the watch on my wrist, I realized it was almost ten, and my mom would be expecting me home.

"It's getting late," I said to Carter. Not that he didn't already know. His grandma had gone to bed an hour earlier.

He nodded, flipping his notebook closed. "We should get some sleep before the test tomorrow."

I nodded, having a hard time moving. But I put my notes in my backpack and stood up.

"I'll walk you outside," he offered.

I didn't decline.

Instead, I let him walk alongside me to the front door of their home. It was a modest ranch-style house, probably built in the seventies, with a big living room for guests and a table inside the kitchen. But it felt like home, with all the photos his grandma had all over the walls.

Walking into the night air was cold in the absence of its warmth.

But Carter stayed beside me, shrugging on his jacket. The sidewalk leading to the street had never seemed so short.

There were so many things I wanted to say to Carter. That I was thankful for him dancing with me. That he'd shown me another world I didn't know existed. That when I danced with him, I felt more like myself than I ever had before.

But instead, the silence stretched on, and I reached my car. Before stepping onto the street, I turned to him. "Thanks, for today. I needed it."

His smile was genuine as he nodded. "I think I did too."

I tilted my head to the side. "It's been a hard couple of weeks, right?"

"Yeah," he agreed, leaning back against my car. "I don't think I made it any easier."

"No. Not really."

He chuckled softly. "Thanks for easing the blow, Addy."

Laughing, I went to lean on the car beside him. On the outskirts of Emerson where his house was, I could see a few stars dotting the sky, including Orion's Belt.

Following my gaze, Carter asked, "Do you know there are some stars that take more than four years for their light to reach the earth?"

I shook my head. I'd only ever heard about the sun taking minutes. Seven or eight, I think.

"I used to look at the stars and think the light that was shining on me came from a time when my parents were still alive." He said it like a whisper. Almost like an admittance.

I didn't know what to say, so I reached for his hand. He glanced at me before returning the gesture and looking back at the sky.

"It made me feel closer to them," he said, a sadness in his voice. "But now all the light I see is from after they died."

My heart hurt for him, and I didn't know what to say. When my grandpa died, I'd missed him like crazy. He'd been my last living grandparent and had always made an effort to be the man in my life the way my dad never really had.

"There are still some stars shining from when my grandpa was alive then," I said, smiling at the thought. Those pinpricks of light held memories I'd forgotten. "Were your parents in love?"

I don't know what made me ask the question, but I felt like it was the right thing to ask.

Carter smiled, confirming my guess. "They were crazy about each other. I can't remember much about them since I was only seven when they died, but I remember them dancing in the kitchen and always wanting to dance with them."

I pictured a little Carter spinning in circles with his parents and smiled. "Maybe that's why you're so good at dancing."

"Maybe." He chuckled, then sobered. "They always told me someday I'd find someone to dance with too." He turned, taking my other hand in his as well. His eyes shined brighter than any of the stars, caressing everywhere he looked so gently.

My heart beat closer to the surface of my skin as if it knew it was the melody to our dance.

"Sometimes in dance," I said, finding my words, "you have to let go."

He nodded, blinking quickly.

Before tears slipped down my cheeks as well, I stood on my tiptoes and kissed him softly on the cheek. Without saying a word, I went to my car and drove away, thinking that sometimes in dance you let go. But sometimes, sometimes, letting go only lasted for a moment before you could hold on tight.

SIXTY-FIVE

THE SCHOOL PARKING lot was only halfway full when I arrived for my first two finals. I had two tests a day until Friday, when I'd finish with my last exam of the year. It was hard to believe I was already heading into my last semester at Emerson Academy. The first semester had gone so differently from how I'd expected, but so much better too.

I went to my locker to put away my chemistry and calculus books and notes, but when I opened the door, I saw something unexpected.

A cupcake box with the Seaton Bakery logo stamped on the outside set atop my shelf. I pulled it out, and a napkin fluttered to the floor.

Good luck on finals this week! You've got this! -Nadira

I smiled at the neat writing on the napkin. Even

though I didn't always feel that way, I was so lucky just to have a few good friends who cared about me.

I opened the box to see a cupcake inside. The frosting was pink and covered in sprinkles. My mouth practically watered, but I told myself I could save it as a treat (or consolation prize) after I took my tests.

Up first was chemistry. I walked to the lab carrying only my pencil, which was all we were allowed to bring into the room.

When I arrived, there were a few people there already, including Carter. He smiled at me as I walked in, and I went to sit with him. Something about this weekend had made things better. Not perfect, but I'd take any improvement after the weird chasm that had divided us.

Mr. Cho came into the room with a thick stack of papers. "Seat yourself in every other chair." He began passing out the papers as the last of the students came into the class. "If I see your eyes on anyone else's exam, you *will* be asked to leave, and you *will* get a zero. Am I understood?"

A chorus of "yes, sir" rang throughout the room.

I gave a final glance at Carter. His eyes were on

the person in front of him, handing him the test. He seemed so serene, so focused.

As if sensing me, he glanced my way and smiled softly, mouthing, "Good luck."

"Thanks," I whispered.

Mr. Cho's chair creaked as he sat down. "Let's get started. You have two hours."

Test after test after test passed in a blur. I barely looked up from my notes to make the most of study time, but my ringing phone distracted me on Thursday afternoon. I was in the final stretch, studying for my very last test before break.

Cori's name was on the screen, so I answered and said, "Hey, Cor, what's up?"

"Ginger's here, so I thought we could meet up to talk about the video?"

My eyes widened. How had I forgotten about the video for nationals? "When do you want to meet?"

"She said we could go to Seaton Bakery together for supper. Then you and I can study while she works on the storyline?"

A relieved sigh whooshed out my chest. "That

sounds amazing. I'm practicing with Carter from four to six, so I can meet you at six thirty?"

"It's a date," she said. "How are finals going?"

I groaned loudly.

"That well?"

"Yours are better?"

She laughed. "Nope, about the same."

I smiled, shaking my head. "I still have another hour of studying before I go to practice with Carter. See you soon?"

"See you soon," she said, and the call ended.

"Practice?" my mom asked at the door, and my heart nearly fell out of my chest.

I scooted back in my chair, covering my heart with my hand. "Mom! You scared me!"

She gave a sheepish look. "Sorry." She held up a bowl of what looked like fresh berries. "I just wanted to see if you needed a snack?"

I nodded thankfully. "I've been forgetting to eat," I admitted.

"I noticed." She came and brushed my hair out of my face. "Have I ever said how proud I am of you?"

"Maybe a time or two." I smiled and reached for a blueberry. "How's it going?"

She shrugged, tugging at the corner of my quilt

on my unmade bed. "I called to tell your dad that you got into Penn State."

"And?" I asked, shifting uncomfortably in my seat. Dad and I hadn't exactly left things on the best of terms, and he hadn't tried to get in touch with me, not even to wish me a happy Thanksgiving. I was surprised Mom was talking to him at all.

She fluffed out the blanket, letting it parachute gently to my mattress. "He said he's proud of you… and told me you went to visit."

My heart constricted. He'd told her?

She spread out the corner and sat, facing me. "Honey, you know if you didn't want Ted and me to adopt, you could have told me."

I shook my head, suddenly feeling heavy, like my shoulders were weighed down with giant stacks of bricks. "It's not that. If that's what you and Ted want, I want you to have it."

"Then what is it?" she asked. "I'd never do anything to hurt you."

My eyes stung. They were dry from so many hours of studying, and the salty tears just hurt more. "I know you wouldn't."

She came and gave me a gentle hug. "I'll let you study. Just remember, I'm here if you want to talk."

Before she walked away, I said, "Wait." I stood from my desk and wrapped her in a hug.

With a surprised chuckle, she said, "What's that for?"

I held her even tighter. "For being the best mom in the world." I pulled back. "I promise, Mom, I'll pay you back for all the time you spent on me for dance."

Her fingertips gently brushed my hair back, and she pressed her lips on my forehead. "You're sweet. But I'm holding out for payback on the potty-training phase." She laughed and waved her arms around. "Pee everywhere. You were like a puppy."

I crossed my heart. "Top-notch nursing homes for you. Nothing but the best for my mama."

She pointed at me. "I'm holding you to that."

"I better get to studying then." I sat down at my desk. "And thanks, Mom, for everything."

SIXTY-SIX

I LEFT PRACTICE WITH CARTER, feeling better than I had in a while, but also nervous. So much rested on us doing well at nationals. Proving Galina wrong. Proving myself right. And potentially creating a career for myself doing something I loved. Not only that, I wanted Carter to see just how much I'd come to care for him over the months. He'd gone from being my dance partner to so much more. I'd never be able to thank him enough for what he'd given me.

I drove the now familiar path to Seaton Bakery and saw Ginger and Cori at the counter talking to the same woman who'd been there the night we caught the kettlebell bandit. She smiled at me and waved.

Cori and Ginger turned then too, waving at me, and the woman said, "You three know each other?"

Cori nodded happily. "She's one of my best friends. You know Adriel, right, Gayle?"

"I sure do," Gayle said.

"Right," I agreed. "She gave Ted and me the most delicious cupcakes I've ever tasted."

Ginger nodded. "You should try the donuts too. Absolute perfection."

Gayle put her hands on her hips and smiled. "If you girls keep being so sweet, I'm going to get a toothache!"

I chuckled. "I might be the one to get a cavity if you keep making such amazing desserts."

Gayle batted her hand at me, and from the kitchen, a guy yelled, "Don't let her take all the credit! The donuts were my idea!"

She rolled her eyes, explaining, "That's my husband, Chris."

Laughing, I called, "Thanks, Chris!"

"Finally, some recognition around here," he called back jokingly.

Gayle smiled, shaking her head. "What can I get you girls?"

We ordered food and dessert, then went back to a corner booth. Ginger looked around nostalgically.

"I don't miss high school, but I do miss seeing my friends around here."

Cori asked, "When are the others coming back for break?"

"This weekend." Ginger grinned. "We get to see a sneak preview of the movie Zara and Ronan have been working on."

My eyes widened. "You have friends who are working on movies?"

"Oh yeah," Cori answered for her, setting down her lemonade. "Zara's an executive producer on this Nattie Jones movie coming out, and her boyfriend, Ronan, got put on the writing team."

My mouth fell open. "*The* Nattie Jones? Like New York Times bestselling author, books in our school library Nattie Jones?"

Ginger nodded emphatically. "That's the one."

"Wow," I said, sitting back. It was hard to believe Emerson Academy had produced so many celebrities years down the line, but Ginger and her friends had just graduated in May. What could I be accomplishing six months from now? The thought brought excited chills to my spine.

"So." Ginger leaned over and got her laptop out of her purse. "Tell me about the guy."

My cheeks instantly flushed, and Cori said, "He's basically Mr. Perfect."

She wasn't wrong.

Ginger waited patiently, fingers poised over her keyboard, and I began telling her everything I loved about Carter. "He's the nicest person you'll ever meet," I said. "Very selfless and giving. And so even-keeled you know you can always count on him. He didn't even know how to dance, had never set foot in a lesson, and he still agreed to help me. We've been practicing for hours a day, and he hasn't once complained."

Ginger nodded, taking notes on her computer.

"He loves his grandma more than anything in the world, and I think that just makes me like him more. He doesn't talk a lot, but when he does, it means something, you know? I can tell that the words coming out of his mouth matter."

"And how do you feel when you're with him?" Ginger asked, typing quickly.

Instinctively, I wrapped my arms around myself. "Being with Carter is like...being home."

My eyes widened as I realized what I had said. Ever since getting kicked out of the studio, I'd felt like a seed drifting in the wind, waiting to see where I'd land, if there was actually fertile ground that would take me. But I hadn't realized my roots were slowly growing, right along with my wings.

Ginger leaned forward, a twinkle in her eyes. "Do you love him?"

"I do." The words were off my lips before I even knew I was saying them. I repeated, in almost a whisper, "I love Carter McCormac."

With a smile, Ginger said, "He's going to see it, in this video. Are you ready for that?"

Slowly, I nodded. Now that the words were off my lips, I didn't know if I could even wait until Saturday for this grand plan to play out. I knew Carter had been scared, and now I understood a little bit more. Love *was* scary. I just hoped he would think it was worth the risk of having your heart on the line.

"Do you have a recording of your routine?" Ginger asked. "And the music?"

I nodded. "I have a video of the run-through we did today, and Carter's friend Griffin is sending us the final track tomorrow."

"Perfect. I'll send you an online folder. Upload the routine and all the photos or videos you have of you with Carter."

"Okay," I agreed, nervous butterflies tickling the inside of my stomach.

Cori squealed eagerly, tapping her feet on the ground. "This is going to be amazing. I can't wait to see it!"

A shiver of excitement went up my spine. For better or worse, nationals was going to be a show to remember.

SIXTY-SEVEN

I SAT on Mom's bed while she packed on Friday afternoon for their flight to Cancun the next day. All of my finals were officially done, with final grades coming in the following Monday. Carter and I had already practiced today. Faith said the shirts were done. Griffin had sent us the perfect song for our dance that morning. Now all there was left to do was compete.

Mom folded a second swimsuit and said, "Are you sure you're okay staying here by yourself? I bet one of your friends' families would love to have you for a few days."

"I'll be on my own in August," I reminded her. "This will just be a good test run."

She sighed and folded a cover-up to go with her suit. "I just worry."

I smiled, leaning back on her plush pillows. "I know. Aren't you excited though?"

"Can you tell?" She chuckled. "I'm pretty sure I'm packing enough to live there indefinitely."

"Good thing Ted works out so he can carry all your bags," I teased.

Laughing, she shook her head. "I haven't been to Mexico since spring break your sixth-grade year. Do you remember that trip?"

I bit my lip and nodded. Mom and I had spent most of the trip laying out on the beach and eating so much good food while Dad worked in the hotel business lounge. Now a part of me wondered if he'd actually been working that whole time or not. "You'll have more fun with Ted. Make new memories."

She turned away from me and went to her closet for another round of clothes. Glancing at her bulging suitcase, I asked, "How much more are you going to put in there?"

"Just the essentials. Do you think I need a winter coat?" she asked.

"For the ride to the airport maybe," I said. "Is Ted packed already?"

She chuckled. "I think he was packed two weeks ago."

"So, he's even more excited than you are."

"Maybe, which is good considering we need to leave here at six in the morning to make our flight."

That was another good thing about their schedule. It left plenty of time for me to get ready. Carter and his grandma would pick me up the next morning at seven so we could arrive and check in on time for our ten o'clock performance.

So many feelings were running through me. Fear, nerves, excitement, hope, and more I couldn't quite identify. And even though I was excited for my mom to get this trip, I would miss her. This would be the first national performance of mine she hadn't made it to. But that would leave room for her firsts too.

Her first honeymoon with Ted.

Her first trip to Mexico since the divorce.

Her first excursion as a wife and not as a mom.

I hope she loved it just as much as I loved her.

I got up early the next day to say goodbye to Mom and Ted before they left for the airport. The house had that blue glow from the scant morning sunlight coming through the windows. Although I was tired, Mom and Ted seemed chipper.

He was carrying their bags out to the car while Mom prepared their coffee in the kitchen.

Mom was wearing an adorable traveling outfit—leggings in her Styled by A line, along with a shirt and a jacket and a shimmering fanny pack around her waist. She set the coffee pot back on the burner and drank deeply from a monogrammed coffee cup.

"Morning, sweetie," she said when she saw me.

I shuffled toward her, still wearing my slippers, and gave her a hug. "Morning." My voice came out raspy, and I rubbed my eyes.

"Want some coffee?" she asked.

I nodded sleepily.

She set her cup on the counter and went to the cabinet to get me one of my own. She retrieved a white mug with a pink dancer on it. My favorite cup. I'd gotten it as a gift from Grandpa on my twelfth birthday, filled to the brim with candy.

I wondered if that was a sign from Grandpa that today was going to be a good day. I sure hoped so.

She filled the cup with black coffee and squeezed

what was left of the honey inside. I extended my hands, wiggling my fingers. "Gimme gimme gimme."

Chuckling, she said, "You're not supposed to be addicted to caffeine until you get to college."

"Tell finals that," I muttered before taking a long sip of the steaming liquid. The second it hit my tongue, I felt better.

She smiled, then closed the cabinet. "So, I put the number to our hotel on the fridge, along with Janice's number. If anything happens, she said you could call her, and she'd be here in ten minutes flat. I also left a credit card for food in the junk drawer so you could order in. Just make sure it goes back there when you're done with it, so we don't lose it."

"You lose a card one time," I muttered. Leaving the card in the changing room at a store last year had been a simple mistake. It wasn't my fault someone went on a shopping spree afterward...

"Uh huh," she teased. "Feel free to have any of your girlfriends over, but if Carter visits, he needs to be out of the house by ten."

My stomach swooped at the idea of having Carter over. Would that be a possibility after nationals?

"Okay?" she said.

I nodded quickly. "I'll be fine, Mom. I promise, no stolen credit cards or illegitimate children while you're gone."

"Ha ha," she said.

Ted came inside, rubbing his hands together. "What's funny?"

My cheeks heated, and Mom said, "Teenagers are *so* fun."

Ted chuckled and said, "Honey, can you go do a doublecheck through the car to make sure we have everything?"

"Sure," Mom said, rubbing my shoulder as she walked past.

As soon as the door closed behind her, Ted said, "So, today's the day?"

I nodded slowly, trying to quell the rush of nerves that statement brought up.

"Are you ready?" he asked. "You and Carter have been practicing like crazy."

"I think so. A lot is going to have to come together for it to go well."

"Like what?" He seemed genuinely interested, and it just made me like him more.

"My friend recorded a song for us to dance to, and another friend made a video for the background display, and another friend is making shirts for everyone to wear."

"It sounds like you have a lot of people in your corner." His words were kind, but there was a look of regret in his eyes that left just as quickly as it came.

"We do," I said. "And Cori's sister is going to film it so you and Mom can see it when you get back."

"Addy, I—" he began, but Mom walked in, saying, "It's all there!" Her eyes were on her watch as she added, "We better get going, or we're going to be late."

Ted cleared his throat and stood. I couldn't help but wonder what he'd been about to say before Mom walked in.

Mom passed Ted and gave me a big hug. The kind that held you together and made you want to fall apart at the same time. How pathetic was I that my eyes were stinging at the thought of my mommy not being at the show.

"Love you, Mom." I hugged her back, reminding myself that this was her time too. If I worked professionally, there would be plenty of performances she wouldn't be able to make it to. This was just part of the gig.

She stepped back and said, "Call me anytime, okay? Any time you need me."

I smiled and nodded. "Have a good trip."

She stepped back, and there was an awkward pause between Ted and me as we tried to figure out what was right. Handshake? Hug? Wave?

He closed the distance and hugged me with one arm. "Have a good week, kiddo. We'll see you Christmas Eve."

"Have fun," I said and watched as he and Mom walked out the door.

Now it was time to focus on nationals, regardless of the strange emotions swirling in my chest. Carter and I had a job to do.

SIXTY-EIGHT

THE DOORBELL RANG, and I reached for my duffel bag with everything I'd need for the day. When I opened the door, Carter was standing there, and I said, "I thought you were just going to text me when you got here."

"Grandma said gentlemen don't honk at the house." He looked over his shoulder at his running car, hot exhaust spilling from the tailgate and lifting until it disappeared into the air. "Apparently texting falls in that category too."

"I think I'm in love with your grandma," I said.

He chuckled. "Let me take your bag or she'll have my head."

I slipped the bag off my shoulder, obliging him, before turning and locking up the house. We wouldn't want that credit card to get stolen, now would we?

"How are you feeling?" I asked as I walked alongside him.

He didn't meet my eyes as he opened the trunk and set my bag inside. "I'm feeling like I messed everything up."

My heart strung tight. "What do you mean?"

He shut the trunk and turned toward me. "What about the grand *jete* we added back in? I can't leap. And the star lift? How am I supposed to emote *and* hold you in the air at the same time? I'm not that coordinated! And I completely wrecked our chemistry after I found out about you and Galina—"

I put a finger to his lips, if only to remind him to breathe. "Carter, now's not the time." Getting worked up now would just make performing together harder. "Remember, Benjamin said your form is alright. It's the emotions we need. And I have something planned that I think will help."

He took my hand in his, sending my heart skittering at a jaunty pace. "I don't want to mess this up, Addy."

I closed my eyes, breathing in the moment. "You won't." When I opened them again, I saw his honey gaze, and my heart melted. How had this wonderful person existed in my world for so long without holding my heart in his hands like he did now?

With a small smile, he said, "My grandma's staring at us."

I turned to look, and she immediately shifted in her seat. A small laugh escaped my lips. "Better not keep her waiting."

"Right," he agreed. He walked to the back door and opened it for me.

I slid into the middle seat so I could see them both and said, "Good morning, Mrs. McCormac."

She smiled at me and handed me a Styrofoam box. "We picked up breakfast for you at Waldo's Diner."

I turned from her to Carter. "Carter... I think I'm in love with your grandma."

They laughed as I took the box, and Carter pulled off down the road. It had been thoughtful of her to get me food. Honestly, my stomach was in so many knots I wasn't sure food could make it through. But I knew I'd need my energy to perform well today.

I opened the box, taking in the spinach omelet

and a small Styrofoam bowl. Inside, there was oatmeal and freshly cut berries.

"I looked on the internet for what dancers eat," Mrs. McCormac said. "Eggs are an excellent source of protein, and oats are supposed to provide long-lasting energy. But eat now, because you shouldn't eat less than ninety minutes before your performance so you don't feel too heavy."

Her thoughtfulness touched me, and I placed my hand over my heart. "Thank you so much."

"Of course," she said. "I made Carter eat the same thing at home before we left."

"She did," Carter confirmed.

I laughed softly and picked up a small piece of the omelet, popping it in my mouth. Waldo's Diner always had the best food. It reminded me of Friday nights after football games and times with my friends. I wondered how our favorite waitress, Betty, was doing and promised myself to go to Waldo's over winter break to find out.

The drive to LA flew by, and before I knew it, Carter and I were checked in and being led back to a small studio where we could get ready. I hadn't done my hair before leaving, so I sat in front of the mirror and began working with the curling iron.

In the space behind me, Carter stretched with

his headphones in. The air had a charge in it, and I hoped we would electrify our performance instead of sparking out. As I sprayed on a thick layer of hairspray, I couldn't help but wish my mom was here, making sure I reached the back of my hair, helping with my makeup.

I did the best I could with my supplies, layering on thick eyeliner and blush that could be seen from stage, and then I put a few extra pins in my hair, just to be sure it would stay in place during our performance.

As if sensing my nerves, Carter said, "Addy, you look great."

"Thank you," I said, turning to smile at him.

He stood with the garment bag that held his costume. "You're welcome," he said. "I think it's about time for us to get dressed."

I checked my watch and nodded. He was right. In less than an hour, we would be on the stage, and we would see whether all of our work, all of the heartache, all of the hope, had paid off.

SIXTY-NINE

A KNOCK SOUNDED on our studio door, and when Carter opened it, there was a man wearing a Dance Dance Nationals shirt. "You're on deck," he told us.

Carter turned toward me, his hand extended. "Ready?"

Silently, I nodded and slipped my hand in his. It was firm and solid as we walked toward the stage. The man led us to a waiting area in the wings, and my heart quickly sank. In front of us were Benjamin and Isabella.

Performing after them could have been our kiss of death, with our strengths and weaknesses standing in such stark contrast to their skill.

It was dark back here, the only light coming

from shadows cast on stage. I could hear music playing loudly, something beautiful and lyrical, but the volume couldn't compete with the pounding in my ears.

"They will announce you on stage after the next act," the man said and walked away.

At the sound of the man's voice, Isabella turned our way and rolled her eyes. "If it isn't Butter and the Beast."

Benjamin gave her a look, but I just rolled my eyes. "Focus on your dance, Isabella. We'll focus on ours."

She looked like she was about to argue, but the song ended, and the announcer called her and Benjamin to the stage.

As they walked away, Carter gripped my hand. "Are you okay?"

I sighed, shaking my head. "I wish my size wasn't an issue to everyone."

He brushed his thumb over the back of my hand. "The fact that you're doing this just proves that it shouldn't be. You're ensuring it won't be for another girl who comes after you."

His words warmed me from the inside out, and I looked up at him in awe. Carter understood. He got me in a way a lot of people didn't.

"Carter?" I said softly.

"Yeah?"

I searched his eyes for a moment, looking for a sign everything would be alright. "No matter what happens out there, I'm glad it's you I'm dancing with."

"Me too," he said.

A sense of finality and peace fell over me as I turned to the stage, watching the end of Isabella and Benjamin's routine. This journey, this adventure, was about to reach the end. I hoped it would be happily ever after.

SEVENTY

THE ANNOUNCER CALLED OUR NAMES, and as we walked onto the stage, an enormous swell of applause greeted us, louder than what I'd heard for Benjamin and Isabella's performance. What was going on? We hadn't even danced yet.

I looked at the crowd, finding all of my friends, all of Ginger's friends, Carter's family and friends, and then...

My mom and Ted.

I stared at them, dressed in matching white shirts with a swirly heart and the letters A+C on the front. How had Faith planned for them to have shirts too? And more confusingly, why had they come here? Weren't they supposed to be midflight to Cancun?

The announcer introduced our dance, and then the opening chords played with the sweet sound of Desirae's voice. Behind us, the giant screen flashed brightly. On instinct alone, I fell into Carter's arms for the beginning of our routine.

It started with a few steps toward him and away to signify retreat, hesitancy. But we quickly found each other again, working through move after move and stunt after stunt, perfectly timed with the rever- berations of the music. With each second that passed, the dance felt better and better until it came time for the big stunt.

I ran toward Carter, and he lifted me in the air. Over the music, I could hear Ginger's voice asking what it felt like to dance with Carter, and me saying it felt like home.

Carter slowly lowered me down, a confused look in his eyes.

Ginger's voice came again. "Do you love him?"

Carter held me close, staring at the screen, the dance forgotten as I looked into the camera. Spread across the giant screen, I said, "I do. I love Carter McCormac."

The music swelled again, and Carter caught me on the wave, blending his emotions with the dance until we reached our final pose. As the chords came to a close, Carter's molten honey eyes stayed on mine. Tears shone in them as he said, "I love you too."

And the entire crowd burst into applause.

SEVENTY-ONE

THE SECOND WE reached the wings, Carter held me tight to his chest and didn't let go. "I love you so much," he said, kissing my cheeks, my temples, the crown of my head.

Tears streamed down my cheeks from the release of the dance and relief of Carter feeling the same way I had tried so hard to resist.

His lips met mine in a tearful kiss that repeated those three words over and over again.

Someone behind us cleared their throat, and I reluctantly pulled away from Carter. I'd forgotten where we were. That there was probably someone here besides us.

A woman wearing a headset said, "You may go

watch the rest of the competition." But as we walked by, she added, "Congratulations," with a wink.

We held hands tightly, leaving the special place backstage and going into the fluorescent lighting of the hallway. But before we could get into the auditorium, a crowd of people burst through the double doors. All of our friends, all the people who had helped us get this far came into the lobby area.

They began cheering for us again, but I only had eyes for Mom, for Ted, as they walked closer to me.

"What are you doing here?" I asked, looking between Mom and Ted. "Why aren't you on the plane?"

Mom smiled at her husband. "Ask Ted."

A genuine smile grew on his lips. "I couldn't let my daughter dance without her family there. I wouldn't have missed it for all the margaritas in Cancun."

All the emotions of the last several months seemed to hit me at once. My heart beat quickly, and I dropped Carter's hand to hug Ted. "Thank you," I cried into his chest. "Thank you, thank you." I looked up at him, into his kind blue eyes and at his smile. "You're more of a dad to me than mine has ever been. Is it okay if I call you Dad?"

His jaw trembled as he nodded and pulled me back into a hug. "You'll always be a daughter to me."

More arms wrapped around us, and I looked over to see Mom hugging us, tears flowing freely down her cheeks.

I let go of my dad, my real dad, to hug her back and said, "I'm sorry I didn't tell you."

She used her thumbs to wipe her tears away even though they just kept flowing. "I'm so mad at you! But I'm so proud of you too."

I gave her a teary grin and hugged her again. "You deserved to go on your honeymoon, Mom. To live your life."

She shook her head. "Don't ever blame yourself for the decisions I made. I settled with your father for a life that wasn't even my own. I used dance as an excuse, when I was really just afraid of failing. But you. You are so brave." She glanced at Carter, who was being patted on the back by everyone within arms' reach. "I can't believe you two did this on your own!"

"Was it good?" I asked, nerves creeping into my voice. Mom had seen enough competitions to know.

She shook her head, and my heart sank. But she said, "It wasn't good, Adriel. It was *amazing*."

As I glanced at Carter and met his honey eyes, I couldn't help but agree.

SEVENTY-TWO

WE MADE our way back to the auditorium for the awards ceremony, taking up two rows in the back. I sat between Carter and my parents, surrounded by all of my friends. They announced the individual winners first, and three dancers from Galina's studio took the top slots. It was the best the studio had ever done at nationals.

When it came time for the couples to be announced, Mom gripped my hand on one side, and Carter squeezed my hand on the other. I knew it was a long shot that we would place, but I couldn't help but hope. After all, so many "impossible" wishes had already come true.

The announcer started by talking about what an incredible turnout they'd had. The addition of the video display to the performances had been a game changer, he said. "Before we start with the awards, the judges unanimously agreed to create a special category for best use of media in combination with dancing. Without further ado, we'd like to announce the very first-ever winner of the AC AV Award for whom it is named! Adriel and Carter, please come to the stage!"

Carter and I stared at each other, open-mouthed. What had we just heard?

"That's you!" Carter's grandma cried, pushing on his shoulder.

He stood, pulling me with him, and we walked together toward the stage.

Applause sounded all around us, deafening and bolstering at the same time. We walked up the steps to the stage and stood with the announcer and the judges. Then the most amazing thing happened.

People began standing while they clapped.

I turned to Carter in shock. "Are they cheering for us?"

"I always knew you were a star." With a grin, he lifted my hand in the air and gestured at me, as if giving me the credit. I soaked in the moment, every single bit of it, from Carter's eyes on mine to my mom and dad at the back of the crowd, to all my friends who'd come together to make this happen.

It was a feeling like I'd never felt before.

We left the stage with the promise of a trophy to be designed and mailed to us, and I could barely focus through the rest of the awards. Benjamin and Isabella won first place in the couples' division, but I didn't care. I felt like I'd won everything I'd ever dreamed of.

That was until I left the auditorium, mingling with the rest of the dancers and families, and a woman came up to me and told me she was from Julliard.

SEVENTY-THREE

MOM, Ted, and I sat at our table, a smorgasbord of food spread in front of us. She and Ted sported deep tans from their short trip to Cancun.

"I think I should have asked for a tan for Christmas," I said, looking at my own pale arms.

Mom finished chewing a bite of her steak. "What, admittance to Julliard wasn't enough of a gift?"

I laughed. She had a point. Not only had nationals earned me the attention of a recruiter from Julliard, but it had also sealed my relationship with my boyfriend. After everything dance had put us through, we agreed we could be boyfriend and girlfriend, but competitive dance partners no more.

That was fine, though, because he still loved dancing in the kitchen.

"Are you excited to live in New York?" Ted asked. "Only a few months left."

Mom swatted his hand. "I told you two already, no college talk at the table. As far as I'm concerned, Adriel is staying here forever and never moving out."

"When will you have time for your new daughter then?" I teased. "She might get a little jealous."

Mom and Ted gave each other a serious look, and my heart sank. I hadn't meant to upset them. I knew my mom would never replace me. Just like she'd told me, I was the one who made her a mom. That would never change.

Ted took a breath. "About that..."

I looked between them, concerned. "Is everything okay?"

"Yes, it's great," Mom said, squeezing Ted's hand. "While we were on vacation, we had a lot of time to think and we decided that our turn is over to be parents."

"That's... wow," I said. "Are you sure?"

Mom nodded. "We're both getting older, and I think we just want to be...us."

Ted leaned over and kissed her on the cheek. "Exactly."

"What do you think?" Mom asked nervously.

"If that's what you want, I want it too," I said honestly.

She reached across the table and squeezed my hand, along with Ted's. "I have everything I want sitting right here."

The doorbell rang, and my eyebrows came together. Why would anyone be ringing the bell during dinnertime on Christmas day?

Mom gave me a coy smile. "Looks like your Christmas present is here."

My eyebrows came together. "We opened presents this morning."

"Answer the door," she said, still grinning.

I pushed away from the table and walked toward the door. I pulled it open to see Carter dressed head to toe in a Santa Claus costume and burst into laughter.

"Now, young lady," he said in a fake Santa voice. "You better check my present bag before I put you on the naughty list."

I stifled laughter as I reached into the red velvet bag he held out. Inside was a small box wrapped in metallic green paper. "For me?"

He nodded, making his plastic beard wobble.

With another laugh, I stepped aside so he could come inside, then began unwrapping the gift. Inside was a clear glass plaque. My mouth fell open. "Our award."

The Inaugural AC AV Award

To Carter McCormac and Adriel Pruitt

There was an image of two dancers etched into the glass, and they looked almost like us.

"Made it here yesterday," Carter said. "They overnighted it." When I looked up, he was holding up another smaller box. "This one's from me," he said.

I took the package and tore away the paper, my heart beating quickly. This was our first Christmas together as a couple. I had a certificate of a star I'd named after him in my room. What had he gotten me?

Forgetting my parents were watching, I began unwrapping gift number two. The paper revealed a velvet jewelry box, and I looked inside to find a necklace with a charm that looked exactly like what everyone had worn on their shirts at nationals.

I covered my mouth, looking from the charm to Carter. "It's beautiful."

"May I?" he asked, reaching for it.

I nodded, turning and lifting my hair.

He had to take off his gloves to get the necklace out, but he easily slipped it over my head and clasped it at my neck. The pendant rested on my chest, the perfect reminder of Carter and all he had done for me. Of all the love that lived between us.

"What do you think?" he asked, smiling under the beard.

"I think," I said, stepping closer, "that you better take off that costume so I can give you a proper thank-you kiss."

Grinning, he pulled down the beard, and I gently kissed his lips, thanking him for the present and for just being him.

Carter seemed to remember my parents were there before I did, because he pulled back, holding my hand.

Mom said, "Carter, do you want to stay and watch a movie? We always watch *Home Alone* on Christmas."

He grinned. "I would love to, but I shouldn't leave my grandma alone too long."

"Invite her too," Mom said cheerily. "You two are family now."

And that's how I ended up spending Christmas night. With my parents and my boyfriend and his grandma, curled on the couch, snuggled under a blanket with my head on Carter's shoulder.

As we watched the movie, I couldn't help but think of all I had to be thankful for, and everything I had to look forward to because of a ripped pair of pants. I wouldn't have traded them for the world.

EPILOGUE

NADIRA

Celebrating New Year's Eve at Waldo's Diner had been Cori's most brilliant idea ever. Not only did they have delicious food and plenty of room for all of us, but we also got to catch up with our favorite waitress and finally meet Chester's wife.

The old man always sat a few booths from the door by himself, drinking coffee and talking about his wife, who volunteered at the local hospital. Today I knew why. They were adorable together, her with her kitten earrings and him with the adoring gaze he gave her.

It seemed like I was surrounded by couples. Cori and Ryker, Adriel and Carter. Even Des had a boy of the night—some guy from Brentwood U who had more abs than brains.

I knew because I was standing across from him and Des, and my mind had been wandering for moments while he talked about the myriad vitamins he took on a daily basis.

"What supps do you use?" he asked me.

I lifted my eyebrows. "'Supps'?"

"Supplements," he said, like I was the crazy one here.

I suppressed a groan and said, "The Flintstones kind." At his horrified look, I added. "Excuse me, I think Faith's calling me." I couldn't get away fast enough. Not just from the inane conversation, but the reminder that even that bozo would be getting kissed at midnight.

I might have been the captain of the Emerson Academy Mathletes, but I felt a million light-years behind all my friends. As far as I knew, they'd all dated, kissed. But me? I couldn't get a guy to notice me if I stood on a corner, waving a sign to sell "supps."

I weaved through the people there, looking for Faith where she stood with Betty by the milkshake machine. Hardly anyone noticed me on the way. Even with a skin condition that took pigment from my black skin, I still blended in. You would have thought the condition was invisibility instead of vitiligo.

"Hey," I said, reaching Faith and Betty.

They smiled at me, and Betty said, "How about a chocolate shake?"

"Was that a rhetorical question?" I teased, reaching for the silver cup she extended my way. "Thank you."

"Of course," she said.

"How's your mom doing?" I asked.

Betty frowned. "She's had a string of bad days lately. I'm worried her Alzheimer's is getting even worse."

"That's awful," Faith said, gently touching Betty's shoulder.

I nodded in agreement. "Anything we can do?"

Betty let out a sigh and shook her head. "She'll come around. She always does." Betty didn't sound quite like she believed her own words.

"I hope so," I said.

The bells over the door chimed, and Betty said, "I'll be right back."

As she walked away, I asked Faith, "Having fun?"

"Oh yeah." She held up her own chocolate shake. "This is way better than a kiss at midnight."

I snorted, leaning back against the half-wall that separated the dining area from the kitchen. "You know, I think New Year's Eve is my least favorite holiday."

"Why is that?" she asked, taking a sip of her shake.

"Where do I even begin? Everyone's running around saying things like 'new year, new you' and making these ridiculous resolutions perpetuated by the diet industry to make more money."

Faith tilted her head to the side. "That's true, but I think there's something kind of magical about the beginning of the year. Like anything's possible."

Maybe Faith was right, but if there was any magic, I wasn't seeing it. "It doesn't help that everyone's supposed to kiss at midnight and there's not a guy within a hundred-mile radius who would be even remotely interested in kissing me. Yet another year being a kiss-virgin."

She lowered her voice and said, "You and me both."

I raised my eyebrows. "Seriously?"

She nodded, not quite meeting my eyes. "Maybe that should be our New Year's resolution—get kissed before we wind up as some kind of spinstery cautionary tale."

I rolled my eyes. "The weight loss resolution is more likely."

With a sly smile, Faith said, "Never say never."

Around us, people began shouting, and I realized they were counting down another year.

"Come on," Faith said. "This is our year. Say it."

I smiled at her shaking my head. "This is our year." The year I would get my very first kiss.

As the clock struck midnight and our friends kissed their boyfriends, I reached for my shake and took a drink. If I was going to ring in the new year single, it might as well taste good.

Want to see Adriel and Carter starting their lives together? Get a peek into their future in the FREE bonus story, Moving Forward!

Use the QR code to read Moving Forward!

Stick with the Curvy Girl Club longer by reading Nadira's story, Curvy Girls Can't Date Soldiers!

Use this code to discover Nadira's story!

The Curvy Girl Club

Curvy Girls Can't Date Quarterbacks

Curvy Girls Can't Date Billionaires

Curvy Girls Can't Date Cowboys

Curvy Girls Can't Date Bad Boys

Curvy Girls Can't Date Best Friends

Curvy Girls Can't Date Bullies

Curvy Girls Can't Dance

Curvy Girls Can't Date Soldiers

Curvy Girls Can't Date Princes

The Texas High Series

Chasing Skye: Book One

Becoming Skye: Book Two

Loving Skye: Book Three

Anika Writes Her Soldier

Abi and the Boy Next Door: Book One

Abi and the Boy Who Lied: Book Two

Abi and the Boy She Loves: Book Three

The Pen Pal Romance Series

Dear Adam

Fabio Vs. the Friend Zone

Sincerely Cinderella

The Sweet Water High Series: A Multi-Author Collaboration

Road Trip with the Enemy: A Sweet Standalone Romance

YA Contemporary Romance Anthology

The Art of Taking Chances

Nonfiction

Raising the West

AUTHOR'S NOTE

Despite having two left feet, dancing has always intrigued me. I love the way people can say so much without saying anything at all. However, as I watched all of my favorite dance movies, I never saw a girl who looked like me.

Why are only perfect bodies allowed to feel the beat? Why are only perfect bodies allowed to shine? And although the athleticism of elite dancers is admirable, why do dancers have to suffer so much to succeed?

I've seen videos of incredibly talented plus-size dancers like Amanda LaCount and Lizzie Howell where they were broken down to tears because someone in a position of authority told them their bodies don't belong on stage.

I'm here to disagree.

When did dancing get relegated to the shadows for plus size girls? If you love performing, you deserve to be in the spotlight, regardless of your body type. Every time you lift your arm or nod or your head or simply breathe, you're engaging in the dance of life. Wherever your stage is, whether it's in the kitchen or in the rain or on the dance floor, I hope you always have the courage to shine and you never let anyone take that away.

ACKNOWLEDGMENTS

Writing a story like this is an incredible journey that I didn't take alone. Between my husband and my children, I have a house full of support and love. My extended family is always there cheering me on.

Some friends become like family—that's Sally Henson for me. She's an amazing writer, and I love having her as a friend!

One of my best cheerleaders is my editor, Tricia Harden. Her feedback on the stories helps me improve as well as lifts my spirits.

I joke that being a full-time writer feels like being in the NBA, but I think it might be a bit of an understatement. I absolutely love what I do, and I wouldn't be able to do it without you. If you have supported me in any way, by joining my readers' group on Facebook or sending me a kind email or leaving a review or simply reading this story, you have no idea how much you mean to me. Thank you, thank you, thank you.

GLOSSARY

Latin Phrases

Ad Meliora: School motto meaning "toward better things."
Audentes fortuna iuvat: Motto of *Dulce Periculum* meaning "Fortune favors the bold."
Dulce Periculum: means "danger is sweet" - local secret club that performs stunts
Multum in Parvo: means "much in little"

Locations

Town Name: Emerson
Location: Halfway between Los Angeles and San Francisco

Surrounding towns: Brentwood, Seaton, Heywood

Emerson Academy: Private school Rory and Beckett attend

Brentwood Academy: Rival private school

Walden Island: Tourism island off the coast, only accessible by helicopter or ferry

MAIN HANGOUTS

Emerson Elementary Library: Where Rory tutors Anna, open to students K-7

Emerson Field: Massive park in the center of Emerson

Emerson Memorial: Local hospital

Emerson Shoppes: Shopping mall

Emerson Trails: Hiking trails in Emerson, near Emerson Field

Halfway Café: Expensive dining option in Emerson, frequented by celebrities

La La Pictures: Movie theater in Emerson

Ripe: Major health food store serving the tri-city area

Roasted: Popular coffee shop in Emerson

JJ Cleaning: Cleaning service owned by Jordan's mom

Seaton Bakery: Delicious dining and drink option in Seaton where Beckett works

Seaton Beach: Beach near Seaton – rougher than the beach near Brentwood

Seaton Pier: Fishing pier near Seaton

Spike's: Local 18-and-under club

Waldo's Diner: local diner, especially popular after sporting events

APPS

Rush+: Game app designed by Kai Rush and his father

Sermo: chat app used by private school students

IMPORTANT ENTITIES

Bhatta Productions: Production company owned by Zara's father

Brentwood Badgers: Professional football team

Heywood Market: Big ranch/distributor where everyone can purchase their meat locally

Invisible Mountains: Local major nonprofit - Callie's dad is the CEO

Dugan Industries: Owns and manages Brentwood Marina, along with other entities. Owned by Ryker Dugan's father, Trent Dugan.

ABOUT THE AUTHOR

Kelsie Stelting is a body positive romance author who writes love stories with strong characters, deep feelings, and happy endings.

She currently lives in Colorado. You can often find her writing, spending time with family, and soaking up too much sun wherever she can find it.

Visit www.kelsiestelting.com to get a free story and sign up for her readers' group!

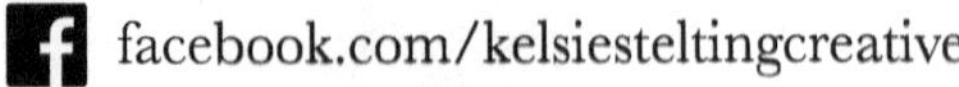 facebook.com/kelsiesteltingcreative

 twitter.com/kelsiestelting

instagram.com/kelsiestelting